THE BLOOD OF PATRIOTS

WILLIAM W. JOHNSTONE
WITH J. A. JOHNSTONE

PINNACLE BOOKS
Kensington Publishing Corp.
www.kensingtonbooks.com

PINNACLE BOOKS are published by

Kensington Publishing Corp.
119 West 40th Street
New York, NY 10018

PUBLISHER'S NOTE
Following the death of William W. Johnstone, the Johnstone family is working with a carefully selected writer to organize and complete Mr. Johnstone's outlines and many unfinished manuscripts to create additional novels in all of his series like The Last Gunfighter, Mountain Man, and Eagles, among others. This novel was inspired by Mr. Johnstone's superb storytelling.

All Kensington titles, imprints, and distributed lines are available at special quantity discounts for bulk purchases for sales promotions, premiums, fund-raising, educational, or institutional use. Special book excerpts or customized printings can also be created to fit specific needs. For details, write or phone the office of the Kensington special sales manager: Kensington Publishing Corp., 119 West 40th Street, New York, NY 10018, attn: Special Sales Department; phone 1-800-221-2647.

This book is a work of fiction. Names, characters, businesses, organizations, places, events, and incidents either are the product of the author's imagination or are used fictitiously. Any resemblance to actual persons, living or dead, events, or locales is entirely coincidental.

PINNACLE BOOKS and the Pinnacle logo are Reg. U.S. Pat. & TM Off.

ISBN-13: 978-0-7860-2808-5
ISBN-10: 0-7860-2808-4

First printing: April 2012

10 9 8 7 6 5 4 3 2

Printed in the United States of America

THE BLOOD OF PATRIOTS

PROLOGUE

Detective John Ward learned a life-changing lesson during his lunch break.

The thirty-eight-year-old had spent the last three hours in Manhattan Federal Court testifying in the matter of the *People v. Alexander Cherkassov*. Questioned by the district attorney, Ward had told a visibly uneasy jury how Cherkassov was flagged by Homeland Security for overstaying his welcome. Russian "visa jumpers" concerned HS because of whispers that the Moscow Mafia was trying to smuggle plutonium to Somalis living legally in the city. What they planned to do with it did not require a physicist to figure out, just to assemble: hold it while they gathered the components for a bomb. The NYPD was alerted and Cherkassov was watched by an undercover team with the Organized Crime Control Bureau under the command of Detective Ward. Though the Russian turned out not to be an intermediary with the Al Shabaab terror organization, he *was* selling guns. Ward explained to the jury how a PSM handgun had been folded inside a copy of the newspaper *Oknó* and handed over in an alley off Pike Street, in exchange for an envelope stuffed with twenty one-hundred-dollar bills. It was a solid bust, everything photographed, no gaps. The crime lab even found a microscopic shred of Cherkassov's tobacco in the newspaper, as a police chemist would explain.

However open-and-shut a case might be, testifying was like high-stakes poker. Ward was aware that a wrong word could cause a mistrial and undo a year or more of surveillance, infiltration, and evidence gathering. Most important, as the DA had reminded him, he had to project an almost supernatural calm to pacify jurors who were afraid of being fingered by thugs in the gallery and blown up as they started their minivans in the courthouse parking lot. Not to mention that if Ward screwed up, the prick would be back on the streets dealing more death.

Nothing would go wrong, he thought as the judge declared a one-hour lunch break. Cherkassov would get twenty years, ten if he spilled on his connections, five if he behaved himself once he was inside.

Ward left the witness stand and made his way quickly through the crowded courtroom. He did not want to look at scowling Russian faces or eager journalists. He wanted to touch the pavement and smell the pretzel vendor's cart and just enjoy the dirty, dangerous world that was a second skin. Ward grew up in Hell's Kitchen on Manhattan's West Side when it was still a sewer, before it became gentrified in the 1990s, when nearby Forty-second Street where his father walked a beat for thirty-five years was a haven for whores and junkies, porn parlors, and burlesque houses. Streets dark with night and illegal commerce fit Ward like soft old jeans. Of course, most of the streets here in Lower Manhattan were like the new Forty-second Street, clean bordering on sterile. Maybe that was why his parents moved to Florida. Pooper-scooper laws, blowing newspapers replaced by neat iPhones and Kindles, chain restaurants and mall stores taking the place of greasy spoon diners, basement dives, and movie theaters that stank of pot. The streets of New York had lost a lot of their flavor, unless one knew where to look. Like down here on Greenwich and Washington streets, thick with Nigerians who hauled around big cardboard boxes filled with handbags made in New Jersey sweatshops that were sold to tourists as authentic Gucci, Hermès, and Ralph Lauren. They were grimy hucksters who only paused when a spotter saw a cop car coming, or when they dragged out their prayer mats to pray to Mecca at least five times a day.

Goddamn hypocrites, Ward thought as he neared the onetime Custom House, a stately Beaux-Arts edifice that was now an Indian museum.

Walking down Nassau Street in his brown Brooks Brothers suit, Ward stood out from the sharp Wall Streeters who were buying lunch-on-the-run from hot dog or falafel stands and stopping every few steps to text something. Ward stood a head taller than most, a sliver under six feet, three inches, and was a few shades paler due to his night and indoor stakeouts. He was also less hyper, and that had nothing to do with the delicate sensibilities of the jurors. Ward had learned long ago that his own anxiety made criminals alert. If an undercover cop seemed hair-trigger while walking a mutt that was actually a police dog or holding the arm of a galpal who was the very married Lieutenant Didi Stone, the bad guys would know it.

Here in the canyons of Lower Manhattan, Ward was never unaware of something else: the shadows he didn't see, the long shapes of what had been the World Trade Center. He did not detour two blocks west to visit the site. There wasn't time to say the proper prayers amid the new construction, and he couldn't afford to let himself become upset.

Ward wasn't hungry, but he was dry from all the talk. He bought a large bottle of water from a cart and walked south into Battery Park. The salt air of the harbor pushed back the smell of delivery-truck diesel fuel that hung in the crooked downtown streets. He had just enough time for a circuit of the Sphere, the large metal sculpture that once stood in the courtyard of the World Trade Center. Dug from the rubble battered and torn, it had been moved to the park as the hub for an eternal flame. It was a survivor. That was what he wanted to see right now.

The voice eased into his ear, like one of the old-time hookers.

"Nice Rolex, cheap."

Ward turned to his left. Just south of the Sphere one of those damned peddlers was selling bogus watches from a briefcase. He held the imitation leather case open in his extended arms, eyes darting from side to side like little machines as he watched for the law. A thin, frayed prayer mat was folded in quarters beneath the suitcase.

Ignore it, Johnny, his own little voice told him. He ignored the voice instead and turned toward the slightly hunched black man.

"Rolex, Rolex."

Ward took a swallow of water and stopped in front of the Nigerian. The gaunt man's dark, sunken eyes held him coldly, his mouth expressionless. Even by con-man standards this guy was as cheap an imitation as what he was selling.

"Nice Rolex, mister, never worn—"

The Nigerian's personal attention was like a dog wetting his leg.

"Where's your vendor's license?" the detective asked.

The man didn't miss a beat. "I forget, leave home," he replied in clipped English. He was already in motion toward the west, along the narrow rectangular plot on which the Sphere was erected. Ward finished his water, tossed the bottle in the trash as he watched him go. The valise was still open, the man still hawking. The Nigerian stopped as a couple of plump middle-aged tourists looked at the watches.

Ward didn't have time for this. Lunch was only an hour. He looked around for a cop or park ranger, didn't see one. He stared at the huckster who was standing in front of the eternal flame.

"Aw, hell," Ward thought.

Ward was moving toward them even before the words had died in his brain. The vendor saw him with those restless eyes but ignored him. The beefy male tourist was turning one of the watches over in his hand and nodding. The thrust of his lower lip suggested approval.

"It's a fake," Ward said. He snatched the watch from the startled tourist, dropped it in the case and slapped the lid shut. The vendor attempted to open it again and continue the negotiation. Ward grabbed his shoulders in order to keep him from sliding off. The tourists left quickly.

"Get out of here."

"You get out," the man replied, shrugging off Ward's grip.

"That's funny," Ward said, his eyes on the Nigerian. Four weeks of sensitivity training flew right from his head. "This is my land. Is it yours?"

"I live here too."

"Legally?"

The man didn't answer. He lowered the briefcase to his side and slid the prayer mat under his left arm. The Nigerian's blank stare had been replaced by defiance. "Who is asking?"

Ward pulled open the lapel of his sports jacket and displayed the shield hanging from his pocket. "Detective John Ward."

"Detective John Ward, you have not the right—"

"Great, great, your handler taught you the profiling mantra," Ward said. "I'm not impressed. I *do* have the right to question unlicensed vendors—"

The man suddenly stepped back. He put down his case and pointed at Ward with a stiff right arm. "Don't touch again!"

Ward stared at him. Something boiled in the pit of his belly.

"He touch me!" the vendor charged. "He *grab* me!"

"Yes, I saw it," said a British accent from behind.

Ward turned. The tourists who had been looking at the watch had returned with a pair of cops: a young African-American woman and an Asian man. They were First Precinct rookies assigned the uncomplicated task of giving tourists directions to the Statue of Liberty ferry and the World Trade Center site. Ward's sixth sense told him that she was a bleeding heart lesbian who hoped to be transferred to the Sixth Precinct, Greenwich Village, after a year while he was a kid from Chinatown who wanted to get back up to the Fifth Precinct to make the hometown safe from gang warfare. Some old-timers said cynically that the NYPD had two priorities: terrorism and diversity, in alphabetical order. Ward knew at a glance that these two were going to treat the illegal with kid gloves.

"Sir, please take two steps back," the policewoman ordered Ward.

"I'm a cop," Ward said. He didn't reach for his lapel; the plebes might shoot him. The Asian's thin hand was already on the snap of his holster.

Two sets of fresh-from-the-academy "ACLU-blue" eyes registered disapproval.

"I need you to take two steps *back*," the policewoman repeated.

She had shifted to the "I need you" phase. They trained cops to use that for emphasis. It was designed to show they were no longer dealing with just a law but a personal command. You slipped that in your verbal arsenal to show *you* meant business.

Ward clapped his lips shut so he didn't say what he felt. He simply did as she asked. The police-woman stopped a few paces in front of Ward. The Asian cop scuttled with studied casualness to the side. It was by-the-book, a thin blue triangle. If he made a move they had him covered.

"Did you assault this individual?" the police-woman asked.

"I did not," Ward replied. He nodded at the tourists and went into his own mantra. "I feared for the safety of these two."

"That isn't so!" the Brit insisted. "We were per-fectly fine. He came over and shook this fellow without *any* provocation."

"I did not shake him," Ward said.

The policewoman's eyes were heavy with disap-proval. "Sir, anything you say can and will be used against you in a court of law." Her eyes slid slowly from Ward to the vendor. "Sir, do you wish to press charges?"

The man glared at Ward. His head was framed by the Sphere. With its sharp angles and torn, golden panels lit by the sun, the monument looked like the headdress of some vengeful African god. "Yes," the son-of-a-bitch replied. Then he covered his eyes with his hands and recited, as though seek-ing to heal his wounded flesh and soul, "Guide us to the straight path, the path of those whom You have favored. . . ."

And in that sick, heart-sinking moment Detective John Ward knew two awful things. First, that his career in law enforcement was on life support. And second, that Alexander Cherkassov would be a free man.

CHAPTER ONE

Before it was a mecca for skiers, Aspen, Colorado,
was a mining center. Founded in 1879 and named
for the trees that spike the landscape, the town
became a resort after World War II thanks to de-
clining silver lodes and unparalleled slopes.

Joanne Ward and her twelve-year-old daughter
Megan lived in nearby Basalt. Located at the junc-
tion of the Roaring Fork and Fryingpan rivers, the
former railroad hub and coal center produced
charcoal used by the smelters in Aspen. The huge
kilns erected for this purpose remain a tourist at-
traction. Today, it is also a destination for trout fishermen, rafters, and campers who enjoy the majestic
mountain beauty.

The Ward women moved there in 2008. Joanne
had divorced her husband after seven years of
marriage—a month of marriage, she maintained,
if she factored out the time her husband spent on
the job. It was a wound that went back to 9/11, a
week after they returned from their honeymoon,

when he spent three solid days digging frantically for his kid brother in the Pile. He found Joseph at dawn on the fourth day—the top half of the young firefighter anyway—under a shattered office sofa. Joanne stuck with him until he got over the loss somewhat. He would always appreciate her for that. She moved in with, and then married, a wildlife illustrator who sold fine art prints on the Internet; they also met on the Internet. John didn't hold any of it against her—it was a common cop-story. He and his daughter Skyped several times a week and she came to see him on holidays. He probably saw her more now than he did when she was a baby. It's one thing when Mommy has to tell a kid that Daddy loves her; it's another when he has to prove it or it doesn't get said.

The day of Ward's arrest he was suspended without pay and released on his own recognizance. Except for the *New York Post* and Fox News—which pointed out that the vendor was breaking several laws at once, and applauded him for trying to clean up the streets of Lower Manhattan—the media called him a Muslim-basher. Grabbing the guy's shoulders to get his attention had translated as "violence." Telling the arresting officers that he was a cop became "emblematic" of corrupt officers who tried to get away with misconduct and corruption. The more charitable articles blamed his actions on untreated post traumatic stress from the death of his brother. Muslims blamed American intolerance, police intolerance, intolerance against undocumented aliens.

Ward remained in his apartment. Neighbors

brought him food. Except for the Muslim ones. Suddenly, the cab driver and his family who lived down the hall, whose kids he had taken to Coney Island when his daughter was in town, didn't want to know him.

Despite a day-long recess, the DA in the gunrunning trial failed in his efforts to conceal Ward's arrest from the jury. The judge ruled that Ward's testimony would have to be stricken and the jury informed about the questionable mental state of the Peoples' key witness. Cherkassov was released the following morning. His attorney had already filed the paperwork that allowed him to remain in the United States.

That same afternoon, before Ward's self-imposed house arrest, he had appeared in a conference room at One Police Plaza—down the street from the courthouse. There, Ward was urged by the DA, the police union, and an NYPD attorney to plea-bargain with the Nigerian huckster: his resignation from the force in exchange for charges dropped. Otherwise, if he were found guilty, the detective faced jail time and dismissal.

"The commissioner doesn't want the illegal immigrant bonfire burning up his workflow for the next six months," the young punk lawyer had told him with the same hard-edged certainty of the arresting cops. He acted as though Ward were a child molester being offered the preferable prospect of chemical castration over ten years in prison.

"And what did the Commissioner promise your pro bono counterpart?" Ward had asked. "Not to bust the other illegal scumbags who are harassing tourists sending American dollars to radicals overseas?"

"That's not your concern."

Again, the smug certainty. Ward wondered how much extra damage he'd incur if he punched the guy square in the mouth. "So I get sacrificed for protecting citizens instead of the asshole who was preying on them."

"That, plus trying to coerce the two officers."

It was a farce without end and everyone knew it, except maybe this manicured clown. The problem was, without a nearby structure to mount surveillance cameras, the memorial was effectively a video blind spot. And despite the best efforts of his Organized Crime Control Bureau brothers who hit the park within an hour, they were unable to find tourists who had caught the incident on video. They left flyers behind on trees, but they were gone the next morning, presumably used to stuff the fake handbags other Mecca-bowers were selling.

"How long do I have to think about it?" Ward had asked.

The attorney then gave him a memory stick, pushed it across the table with his fingertips like it was a cyanide pill. "The regulations and your resignation letter are on there," he had said. "We've got the weekend coming up but I wouldn't give it past Tuesday."

Of course. The commissioner telling the press, "We're looking into the matter" wouldn't hold them off much longer. "We'll have a statement to make early next week" would get the media off his back, especially if he gave them one of those characteristic half-smiles that let them know it would be a dead issue by then.

Ward didn't bother to go home and pack. He took an underground passage to the subway, rode out to the Jamaica terminal in Queens, and cabbed to the airport from there. He could have used his driver's license as an ID but used his shield instead to buy the plane ticket. In fact, the clerk said the airline seemed happy to have him aboard. Her smile told him she was sincere. Right then, that mattered to Ward. He wanted to feel good whenever he thought back to the last time he used it.

Joanne had already heard the news. A friend in New York had sent her a link to the NY1 Web site. But Ward hadn't returned her call until he was at the gate and about to board. Her message had expressed measured concern for his well-being, cautious because for all she knew he might well have gone off the tracks. Finally. This was something he wanted to discuss in person. When she didn't pick up, Ward left a message saying only that he was on the way. That wasn't her favorite news at the best of times. But she'd see him or, at least, she'd let him see their daughter. That was what he needed right now. To get out of the city and hang with someone to give him unconditional love.

And what will you give her in return? he had asked himself. For that he had no answer. This was a lot to lay on a kid.

Now he was in Aspen listening to clerks nattering about a terminal-clearing false alarm the day before as he rented the only midsize they had, a white Prius.

"What kind of false alarm?" Ward asked, the cop in him unable to not wonder.

"There was a shell casing beside an insurance dispenser," the young man told him.

"Do you get a lot of those? False alarms?"

"I've been here a year and this was my first," he said.

"We don't get the kind of traffic volume that puts us on the A-list," said the chatty young woman he had been talking to.

"Vegas, baby!" replied the other.

Obviously, security training was thin this far from the gates. Staff shouldn't be joking about terror targets. "It's numbers, not lifestyle," Ward said.

"Pardon?" the woman asked.

"Never mind," he said. "I'm a cop. Police talk."

That was one of the formulas law enforcement used to conduct risk assessment. Terrorists preferred mass casualties above all. To hit a movie star on vacation was next-to-pointless; many people would be happy to see some spoiled hunk get his Carradan skis splintered and move on. Second on the list was to strike at so-called decadent targets: amusement parks, casinos, film and TV centers. Third were national symbols. It may have been said in jest, but terrorists would achieve two of those three goals by striking at Las Vegas. A concurrent hit at nearby Hoover Dam would give them a hat trick. Aspen would be a B-list target, and only then if they could get a slew of celebrities or international jet setters at the height of the season—which this was not.

Ward didn't much care for the resort. It was like the Hamptons with snow, a place to show off what you could afford on and around you. He was hungry and he was tired, but he was on 82 heading northwest within fifteen minutes. It was off-season and two hours before the evening rush—he wasn't even sure they had one here—and the highway was empty. He made the trip in just under a half-hour.

Ward hadn't been to Colorado in nearly a year, since he visited Megan the previous Thanksgiving. Still, as soon as he got off on Basalt Avenue he knew that things weren't right. The last time he was here a new Pullet 'n' Pork had just opened at the corner of Two Rivers Road. He remembered chuckling at the dancing chicken and pig sign off the driver's side of the car. The restaurant was gone, replaced by something called the Al Huda Center. As Ward drove by he felt the small of his back tingle. This place wasn't honoring some civic hero named Al. Beside the ornately carved wooden door was a brass plaque with Arabic characters.

His eyes followed the low-lying structures of the small strip mall. Adjoining the Al Huda Center was a day care facility. Next to that was the Fawaz Dry Cleaner. A pizza parlor, Papa Vito's, sat on the far side. That was where all the dented, dirty trucks were parked.

"This is a joke," he muttered. Basalt did not have a significant Muslim community before, at least not that he noticed.

As Ward passed the strip mall he thought he saw a familiar figure in his rearview mirror. "Angie?"

Ward swung the car around and pulled into the parking lot. He looked more carefully at the young woman who was climbing into a small white Fawaz delivery van. It had to be her, the girl who used to babysit his daughter. He rolled down the passenger's side window as he pulled in.

"Angie Dickson?" he asked before she shut the door.

The teenage girl looked over, her blue eyes wary, her blond ponytail swinging behind. "Who's asking?"

"It's Megan's dad, John Ward."

The pretty face erupted in a smile. She slid from the van as Ward swung around the front of his car.

Angie was the daughter of Earl Dickson, manager of Fryingpan Savings and Loan. Ward had spent time with Angie when she brought Megan to New York one summer. It was the first time the then-sixteen-year-old had been out of Colorado.

He kissed her cheek and stepped back. The tall, slender teenager was dressed in a plain white blouse and black skirt. Neither was particularly flattering. But what struck him most were her eyes. Always lively, eager to take in everything around her, they seemed flat, purely functional.

"How have you been?" he asked.

The smile matched the eyes now. It became pinched and a little less inviting. "Same as everyone."

"That doesn't sound good."

She shrugged a shoulder. "People aren't happy."

"I thought you were going off to college," Ward said.

"I was accepted to UC Boulder but I decided to wait a year," she said. "Y'know, the economy."

"Your dad's bank okay?"

"It's picked up the last few months but it was hurt like everything else a few years back," she said. "Not as bad as tourism. That was hit hardest. We've got a lot more people fishing for food than for recreation."

Ward cocked his head toward the dry cleaner. "Is that the reason for all this?"

"The mussacre?" she said softly.

"The what?"

"The Muslim massacre. That's what folks call it." She laughed nervously as she gave a quick sideward glance. Ward recognized the look. It was the same one drug dealers and those goddamn hucksters flashed when they were checking for cops.

"Tell me about it," Ward said.

"Happened about—let's see. Five months ago," she said, looking up as she counted back. "Yeah, April. Right after tax time. Things went from bad to super bad when the summer bookings didn't start to happen. A group came in and bought up this strip mall and another, along with a bunch of short-sale homes."

"A group?"

"They were just investors from Chicago, called the Midwest Revitalization Initiative," she said. "We didn't know they were Muslim. When we found out people were joking that it should have been called the Mideast Relocation Invasion."

Ward knew that wasn't a joke. There was no humor in her voice.

"My dad could tell you more. All I know is that the developers of these places needed cash to finish other projects, homeowners were struggling and looking to sell to the transplants, so the money was offered and they took it."

"I can't believe things got so bad so fast," Ward said. "That new place seemed busy last time I was here, the Pullet 'n' Pork?"

"Oh. They had a fire. Never reopened. Mr. Randolph—he lives up the mountain, provided all the pork—he thought it was suspicious."

"Because?"

"Dad says he's just a suspicious guy. Anyway, everyone had their own stuff to worry about. The police said it was a grease fire and that was that."

Ward looked at the white van. "So now you work for the new owners."

"They needed someone who knows the area and didn't have an arrest record," she said. "They pay over the hourly and the checks don't bounce. My dad said those are good reasons to work for anyone these days."

"At least they don't make you wear a head scarf."

"I know, right?" Angie chuckled. But the smile was gone now. "Some folks might not even object to that if they had jobs. They say we should be grateful. The prices were fair and without the bailout these places would all be boarded up. Except for Papa Vito's. You can't beat his price for a pitcher of beer, and people are drinking a lot of it. He refused to sell his lease, so he'll be here at least till the end of the year."

Angie saw a face in the shop window and turned back to the van. "Hey, I've gotta make my deliveries. How long are you here for?"

"A day or two."

"Maybe I'll see you around," she said. "Give Meg a hug for me."

"Will do."

Angie shut the door and drove off. Ward waved as she left then turned toward the dry cleaner. The face in the window was gone. But not the fire in the small of Ward's back. If anything, the sense of danger was even stronger now. He wanted to see his daughter but he was suddenly having butterflies. He wasn't the same gangbusting crusader-dad she had known; he wasn't sure what he was and he didn't want to show that to his kid. He needed to get his man-legs under him, fill his new, emptier self with something useful.

He crossed the river, made a right onto Midland Avenue, and looked ahead toward the city center. He saw the sign of the stand-alone building on the right and headed for the Fryingpan Savings and Loan.

CHAPTER TWO

Ward parked and entered the bank with no clear idea what he wanted to ask or say. He didn't know Earl Dickson, wouldn't know him if he saw him, but he wanted to know more about what had happened here. He wanted that because he was a detective and detectives asked questions and observed people and drew conclusions. Even if it were just an exercise, he needed to move those muscles. Until now, he hadn't realized how much just a few days alone in his apartment, ostracized by all but his team, had compacted and crushed him.

The tellers were busy and there were several people sitting on cheap vinyl sofas beside the door. There were three officers. Two had cubicles and the third had an office. Two were busy with clients; the other, an older woman, was on the phone. Ward didn't have to read the nameplate on the door to know who the office belonged to. The door was shut and there was a middle-aged couple inside. The woman was touching a handkerchief to her eyes.

The man's shoulders were rounded. They were losing a home or a business. Earl Dickson was showing them where to sign papers.

Ward studied the man. He was stout, balding, with close-cropped graying hair on the sides. He was wearing a three-piece suit and a grave expression. It was set, a mask, like the simulacrum of grief worn by a funeral director.

"Can I help you?"

The woman who had been on the phone was walking over. She was tiny, older, with sparkle in her voice. Her eyes, though, seemed tired.

"I'm waiting for Mr. Dickson," Ward said.

"He may be quite a while. They're all waiting for him." She indicated the others on the sofa.

Ward looked down the line. "None of these folks look very happy."

"My name is Deb," she said, ignoring the comment. "Perhaps there is something I can do?"

"Actually, I just wanted to introduce myself. My name's John Ward. His daughter used to babysit my daughter—just bumped into her down the street, thought I'd say hi."

The woman seemed surprised. "You're Megan's father?"

Ward nodded.

"We read about you," Deb said.

"Oh?"

"In the New York Times online."

That figures, Ward thought.

"You had a run-in with some Muslim man in the park," she went on. "I'm glad they let you out."

"Of what, New York?"

"No, I mean—" she seemed embarrassed now. "I understood from the article you were in trouble for that."

"It's only trouble if I let it be," he said. "It's sort of complicated."

"I see," she said, though her confused expression said she didn't. "Well, if you'd care to have a seat—or perhaps there's a number where he can reach you?"

"Y'know, I'll just come back some other time," Ward said.

"All right," she said.

There was a moment before she turned when Ward felt she wanted to say something else, or take his hand, do something supportive. But she obviously thought better of it and went back to her desk. Ward watched her go and headed for the door. He paused beside a young man sitting on the edge of the sofa. He wore a flannel shirt and jeans. A manila folder sat on his lap, his hands folded on top of it.

"Good luck," Ward said.

The man snickered. "With the gunslinger?"

"That bad?"

"You must not owe him anything," the man said. "If you're behind two months, you go in that office and beg for your life looking into the barrel of a twelve-gauge. And when you're done he pulls the trigger, like he's doing with the Pawleys. They've got a fishing supply store and not enough fishermen."

"What about you? Home or business?"

"Mister, I got the trifecta. Home, business *and* truck. I'm hoping I get to keep one of them so I'll have a place to sleep."

"There's always Al's place," said the man sitting to his right. "It's a center for the community, right?"

They both smiled thinly and that's when Ward got it: they were joking about the Al Huda Center he'd seen at the edge of town.

Ward left. Despite the warm sunlight filling a cloudless sky, and air pure as heaven's own breath, the place felt like the devil's armpit, close and foul.

And he had been there less than an hour.

CHAPTER THREE

Being an undercover cop, it felt strange to Ward to suddenly have notoriety. He wondered what kind of reception awaited him at Joanne's house.

"She'll hear me out," he said to himself as he stopped to book a room at the Basalt Regency Inn then drove up Ridge Road into the Rocky Mountain foothills. Joanne was still angry at Ward but she didn't hate him. "Guarded" would be the best description of their exchanges.

He drove with the window still open, past the tall lodgepole pines and taller Scotches—some of them looked dead to him—and the slopes covered with Cascade Purple rock cress. The carpet of perennials went on for acres in all directions as he ascended, adding a fragrant tang to the air. He didn't dislike the aroma, but it didn't speak to him. He preferred the smell of hot asphalt being laid over a ruptured pipe hole. He had always responded to brick and concrete, the fingerprints of human industry, rather than the seasonal, third party works of nature. Cities were constantly evolving to suit people. Nature demanded that you adapt.

The homes on the ridge had plenty of land and shade from both the peaks and trees. The temperature had dropped noticeably as he reached the large cabin. The valley and river below were still sunlit and he took a moment to take in the view. That was something else cities had over nature. When there was trouble somewhere, even from this distance, you knew it. The way traffic flowed, the speed and density of the pedestrian population, the telltale haze of a fire, the sounds of sirens. From here, everything in Basalt appeared just fine.

He turned into the gravel driveway. Joanne came out to meet him, alerted by the crunch of the tires.

She looked better than ever. Tall, slender, red hair held on her head with a clip. Even in a sweatshirt and torn jeans, she had an elegance about her. But her skin was a healthy color, not the pallor it had in the city, and she wasn't hurrying. She was smiling slightly—a good hostess smile, not an I'm-really-glad-to-see-you one.

He got out and they kissed on the cheek. There was no embrace. She took a step back and folded her arms.

"Megan is out back with Hunter," she said. "I wanted to talk to you first."

"Okay."

"What happened?"

"I wasn't acting out or anything—"

"I'm not charging you," she interrupted. "I'm just—asking."

"Sorry. It's been all defense the last few days." He sucked down a breath. "I was trying to get an unlicensed vendor to move along. I put my hands on his shoulders. Rookie cops busted me for assault, the media tried me, here I am."

"The news reports said you were asked to resign."

"It was recommended," he replied. "But—we haven't talked about what part of my pension I get to keep. It's all on a disk or chip or whatever the hell it is that I haven't looked at yet. Don't worry, though. I know what my responsibilities are."

"I wasn't thinking about that," she said.

The alimony had ended when she remarried, but he still had child support and college to go with Megan.

"Megan know?" Ward asked.

She nodded.

"How'd she find out?"

"In the car, coming home from school, on her iPhone," Joanne said. "I couldn't tell her not to read it. We looked at a few of the articles together when we got home."

"Anyone give her a hard time?"

"No," she said. "Not for what you did. Or rather, who you did it to."

"Ah. I have street cred in Basalt."

"But she's embarrassed," Joanne said. "I guess that's not the best word. Uneasy, maybe? She doesn't know how to be around you."

"I'll take that up with her," he said. "Look, I'm embarrassed and uneasy and *scared*, too. I came here because I needed to connect with the only people on the planet I thought would give me a fair hearing."

She nodded. "What did your folks say?"

"They're in China. I'm not sure they've heard about it."

"Are they okay?"

"They've got their health and they've got *their* pension," Ward replied. "They're fine. Thanks for asking."

Joanne turned quickly. He knew the move well. She did it when she wanted to yell at him for being stupid but didn't feel like fighting. Ward followed her up the walk.

"I noticed the town's undergone a few changes since last year," Ward said.

"Towns do that. A lot of people want to make more of this than it is."

"Tough not to. The first three places you see when you enter town have signs that have to be translated. That's a pretty big change."

"Better they should be boarded up?" she asked. "And don't talk like that in front of Megan, please."

"Like what?"

She stopped and turned on him. "Disparagingly. Would you have said that if they were in Chinese or Spanish?"

"If I were in Tibet or Arizona, maybe," he said.

"Megan has Ute friends and French-Canadian friends and I hope she will have Muslim friends as well," Joanne said. "Do you understand me, John?"

"No, but I hear you," he replied.

The Vassar College liberal lion was in full roar. Ward backed off. It all came back, the whole marriage, like undigested sushi. The differences you overlooked for months because you thought she was really smart and hot and she thought you were brave and studly. And then you were parents and all the illusions ended.

They walked around the side of the inverted-V roof, along a slate path. Every second slab was glazed with a painting of a bird underneath. Ward wondered how many owls broke their necks dive-bombing the cartoony suckers. He experienced a sudden deep longing for New York sidewalks with gum, chalk art, and real pigeon droppings.

Hunter and Megan were grilling corn, red pepper, and eggplant on a firepit. Joanne took the tongs from Megan, who ran over and locked her spindly arms around her father, her cheek pressed to his chest.

"Hi, Daddy—"

"Hey, Princess," he cooed.

She had grown taller, and stronger. It was no longer a little girl who held him.

"I hear you've been surfing the net," he said.

"I was worried about you," she said. She chuckled through a sob. "You're a superstar on Fox."

"Me and Homer Simpson."

"Actually, it's Hannity," Megan told him. "They said they've been trying to get in touch with you."

Ward hadn't bothered to check any of his cell phone messages. He didn't want to hear from attorneys or officials and he certainly had no intention of giving interviews; there was nothing to be gained from intellectualizing a moment of conviction or living it over and over—though now that he thought of it, maybe his next career could be as a talking head or radio host or blogger. Part of him, a big part, still hadn't accepted the idea that he wouldn't be going back to his old life.

Megan continued to hug her father in silence as Ward cradled her head. He didn't want to look over at his former wife and Hunter but he did, anyway. The shouldery, bearded man had taken Joanne's hand. His big-as-all-outdoors compassion made Ward feel inadequate and angry. Mostly angry.

Father and daughter released one another and walked hand-in-hand to the firepit.

"Hunter," Ward said, offering his hand.

The big man took it. "Welcome," was all he said.

Hunter McCrea was a lumberjack of a man, three inches taller than Ward, with gray eyes set deep in his broad, bearded face. There were paint splotches on his apron—it obviously doubled as a smock—and flecks of red and yellow in his curly salt-and-pepper hair. He looked like one of his colorful birds that had mutated.

"Daddy, are you going to stay for dinner?" Megan asked.

"Actually, I was kind of hoping I could steal you for a couple of slices at Papa Vito's," he said. He was talking to his daughter but looking at Joanne.

"We never really go there," Joanne said.

"Except for parties, when I only have a little cake and tea," Megan said.

"Just like one of your old doll house fiestas," Ward said, adding pointedly. "When you were five."

"We're vegetarians," Hunter explained. "People understand."

"Where's the brawn come from?" Ward asked, using his chin to point at Hunter's shoulders.

"Soy milk, peanut butter, beans and unprocessed tofu are all great sources of muscle-building protein."

"Sometimes Hunter sounds like a cable TV ad," Megan chuckled.

Hunter grinned but Joanne looked unhappy.

"So what if we get a cheeseless pie with onions, olives, mushrooms—that kinda stuff?"

"That works," Hunter had to admit.

Megan made a face. "Except for the olives," she said. "I don't like them."

As they were speaking, Ward became aware of a distant buzz, like a lawn mower. He wouldn't have thought much of it if Megan hadn't shot her mother a look.

"Just ignore them," Joanne said.

"Who are we ignoring?" Ward asked.

"The off-roaders," Megan told him. "They cut through Mr. Randolph's place to get to the field."

"Should they not be there?" Ward asked. *Randolph. The name was familiar—*

"We learned in school how it cuts rivulets in the earth and changes the flow of the runoff from the mountains," she said. "*That* starves the fields off Ridge Road."

"Yeah, I saw them. They looked a little parched," Ward said. "Can't the police do anything about it?"

"They never get there in time," Megan said.

Ward heard a gunshot. Then another.

"That's new," Hunter said.

"Mr. Randolph?" Ward asked.

"That sounded like one of his blunderbusses," Hunter said. "He sometimes shoots at coyotes."

"Not this time," Ward said. "What's got him so upset?"

"Scott's got a ninety-four acre hog farm and he says the noise scares his pigs," Megan said, proud of her knowledge.

That was where Ward had heard the name. From Allie. He used to provide the pigs to Pullet 'n' Pork.

"Maybe we should call 9-1-1," Ward suggested.

Hunter considered then dismissed the idea. "They'll still be gone before the police get there."

"From up there you can see them coming along East Sopris Drive," Megan said. "That gives the riders enough time to leave."

"You're a regular detective," Ward said to her.

"And the chief may not look kindly on Randolph firing at people," Hunter added. He took the vegetables from the grill and put them on the pita pockets. "Don't get me wrong. It's upsetting. And Scott used to call 9-1-1. The law is on his side, there are trespassing and noise violations. But as Meggie said, the police never catch anyone."

"They're probably kids, and kids do stupid things," Joanne said, in a voice intended to be the final word on the subject.

"Some kids," Megan corrected her.

"Sorry, honey," Joanne stroked her daughter's hair and smiled apologetically.

Ward looked through the trees toward the ridge above. "Does Ridge Road go to Randolph's place?"

Megan said, "The dirt road beyond the fence does—"

"No!" Joanne said.

Ward fired her a look.

"You're not going up there. Scott might shoot at *you*."

"In a Prius?" Ward said.

"John, *don't*," Joanne said. "This has nothing to do with us or you."

There was a thick, unpleasant silence. Ward turned and started toward the painted slate path.

"I'll just go and check it out," he said. "Maybe I'll see something that'll help the police. A license number, something." He glanced at his daughter as he was about to turn the corner. "Be back in a little bit. Don't fill up on chick peas."

From Megan's expression he couldn't tell if she was eager that something was being done or anxious that he was doing it. Not that it mattered. Only part of him was doing this for her approval. He was going up there because he couldn't help himself.

Ward was jogging when he reached the front of

the house. He jumped in the Prius and tore from the driveway. A wooden-slat fence marked the end of the city-managed street. It was easy to maneuver around it. Flooring the pedal, Ward spun a cloud of dirt behind him as he raced up the road.

CHAPTER FOUR

It wasn't exactly the *Bullit* car, but the Prius had better pickup and maneuverability than Ward imagined. He picked his way along the path through trees that bore a hint of twilight on their trunks. There were no foothills like the one through which Ridge Road ran. When he reached the plain, that was it. Beyond it, the Rocky Mountains rose straight and mammoth. If Ward had a poet's vocabulary something would have occurred to him to commemorate the moment. The only phrase that came to mind was "freakin' big."

Before them, the punks seemed trivial. The noise was loud, though, echoing and nondirectional. Ward could barely make out the bikes in the setting sun. As his eyes adjusted to the dark under the peaks he saw the sparks of the engines. Those could probably cause a helluva brushfire. He also saw the lights of the Randolph home and just once the flare of his gun. He heard the crack a moment later. There did not appear to be a functioning fence between Randolph's spread and the field, just a few old posts that had fallen to the ground and rails that had long since rotted from the posts that were still standing. Before this, Randolph probably hadn't needed one.

Ward had driven up without his lights—*stealth mode,* he thought whimsically. The car was nothing if not quiet; he doubted anyone up here was aware of him. He took that advantage to reconnoiter. The field where the four ATVs were humming lay on the west side, Randolph's hog farm was in the center, and the slope down to Ridge Road and the valley beyond was on the east. The lights of Basalt were visible beyond; they were just starting to twinkle in the dusk.

Ward turned left from the dirt road onto the field. He proceeded slowly, trying to pick out any boulders or pits that could stop the car. The riders were turning circles and wide figure-eights. Randolph wasn't firing anymore; in the fast-deepening darkness, Ward could not tell what the farmer was doing. He was a shadow among larger shadows.

The sparking motors of the ATVs seemed to align for a moment before the vehicles revved and, as one, began racing toward the west in the direction of Randolph's place. They might veer off before they came within range. Then again, they might not. Maybe this was some idiotic Basalt version of Chicken.

Ward wouldn't be able to reach them in time to intervene but he felt he might be able to distract them. He fumbled for a switch to turn on the headlights and was relieved to find them come on by themselves as dusk settled in. Now that he could see the field he cranked up the acceleration. He sped toward the riders and not the farm so that Randolph wouldn't think he was with the bikers.

The ATV riders stopped; first one then the other three. They'd know he wasn't a cop since there were no flashing lights. But they couldn't know whether Randolph had an ally who might have been waiting for them. Three of them didn't stay to find out. They cut diagonally across the field, toward the road—not the one Ward had taken but the real one, below the farm. Now that Randolph was armed, they avoided what the fence remnants suggested was the boundary of the farmer's property, staying to the outside. Ward used to tell students at a firearms class at the local YMCA: "If you ever use deadly force on your property, be sure to tell the investigating officer these words: 'I feared for my life.'" He was sure the same dictum held out here. Those three riders were being cautious.

The fourth rider was not. He spun his ride ninety degrees to face Ward. He seemed to be weighing a run at the Prius.

I've got two tons, insurance, and an airbag, Ward thought. *I'm good for a game of Chicken.*

The ATV engine roared once, deeply, and took off toward the detective. Ward accelerated as well, hard. The idea of Chicken was not to see who veered off first. That was the result. The best tactic was to narrow the window your opponent *thought* he had to make a final decision, to speed things up so that his instinct for survival overrides his bravado. Ward crushed the pedal to the floor. There was no accompanying howl of horsepower but the dim outline of the ATV got larger faster, and his own headlight would be doing the same. There were less than five seconds to impact. Ward had stiffened his arms on the wheel; he relaxed them, relaxed his body, so it would be flexible, no bones braced to snap in the ensuing collision, if it came.

It did not. Ward kept going, surprised by his own apparently suicidal resolve, but the ATV swerved around to the driver's side, passing Ward like a missile. He picked it up in his rearview mirror, watched it pivot and swing back toward him. Now Ward had him. The rider closed on the Prius, obviously intending to bump Ward in the rear. The detective watched the ATV carefully then mashed the brakes and immediately jammed the gas. Rocks and dirt flew in a sheet behind the car and the rider was close enough to catch them full-on. Ward crushed the brake again, sped up again, and sent another wave flying behind him. He only needed to do it twice. The ATV swerved and swung away, toward the ridge, toward where the other bikers had stopped to watch. The leader, their champion, couldn't have been happy with what they saw. When he reached them they left together.

The sound of the ATVs faded not long after they disappeared over the ridge and headed down the slope to East Sopris Drive. Ward turned the Prius toward the house. He would have flashed his lights as some kind of signal if he could have figured out how to do so. Only as Ward thumped across the lumpy terrain did he realize his heart was beating rapidly, as it did just before he made a bust. It felt good to be in business again, even without portfolio. He passed through a broken stretch of fence and slowed as he neared the farm. It was dark now and he couldn't see Randolph. But he suspected the hog farmer was there. As the lights of the house revealed the dim silhouette of a man standing out front, Ward stopped the car. He did not turn it off but left the headlights shining ahead. He got out and walked into them, his hands slightly raised. Now that he was outside, and the bikers were gone, he could hear the pigs squealing on the other side of the farm. The detective had no idea what a happy pig sounded like, but these seemed agitated.

"Mr. Randolph?" he said softly. "My name is John Ward. I used to be married to Joanne McCrea who lives down on Ridge Road."

"You took quite a chance there," the man said from the darkness. It was a hard voice, like shale. He was near, maybe a hundred yards, and coming closer.

"No one ever accused me of being smart," Ward replied. "I was down there and heard the noise. Joanne told me what was going on—thought I'd check it out, see if there was anything I could do."

"Sir, I'd say mission accomplished," Randolph said.

"An honorable phrase that's fallen out of favor."

"Among some," Randolph said. His voice was much closer now. Ward could hear the crunch of dry scrub and then the farmer was in the cone of the headlights. He was slightly shorter than Ward, rounder, and about twenty years older. He had a thick head of wavy gray hair beneath a beaten old Stetson, and dark eyes that had some steel in them. He tucked his shotgun under his arm and offered a big, raw hand. "Scott Randolph. Pleasure to know you."

Ward felt his heart slowing. "Likewise," he said with a smile.

Randolph reached into the pocket of his denim jacket and pulled out a tobacco pouch. He offered some to Ward, who declined, then tucked a pinch in his cheek. "You're the New York cop, aren't you? The one who got busted."

Ward nodded.

"Tough break," Randolph said. "Can I interest you in a Coors?"

"I was supposed to take my daughter to dinner."

"Understood. Another time, then."

Ward hesitated. He wanted to know more about what had happened up here and what, if any, repercussions there might be—not just against Randolph but against the stranger in the white Prius. And, there was something more. Ward felt good right now, planted. He wanted to hold on to that a little longer, bring a better dad back to Megan.

He took his cell phone from his pocket and called Joanne. She was neither surprised nor happy to hear from him.

"Is everything all right?" she asked.

"Yeah. I'm going to stay with Mr. Randolph a bit."

"Of course you are," she replied. "The job is still keeping you away."

"It's not like that," Ward said. It wasn't. It was bigger than that. Ward looked at the farmer standing in the white glare of the headlights, his backbone straight and his red neckerchief rustling slightly in the breeze. His eyes were turned to some distant vision, as the gaze of American farmers have always done. A chill ran up Ward's spine to his skull. "I'll come by in a little bit. You've got dinner there— I'll take Megan for dessert."

"Don't bother," Joanne said.

"I'll be there in less than an hour," Ward said firmly—to dead air.

Ward folded the phone slowly. He considered calling Megan herself but decided against it. This was something you discussed in person. It wasn't an apology, it was an explanation. What was the old song or saying or whatever the hell it was about being good for yourself first before you can be good for somebody else?

He tucked the phone in his pants pocket. "I guess I've got some time," he said.

"Joanne—she's a tough one," Randolph said.

"She's a Brooklyn girl," Ward replied. "You drive a car at *them,* they'll just stare you down."

Randolph let loose another throaty laugh and slapped his companion on the back. Ward turned off the car and followed Randolph to the house, the headlights lighting their way before winking off.

CHAPTER FIVE

The wood-paneled room was lit by the shaded glow of a single desk lamp. Aseel Gahrah, director of the Al Huda Center, sat behind the large, clean, mahogany desk, stirring tea. His round face was serene behind his neatly trimmed salt-and-pepper beard. He felt comfortable here and, despite the news, he felt comfortable at this moment. He understood that few plans run smoothly and that corrections were sometimes necessary. Results were more important than expediency.

Nineteen-year-old Hassan Shatri had not yet learned those lessons. He stood shifting from foot to foot before the desk, his expression grim bordering on angry, his fingers curled to fists. Now and then his eyes flashed on the darkness behind the desk before quickly dropping away; two pinpoints of light seemed to hover there, like stars.

Gahrah listened impassively as, with flourishes of self-reproach, the young man told him what had happened.

"We didn't know who it was," the swarthy young man said. "The decision to challenge him was mine. The others did not wish to take a chance that the car belonged to an off-duty police officer, someone Randolph might have hired to—"

"But *you* did," Gahrah interrupted. "You were willing to risk being arrested or slain, exposing us all, inviting scrutiny."

"You gave us a job, Uncle. I wanted to make sure we finished it." His voice dropped. "I had hoped to make you proud."

"By running yourself at an oncoming car?" The man's face remained calm but his voice had an edge. He did not want to beat the boy down, merely make him aware that not everything could be solved by frontal assault.

"I did not want to shame you with cowardice," Shatri replied.

"Courage is not merely in the sinew of a man," Gahrah told him. "Many fools have that. As our brothers-in-arms in the Holy Land learned centuries ago, one must also have the judgment, the wisdom, the *patience* to know when a retreat today is the groundwork for victory tomorrow."

The boy considered that. "It is difficult to know this in the moment," he answered.

"Hindsight is useful," Gahrah said. "I know that your passions have been raised by the imam. There is good and there is danger in that." The director had turned his head slightly to the side when he said that. "Let us agree that if a plan is to be changed, unless you can tear the eyes from all who might see you, and deafen all who might hear you, the wisest course is to withdraw. Yes?"

The young man hesitated then nodded once. "Yes, Uncle."

"It is done," Gahrah said, softening. "Your identity was not revealed and your actions *did* tell us something. Whoever was on that field tonight was not a tourist, someone who came upon you by chance."

The young man's interest perked. "Then you think the farmer has hired someone?"

Gahrah shook his head. He smoothed his beard with a hand while he considered what had happened. "Private security would not have been permitted to intervene on public land. Not in the way you describe. No, this was someone who was willing to become involved either by design or chance."

"A friend of Randolph's?"

"Possibly. But waiting in the field? No. Randolph fired at you. I believe this person was passing by." Gahrah thought aloud. "In any event, they may be emboldened by this. We cannot allow them to unify and start patrolling the field." Gahrah raised both hands and set them down, indicating the matter was closed. "Join your brothers. We will speak of this no more tonight."

The young man bowed slightly then left the room. When the door had shut a short figure emerged from the shadows to the left of the desk.

"A disappointment," a soft voice said.

"Not entirely," the director replied. "The farmer did fire on them this time, Imam. The boys achieved that much."

The imam raised an eyebrow. "You assume I was referring to the boys?"

Gahrah frowned. "You give them fire without a torch to hold it. That can be dangerous. He needed to hear what I had to say."

"Wildfires can be useful," the imam replied.

"And unpredictable," Gahrah shot back. "The plan was to provoke the farmer to go after them in public. When he does that we will have the arrest we desire."

"A hate crime."

"That *was* the goal," Gahrah reminded him.

The imam shook his head slowly. "It is no longer enough."

The imam shuffled around the desk, his slippered feet whispering along the rug. He stood by the room's one window and looked down the main street toward the mountains. He was a tall man with hunched shoulders and hawkish eyes peering from beneath thick gray brows. His skin was deeply wrinkled and his white beard came to a sharp point just below his thin neck. Bony fingers locked behind his back as he stood there.

"What we need are *basijis*," the holy man said, almost wistfully. "Then we would have results."

The holy man was referring to the undercover operatives who mingled with the civilian population in Iran. When suspected anti-government activists were found, the secret police would draw them out by pretending to be fellow revolutionaries.

"That would not work," Gahrah pointed out. "You have not been here long enough. You do not know Americans. The citizens of this town know each other, they only trust each other."

"Your banker?"

"He trusts money," Gahrah replied. "He is the exception."

"These Americans," the imam said disdainfully. "That boy fights against his instincts and you encourage that. He has been raised in a country where men are taught to be like women and women to be like men. It is a sin against the order of things."

The director had a sip of tea then sat back. He did not agree with the imam. The young men had been following the plan the director had laid out for them: to get a judgment against the farmer, then convince him to sell the farm in exchange for the charges being dropped. The land was the immediate goal, not ideology. Gahrah was aware of the laws and the ways to manipulate them in a way the imam was not. But the holy man was nearly eighty. For him, patience was a weakness. Inactivity showed a lack of faith.

"The swine must be gotten rid of," the imam said suddenly.

"The pigs," Gahrah clarified.

"Yes. I have lived these weeks with those creatures of the devil and with the stubbornness of their owner." The imam was silent for a long moment then fixed his gaze on Gahrah. "Do it tonight."

Gahrah regarded him with open surprise. "Are you certain?"

"I am certain that we shall be the victors in this, and I tire of waiting," the imam said.

"Imam, I understand," Gahrah said. "But the boys are needed for the other mission. If we were to lose any of them now—"

"'Those that have left their homes and fought for God's cause with their wealth and with their persons, it is they who shall triumph.' What the boy did tonight was rash but his heart was true. Let ours be likewise, tempered with the tactics of our *jihadi* brothers. If the time and place are unexpected, we will bend events to us, not the other way around."

Gahrah mouthed his silent accord as the imam retired to the adjoining prayer space of the community center while the director considered how they should enact the will of their partners. One turned to God for guidance; one turned to the Internet for practical applications. Gahrah took his laptop from a drawer, opened it, and studied the map of Basalt. It was marked with virtual pins: property they owned was in red, property they wished to own was in green, public lands were in white.

The colors of the flag of Iran, their native land. A country they had not seen in over a score of years—the young men, never. They had lived their lives among the Arab community in and around Michigan Avenue in Chicago. It had been necessary that the group not travel, that they remain invisible to airlines and immigration officials, especially in the aftermath of the September 11 strikes.

Gahrah brought up a Google Earth image of the Randolph farm. He studied it for several minutes. There was only one way the thing could be done. He would inform the boys after dinner. They would prove to the imam that they were not afraid. They had, all of them, embraced the imam's dream, the vision articulated by the late Ayatollah Mohammad Zarif, the Islamization of the west in a single generation. So ordered, they would do whatever was necessary.

The director shut the computer and looked around. Yes, he was comfortable here. The room reminded him of the religious center where he had studied in Tehran. Books were brought to students at a desk and, there, one was transported to Paradise and the presence of God. What greater comfort could one know than that?

Perhaps the imam is right, he thought. He was the spokesman of God, and perhaps it is God's will that everyone know that joy as soon as possible.

Either they would know joy, or Hell would be their home.

CHAPTER SIX

When John Ward was ten years old, his parents took him on their only real vacation together. They went to Yosemite and stayed in a cabin at the Ahwahnee Hotel. They had booked one of the cottages and what the young Ward remembered most about the visit wasn't the scenery or the wildlife, the Native American guides or the sky drenched with stars. Even then, big buildings full of light impressed him more than distant pinpoints in the sky. What stuck with him was the smell of the cottage. It was like nothing Ward had ever experienced, a mixture of smoky wood and volcanic soil you could literally feel at the back of your throat, of air filled with fragrances he couldn't place blended in a way he could never have re-created. That smell was just a memory until he entered Scott Randolph's home.

Maybe because his nose was more sophisticated now, Ward could pick out the pine from the lavender, the smell of the horses from the pigs, the old leather of the chairs from the adobe used to build the chimney. But it was still a blend that transported him to his childhood. The feeling was a sense of wonder tinged with caution and fear because he felt—he *was*—so clearly an outsider.

The floorboards creaked as the two men entered. Even that was different from the way New York hardwood sounded. He glanced down. The slats were wide and held firmly in place with wooden dowels. The pegs had been there so long they had become a part of the wood around them.

"You built this place?" Ward asked.

"Put it up with my dad in 1960," Randolph said. "His father owned the property—oh, it was about three times larger then, but a bunch of it was sold off in rough times to build the houses where your ex-wife lives now. The family lived in a real small place next to the barn. Thing fell to hell about 1970. The hog shed is still the original, though I've had to fix the roof a coupla dozen times." He laughed. "But the rest is all new. Well, newer than what Grandad built in 1930."

Randolph spit his chaw into a real brass spittoon, then went to the kitchen and grabbed a couple of beers. Ward just stood on a bearskin rug—unashamedly real, the teeth yellowed and eyes stone-dead—and turned a slow circle. This was a home. Ward had never really had one, other than the city itself. An apartment was where you showered and slept, the bars were where you watched TV, and the streets were where you lived and worked.

For the second time that night his backbone felt

a chill. A familial home and the values, the survival traditions that got you there. Those were worth fighting for.

"Sit," Randolph gestured to an armchair with a beer as he handed the bottle to Ward. The farmer pulled over a rocker and sat facing his guest. "I hope Megan will forgive me for holding you a bit longer."

"I think that engagement is on hold till I can square things with her mother," Ward said ruefully.

"Your daughter—she knows about what happened back East?"

Ward sipped the beer and nodded. "She knows what people *say* happened and what everyone thinks."

"About half of which is BS?"

"Depends," Ward said. "I'm guessing they got it right on Fox. I'll explain it to her before I go. What about you? Any family?"

Randolph shook his head. "I had a wife. Boston gal. Met her when she was out here taking photographs for college back in the 1970s. She thought it would be neat to live in the mountains. That lasted about a year. I used to date a gal in Aspen, but she ran off with some European asshole name of Franz. Last I heard she was alone and tending bar in Italy." He shrugged. "It's okay. I got my hogs, I got my horses, and I got Papa Vito's when I feel like a game of pool. I've got a cabin in the mountains when I want to go hunting. I like not having to answer to anyone except my pigs."

"What about those off-roaders? How long has that been going on?"

"About three, four weeks," Randolph said. "Damnedest thing. I can't put a finger on it, but I don't think this has anything to do with recreation or their goddamn bikes. I feel like they're baiting me."

"Why?"

Randolph shrugged. "Ornery? Vegans? Got a grudge I don't know about?"

"Do you know who they are?"

Randolph shook his head. "They come when it's too dark for me to see their faces, and they all dress in black. If I had to guess I'd say they're young Muslims."

"What makes you think that?"

Randolph finished his beer, went to get another. "I know all the kids in town here. None of them would behave this way. Besides, a bunch of Arab kids moved into town shortly before all this started. It was after that strip of Muslim places opened. The newspaper reported that some group from Chicago picked up a string of foreclosed homes over on Floating Fork Court. Quiet cul-de-sac, very private. Some of the places were for families and some are like frat houses, all young men."

"Or barracks," Ward mused.

Randolph shot him a look from the kitchen. "Are you serious?"

"I didn't think I was. At least, I hope I'm not."

The idea hung there as each man processed it. Randolph sat down and leaned back, the chair dipping slowly. Ward held the beer on his knee and looked at the bottle. The big picture wasn't coming together from the parts they had.

"I don't know what's behind this," Randolph

said. "Maybe they just don't like the idea that I'm a pig farmer. They got a strong dislike for pork."

"It has to be more than that," Ward speculated.

"Why? These people are funny. You draw their prophet in a cartoon and they want to cut your head off."

"True," Ward said, "but I still think it has to be more."

"Some folks think they torched the Pullet 'n' Pork because of that."

"I heard that was a grease fire."

"The fire alarm had been disconnected," Randolph said.

"How was business there?"

"So-so," Randolph admitted. "Tough going up against Papa Vito's."

"Well, that's a reason too. Besides, wouldn't they have struck you first? Choke the supply line at the source?"

Randolph took another chaw and chewed it thoughtfully. "Possible, I suppose."

"Is there anything special about your property?" Ward asked. "Size? Location?"

"Both," Randolph said. "Highest in Basalt and single biggest privately held chunk of land."

"Those are more likely reasons to try and get under your skin."

"More likely, but not practical. There's no way in hell they're gonna chase me from my home."

"Has anyone tried to buy it?"

"Nah," Randolph said. "People try, but most know better. Dickson would've told them. I mean, look. I don't owe anyone anything, and the farm provides me with a sufficient income. What I don't shoot during hunting season or catch in the river I'm able to buy. What the heck reason have I got to leave?"

"No kidding," Ward said, a little envious. "I guess the other question would be why Basalt?"

"I think that should be obvious," Randolph said.

Ward was missing it. He waited.

"We're the heartland," the farmer said.

Ward couldn't dismiss the symbolism of that, though his gut told him it had to be more. "You got someone to watch your back if these guys come back?"

Randolph dismissed the idea with a wave. "I can look after the place. They know I wasn't shooting at them before, but they know I can. I'll be okay."

"Well, if these guys do come back tonight don't get carried away," Ward cautioned. "And I'm speaking from experience here. Minorities have a way of turning public opinion against a man."

"John, I'm pissed off and I'm worried but I ain't stupid," Randolph assured him. "I hold my water unless there's a real fire."

Ward grinned and finished his beer. Randolph saw him to the door. The farmer clasped his hand and didn't immediately let go.

"You reminded me of something tonight," Randolph said. "That true Americans, wherever we're from, whoever we are, are in this together. It's not 'you give this to me' but 'what can we do together.' That's one of the things that distinguishes us from other people and it's one of the things we're in danger of losing."

"Too many hyphenates," Ward agreed.

Randolph frowned. "I don't follow."

"Korean-American, African-American, Gay-American, Muslim-American," he said. "We've got more tribes than Afghanistan."

"Amen," Randolph nodded. "Hyphenates. I'll forget the word in about two minutes, but I like it."

Ward grinned and returned to his car. He switched from green to gas. Driving without engine sounds was like trying to walk down the stairs without looking at your feet. You didn't get the full feel of what you were doing.

He sought out the illuminated clock on the dashboard. He had left the house forty minutes before. If her mother didn't push, there was a good chance Megan wouldn't hold it against him. He leaned into the gas and crossed the field and got down the dirt road as quickly as the streamlined little car would allow.

CHAPTER SEVEN

Ward pulled into the driveway, not sure at first that he had the right place. There were no exterior lights and the shades were drawn dimming what illumination there was inside. It was almost as though the house itself had vanished. Either he wasn't expected or he wasn't welcome.

He didn't bother turning off the engine. He wanted his getaway car ready. Whichever way this went, he wouldn't be long.

It was shorter than that.

He punched the bell with a knuckle, heard footsteps—a long slow stride, not Megan's—and Joanne was at the door. Her open face was expressionless.

"What, John?"

"The man needed help," he said flatly.

"People always need help," she said. Her voice was tense but soft. She obviously didn't want Megan to hear. "That's why we're no longer together, remember?"

"You won't let me forget."

"Oh, right. This is my fault."

"It's nobody's 'fault.' It's just the way things are. But Megan doesn't have to suffer because of what went on between us—"

"No," Joanne agreed. "And she's not going to suffer for what you do now, promising to take her somewhere, then running off."

"This is *her* community—"

"And you were trying to fix it, I know. God, I'm so sick of that. Would anything have turned out differently up there if you'd skipped the testosterone rush and taken your daughter out when you said you would?"

There was no point trying to explain to Joanne what had transpired, how it had made him feel. And even if he could communicate that, she wasn't wrong; he had done this at Megan's expense.

"Is she coming?"

"She's doing her homework," Joanne said.

Ward pressed his lips together and glared at Joanne and stood there waiting for her to come up with something less ridiculous. She yielded somewhat.

"Are you staying over long enough to have breakfast with her?" she asked.

"Yeah," Ward said. "What time does school start?"

"Eight."

"I'll be here at seven," he said. "Little picnic, then I'll get her to school."

"Fine."

Joanne started to close the door. Ward stopped it with the heel of his hand.

"You make me feel like a bad man," he said. "I'm not."

"No, you're not," she agreed. "But that's not the same as being a *good father*. Or husband."

Joanne leaned into the door and Ward removed his hand. It shut with a gentle click. Ward stood on the small wooden patio, surrounded by loneliness, the soft vanilla scent of wisteria hanging from the pergola, and the feeling that despite all that supposed testosterone, he was somehow half a man. He was pissed that his former wife still had the power to make him feel that way.

That's why athletes and movie stars get trophy wives, he thought as he stalked back to the car. *After you agree to an allowance there's nothing left to debate.*

Ward drove back to the Basalt Regency Inn and ate at the small coffee shop in the back. He considered going to Papa Vito's but decided he was too tired to listen to tales of the town. Besides, he didn't know if he wanted to be that close to the Al Huda Center. Not just now. Most important, he wanted to think. Since the confrontation in Battery Park he hadn't stopped moving—from Muslim accusers, from cops who were for-or-against him, from reporters. He had walked, flown, driven almost nonstop with no real idea where he was going, only what he was leaving.

Now he was still. And in those first moments of

calm, waiting for his dinner in the nearly deserted café, he realized several things. For the second time in his life, a chapter had closed. The first was his divorce; now, for the first time in his adult life, he had no job, no career. He was one of the vast unemployed of the ailing nation. He wasn't simply a visitor in Basalt, someone just passing through a quaint Midwestern community. They were, all of them, hurting, floundering Americans—

Don't do this, he thought suddenly. *Don't wallow.* Despair was counterproductive. *Just get some sleep, see your daughter, and think about what you'll do when you get back. Either fight the charges or put the NYPD in your rearview mirror and get a job in security somewhere. Or do what you joked about not doing, blogging or becoming the voice of sanity on FM radio somewhere.*

His cheeseburger and french fries arrived. The meat was plentiful and the trans-fat ban obviously hadn't reached Basalt. Half of what was on the plate took care of him. Paying, he found out the diner opened at six in the morning. Ward put in his order now so he could grab it and run up to collect Megan.

He dragged himself down the long corridor to the lobby and then up the single flight of stairs to his room. As he did, he was only dimly aware of the low-beams rushing toward the foothills.

CHAPTER EIGHT

For the first time in weeks, Scott Randolph didn't feel alone.

Lying in bed, staring at the ceiling, Randolph reflected about John Ward and how he wasn't like the men who sat at Papa Vito's and grumbled about life and wrote things like aMEriCCA on the place mats. He also wasn't like those people who had jobs and didn't want to make waves. He wasn't politically sensitive to the point of paralysis. Ward had smelled something wrong and came up to investigate and took up the cause of a man he didn't know. That was rare these days. Randolph knew that pride and fellowship were simply dormant in his fellow townspeople, and he missed it.

A hint of milky white light, like the first arc of moonrise, hit and then played swiftly across the ceiling above his bed. Randolph listened. The only lights he ever saw up here were police choppers looking for hikers who had failed to come home. He didn't hear a rotor or an engine. If it was a vehicle, it was gone. Sometimes kids would come up to the field to make out, but the lights were followed by the distant sound of music or beer bottles being hoisted from a cooler. He heard none of that. He considered investigating but his eyes had other ideas. They shut slowly.

A few minutes later the pigs began to snort. Randolph was instantly awake. It wasn't their usual sound, when one of them wanted a corn cob another had taken or tried to nose into a spot where another was sitting. It wasn't an aggressive sound, but, like this evening with the ATVs, they were grunts of annoyance. The farmer raised himself on an elbow. The barn was far enough from his room so that he couldn't ordinarily hear them moving about, bumping against the wood of the stalls, flopping over in the soft earth, or moving through the hay. But he heard something that suggested movement—creaking, the sucking of muddy earth, faint, faint whispers of activity.

Then Randolph heard a squeal that could only be one thing. A pig was hurt.

He threw off the blanket and jammed his feet into the slippers beside his bed. In the same motion he grabbed the shotgun leaning against his night table. The gun was always loaded. As he hurried to the bedroom door that opened into the back of the property, he flicked off the safety with his thumb. The door squeaked as he opened it but anyone who was inside the barn wouldn't hear it. There was no moon but he knew every inch of his land. He stepped from the small wooden stoop onto short grass made brittle by a parching summer. His eyes

were on the barn, on the open door through which
someone had entered.

Which was why he didn't see the man standing
on the other side of the door. He only felt, for a
moment, the tire iron as it came down on the base
of his skull—

It was still dark when Randolph woke. The back
of his neck was cold; it was more than a cool night
breeze washing over it. A sharp, throbbing ache
stretched from ear to ear. When he tried to move,
electricity fired through the back of his skull. He lay
still, his eyes looking out at the barn. He struggled
to remember. It was just the way he had last seen it,
the door on the north end opened inward. Only
now, there were no sounds coming from within.

He put his palms on the ground, felt the shotgun still lying beside him. He moved his hand
from it, pushed up very slowly while he raised his
head from the grass. He moved his head tenderly
from side to side, as he would if encouraging a
newborn piglet to breathe. He didn't have a lot of
mobility. There was a lump the size of a lemon. He
was able to get to his knees without bringing back
that searing pain. He waited there, breathing
slowly, feeling moisture run down the collar of his
pajamas. He closed his right hand around the gun
barrel, felt for the safety, locked it and used the
weapon like a cane to push himself up.

The world turned round as though it had been
swept up by a tornado. Randolph shut his eyes and

let his body adjust to standing. His mind was already replaying what had happened. He had let himself get cold-cocked. Hopefully, that was all the intruders wanted. Anyone from around here knew he had nothing of value in the house. All he owned were two-dozen pigs of varying size, from newborn piglets to full grown 250 pounders.

"Jennifer? Sharon?"

Those were two of the four young sows he kept for breeding. They tended to be the most vocal.

There was still no sound save for ringing in his ears. He had to get over there and see why they were not responding. Even sleeping pigs made occasional sounds. Randolph took a tentative step. Flame shot from the base of his neck up his skull. He winced, took another step, then another. Whirlpools of brownish-red swirled in front of him. He felt his supper rise in his throat. He kept going.

The farmer knew something was wrong when he was still twenty yards away. He couldn't hear and he couldn't see but he could smell and feel. The soil grew damp beneath his slippers. Each step released a faint metallic smell, like rusted iron.

"Oh, no."

The farmer increased his pace despite the lancing pain. He reached the door and, breathing heavily from the exertion, he snaked a hand around the frame and tugged the string of the wall-mounted lamp.

Covered with dust and spots of mud, the bulb threw a pale, murky light on the nearest of the pens. Everywhere Randolph's eyes moved, it looked

like one of Matthew Brady's photos of the Civil War.
Bodies were strewn here and there, each of them
nestled in a puddle of blood. Boards had been ripped
from the stalls and used to beat the pigs before they
were slain; he could see the bruising, the places
where nails had penetrated their flesh. There were
ragged tracks leading from each point of impact.
Struggling to get away, they had been ripped deeply
by the rusty nails. But that was just for fun. The pigs
died from having their throats slashed ear-to-ear.
He could tell they had struggled for breath: there
were deep indentations under their bodies. They
had flailed up and down, unable to rise, unable to
breathe, for the long seconds it took for them to
fall unconscious.

The pen doors had been opened so they could
be chased and beaten. He could see the prints their
flight had made in the earth. Now the pigs lay
helter-skelter as far as the light could see. Flies flitted
around them. As his hearing returned he could
hear their buzzing. It occurred to him to look for
human footprints. A flashlight hung from a nail on
the wall under the light. He switched it on, cast it
along the ground.

There were large, vague impressions in the
earth—not so much footprints as depressions.
The attackers had probably worn plastic bags on
their feet. This wasn't a drunken assault. It was pre-
meditated.

Why?

It was the only word, the only question he could
think of. Randolph looked away. He began to sob.

The tears were partly from the pain in his head, partly from the loss of his herd, but mostly for the unfathomable cruelty of the people who did this.

He finished turning around, walked back to the house, and called the police.

The tears were partly from the pain in his head, partly from the loss of his nerve, but mostly for the unfathomable cruelty of the people who did this.

He finished urinating, turned, walked back to the house, and called the police.

CHAPTER NINE

Ward was tired but he couldn't sleep. The reality of his situation had begun to take hold, and with nothing to do but think about it that's what he did. Fear had never been a part of his world, even on the most dangerous undercover operations. Those had been marked by an adrenaline surge, hyper-alertness, hair-trigger reflexes—but he was never afraid. He could live with being wrong but he didn't think he could live with being beaten.

What if he had no choice? What if the system was just too strong, stacked too heavily against him? The NYPD brass wasn't a gunrunning operation he could simply wait out, watching for a slip-up or encouraging them to take this bait or that. It was, like any government agency, a self-preserving monolith that didn't take risks. It was a hive that protected itself from bears even if it cost a few stinging drones.

Ward was turning over yet again when he heard the sirens. It took a moment for him to remember that it wasn't just New York background noise and to realize they were heading into the mountains. That could mean absolutely nothing. Or it could mean the ATV riders he'd scared away had gone back to the field to bust Randolph's hump. Randolph, the man with a shotgun. The riders, who might have their own drones to sacrifice for a cause.

The detective pulled on his clothes, ran out the door, and peered out the inn's side entrance. He saw the patrol car's flashing lights as they made their way into the foothills. He jumped into the Prius and followed them.

The red-and-blue light bar was just below the ridge, the glow visible from the road that ended at the field. The patrol car was definitely in the vicinity of Randolph's farm. Ward gave himself a mental kick for leaving the man alone; it was a good fit with the rest of his down-on-John mood.

Ward listened carefully over the silent motor. He did not hear an ambulance and hoped Randolph was all right. It also meant he probably hadn't shot anyone. When he arrived Ward parked beside the police car. He strode over, rolling his shoulders like a fighter to generate some warmth in the cold night air. He watched the play of a flashlight beam across the inside of the barn. As Ward neared, he saw—and smelled—the carnage. It was like arriving at a homicide crime scene where voices were muted as investigators sought to preserve their own quiet dignity, a veneer of humanity as they sought purpose and clues in the face of bloodshed. Only a police officer and Randolph were inside.

". . . back to the car to get the camera, take pictures for our files," the cop was saying. "You ought to take some for insurance, too. And you need to get that bump looked at."

"I will," Randolph promised.

"Need a ride to the hospital?" Ward asked.

The men turned as Ward spoke.

"John," Randolph said. There was relief as well as pain in that one word.

Ward only gave the dead animals a passing look. "They came back," he said.

"Who are you?" the officer asked. He stood about six-foot-five, a beanpole of a man who made up in height what he lacked in breadth.

"John Ward. I'm here from New York to visit my daughter." He added, "Joanne McCrea is my former wife."

The officer relaxed slightly at the mention of her name. He tucked his flashlight under his arm, jotted the name in a notepad he carried, and marked the time with his watch.

"Who was it?" Ward asked Randolph.

"We don't know, Mr. Ward," the officer said.

"*I* know, Harry," Randolph said.

"You don't," the officer replied.

Ward stopped beside Randolph. "Where were you attacked?"

"By the bedroom door," Randolph said, pointing.

Ward studied the large wound in the dull lamplight. "We know this much, officer. The assailant was about five-foot nine or ten, left handed, and used a metal object, probably a tire iron or a crow bar."

"And you know that how, Sherlock?" the officer asked.

"Because he's a New York City *detective*," Randolph said.

Hawks—by his nametag—was in his late twenties, Ward guessed, now that he had a close look at him. He was more full of training than experience.

"The upward angle of the swing is marked by a gash in the center of the lump," Ward explained. "The bruise starts on the left side which was the point of impact—I don't think the attacker reached around to hit his victim. And the cut itself is a tear. Baseball bat or blackjack doesn't do that." Ward borrowed Randolph's flashlight and walked over to the door. "With a wooden club wound, the skin may pop from internal pressure but that's not what happened here." He squatted and cast the light across the ground by the door. He found the bloodstains, looked around. "There," he said, shining the beam. "Narrow drag marks where the perpetrator wiped off the blood. Tire iron for sure."

A siren reached them and Ward rose. Moments later a Toyota Camry arrived with a red light spinning on top. A woman in civilian clothes got out. Ward saw the other officer straighten slightly. The woman was nearly two heads shorter than the officer but broad-shouldered and walked with a natural swagger. She looked to be in her early forties. Her long brown hair was held in place with a large plastic clip, done hurriedly when she received word of the attack, Ward surmised. Her eyes were alert.

"Chief Brennan," the officer said.

"Officer Hawks," she replied. "Why don't I hear an ambulance siren?"

"Mr. Randolph wouldn't let me call one," Hawks informed her.

She faced Randolph. "Why not?"

"When I leave here it's gonna be upright, lest I'm dead," he said. "Except for a tomato on the back of my neck I'm fine." His voice caught as he spoke. He cleared his throat, wiped his eyes with his sleeve. "It's my pigs, dammit. They all been throat-cut."

The police chief gave his upper arm a reassuring pat. She noted the mud on his shoulder and jawline. She looked at Ward. "Who's our guest?"

Ward introduced himself. He stood where he was, instinctively protecting his corner of the crime scene.

"Right—I read about you," Brennan remarked. There appeared to be caution in her tone. Ward couldn't be sure; it was all she said to him. She spoke to Hawks over her shoulder. "You get photos?"

"I was just about to take care of that, Chief," Hawks said.

She shooed him with a cock of her head then looked at Randolph's wound. She told Hawks to get pictures of that as well. "You want an ice pack?" she asked Randolph.

"I want the guys who did this," he snapped.

"We all do," she reminded him. That seemed to

calm the man a little. "Dispatcher said you told him there were riders up here earlier. Same drill?"

"Yeah, except that John here showed up and apparently scared them off."

"How'd you do that?" she asked, surveying the ground outside the barn.

"White Prius," he replied.

The chief's eyes snapped to him. "I'm sorry?"

"Those engines are quiet. I heard shots and started across the field. Scared them to have company, I think."

She nodded. The caution seemed to have acquired a touch of admiration. She took a wide turn around the crime scene, avoiding the places where the perpetrators had stepped. The chief shook her head as she walked. Ward knew why. Not only were there no footprints, the impressions crisscrossed each other so that it was impossible to tell how many individuals had been here.

"I'll have sanitation come in the morning and take the animals away," she told Randolph. "I'll want one or two for the lab."

Randolph nodded.

"I'm real sorry, Scott."

"Thanks." The farmer fell dead silent for a moment, as though the enormity of what had happened was just sinking in. He forced himself out of it. "John had some thoughts about whoever hit me."

"Oh?"

Ward told her what he had told the others. She took it all in then said, "We've got a lot of guys in town who are five-nine or -ten, but it's a start. Thanks."

"While you're looking, keep an eye out for clean boots," Ward suggested. "Those ATVs kicked up a lot of dust. The perps would want to brush off the evidence."

"Or change their shoes," the chief said.

"Not likely," Ward said.

"Oh?"

"Shorter guy would like the big heels," Ward told her.

She grinned. "Need a job?"

Hawks, who was in the barn taking pictures, looked back like a kid who was no longer hall monitor.

"I *am* currently unemployed," Ward admitted, "but I'm not sure my references would pass muster."

"I'm not sure I'd care," Brennan smiled. She looked at Randolph and her smile faded. He wavered a little and she took his elbow in her hand to support him. "Time we got you to the hospital. We need X-rays for the file and you need medical attention. I didn't overrule you on the EMS, but you are gonna ride with the seat down."

The farmer nodded weakly. The shock had propped him up. Now that it was passing, it was as though his will had been sapped. Ward noticed that his knees were shaking and his shoulders had drooped. For a moment it looked as though he would fall forward. Ward put the flashlight down and jumped over to assist. They each took an arm and walked him to her car.

Randolph leaned against the hood as she lowered the seat. "I'm taking him to Mid Valley if you want to check on him." She leaned nearer. "He won't be coming home tonight."

"Gotcha," Ward said. He helped her put Randolph in the passenger's seat.

"I'm sorry to be trouble," Randolph said. He was wincing now, chronically. The short walk to the car had taxed him more than he'd admit.

"You can make it up to us when you're better," Ward said as they shut the door.

"I'll call when I'm leaving the hospital," she told Officer Hawks as she ran around to the driver's side.

Ward watched until the car was out of sight. Then he picked up the flashlight and went back to his car. Hawks continued taking pictures, looking over frowningly as the Prius pulled away. Ward didn't take it personally. The kid felt threatened. He'd get over it. Ward didn't think Brennan's offer was sincere. Whatever she thought about what had happened in New York, it was just her way of extending support to a fellow officer who had taken flak in the line of duty.

Ward drove to the road and parked, leaving the headlights on. He got out and walked slowly along the middle of the road. He was scanning the rocky soil just beyond the asphalt curb that ran along the side. After a few minutes he found what he was looking for. He took several pictures with his cell phone.

When he was finished he drove back to the inn, confident now that he'd be able to sleep. Before turning out the light he called the hospital to check on Randolph. The nurse said she was only permitted to give information to family, but did say he was "resting very comfortably" so she could not put the call through. Ward thanked her for that.

Within minutes he, too, was resting very comfortably.

CHAPTER TEN

It wasn't a long sleep, but it was the first restful night Ward had enjoyed in a while.

The alarm went off at 6:15 and, before showering, Ward called over to the diner to make sure his take-out breakfast would be waiting. Half an hour later he plopped the bag on his seat, his cell beside it, and was on Ridge Road a half-hour after that, in plenty of time to pick up his daughter. There was no point calling the hospital again; he would stop by after breakfast.

Ward cranked down the windows as he drove. It was cold, but the air had an invigorating quality that chased away lingering sleep. As he climbed the road, his eyes were drawn to the ridge that marked the start of Randolph's property. He couldn't see the house or farm from here but he passed the spot where he had taken the picture. He slowed. In the light, he saw something he had missed the night before: flecks of blood on the ground. That made sense. The intruders had wallowed in the stuff back

at the barn then paused here to remove the bags
from their feet. Some of the blood would have
come off. He pulled over and crouched by the spill.
There was nothing but what he had seen the night
before: a partial footprint. The blood spots satisfied
him that the shoe belonged to one of the pig-
killers. The print was left when he put on or took
off the bags—the plastic grocery store sacks, most
likely—that were used to distort any footprints left
behind.

As he squatted there, Ward saw a black van coming
up the road. He hurried to the Prius, punched up the
map screen, and pretended to study it. The van
stopped behind him, but only for a moment. It pulled
around him slowly and he looked up at the dark windows. He could see nothing of the inside as the van
continued on up the road.

"Too many years on the streets," he muttered.
There, everyone was a potential criminal from the
homeless guy who might shiv you to the fellow
officer who might shiv you without a knife, or
worse. He pulled from the curb and continued up
the road.

The van had pulled around the fence and was
going up the dirt road. No one lived up there but
Randolph. Ward slowed. There was no one watching the farmer's place. He didn't know if these
were the perps, what mischief was intended, or
even what more damage could be done.

"But you'll never know if you don't follow them,"
Ward told himself. He looked at the clock. Twenty
minutes past seven. Swearing, he went around the
fence and followed the van at a distance.

The big, black vehicle wobbled across the field as Ward had done the night before. It stopped well short of the Randolph property, its surface shining like marble in the early morning sun. The back doors were facing Ward. They opened and four young men emerged. They were fussing about something in the van but it was too far for him to see inside the shadowy interior. He didn't know whether they had bikes with them or picnic baskets. Ward drove slowly onto the field, his heart racing with a familiar rush.

First one, then all four of the men stopped and looked at the Prius. He drove closer, saw that they were swarthy. He put them all at between sixteen and nineteen, ranging in height from five-six to the leader who was about six-one. The four had what appeared to be Asiatic features. They stood proudly, not as interlopers but as though they belonged here. Just now he noticed a bead necklace around one of the men.

Of course. Ward stopped the car some twenty yards from the group. He got out. "Good morning," he said. These guys were Native Americans. Probably not the ones he was looking for, but you never could tell without checking.

The others stood in silence. Then, at a signal from the man with the beads, they resumed their activities. These consisted of pulling blankets from the van and carrying them to the other side. Ward approached cautiously, not from fear but from respect. They worked in silence. The men had just finished spreading the blankets on the ground when the leader turned on him.

"What do you want?" the youth demanded.

"I was curious," Ward said.

"About what? Us? Life? Why the universe has turned against you?"

Ward was not expecting attitude. "Slow down," he said calmly, as if he were addressing a crackhead in an all-night bodega.

"You are the one who is rushing," the young man replied.

"Am I? Okay, we can do this your way. Why is the universe against me?"

The youth scowled. "This is a joke to you."

"Trust me, friend, there is nothing funny in my world right now. Buddy of mine was roughed up here last night, his pigs slaughtered. I was up here looking for clues—tire tracks, discarded cigarettes, that sort of thing."

"Yes, you mistrust like a policeman" the man said.

"Do I?" Ward replied. Though he had to admit the man was right.

"I don't recognize you," the man said.

"I'm not from around here," Ward replied. "You?"

"We were here when the land was new," the young man said. "We are Ute."

"Do you come up here every day?" Ward asked. "Some kind of ritual?"

"We heard of the deaths and came to pray for their spirits."

That was one Ward had never heard in New York. "I see." He didn't know that animals had spirits.

"Would you care to join us?" the man said after a moment.

"I, uh—I have to meet someone." He lingered a moment, heard himself say. "I'm sorry I intruded."

"I believe you."

Ward was surprised by his own reaction. In New York, passing a house of worship had no effect on him. Here, he felt like he was tromping on something hallowed. That was the difference between spirituality and institutional religion, he guessed.

"How is Mr. Randolph?" one of the men asked.

"He's in the hospital. Took a bad blow to the head. I'm going up there soon. I'll know more then."

"Tell him Thomas Chapoose sends his breath," said the shortest of the youths. "I worked with him on the farm last summer. He is a good man."

"He is very good." Ward agreed and took a few steps closer. "Do you have any idea who might have done this, or why?"

"The who and the why are one," the leader said.

"I don't follow."

"This is sacred land."

"To—?"

"Our people," he said.

"Why would that matter to anyone who isn't Ute?"

"Our people used to honor the sun from this spot. We celebrated its rising and, when it set behind the mountains, we thanked it for the light. It was then the animal spirits converged and spoke to those who wished to hear them."

Ward looked around. Something clicked. "The high ground," he said. "You can pretty much see everything from this spot."

"The spirits had room to gather, along with the people who communed with them. And from below, those who could not climb could still see and be seen."

So Scott Randolph had the highest private, most visible property in the region. That was a possible "why."

"Is there anything *else* you wish to ask?" the shortest man asked.

It was a leading question. Ward decided to tug the thread a little. "Is there anything else you want to share with me?"

The youth said, "This land we're standing on is public land. We come and go as we please and, once here, we obey the law. We have no need of Mr. Randolph's property."

"Does everyone feel that way?"

"We do not know 'everyone,'" the youth replied. "Only our own people. Over the decades the Randolphs have given us food when we've needed it, and jobs. It would dishonor all if any one did him harm."

"Do you have any idea who might not feel that way?"

"If we knew that, we would be summoning a very different spirit for a very different purpose," the leader replied.

Ward nodded. The detective wasn't sure he

understood but he absolutely respected their conviction.

The leader rallied the others with a cock of his head and they carried their blankets beyond the van and spread them carefully on the grass. Ward crouched—it felt rude to stand, hypocritical to kneel—and watched as they knelt toward the sun and raised their faces and arms to the sky. The wind carried the small sounds they were making in a tongue he couldn't understand.

After a few minutes he returned to the car, feeling strangely settled. But then the old John Ward returned, focused on the information he had picked up and disturbed at the way it fit with the rest of what was happening in Basalt.

CHAPTER ELEVEN

Joanne opened the door. Disgust was apparent in every line of her face. "You're late. Again."

Ward looked at his watch. "Yeah, a little. We'll eat in the car. I'll get her there on time."

"You still don't get it," his former wife said. "You say you'll be here, you should be here. Not ten or even five minutes later."

"It couldn't be helped," he said. He saw Megan sitting in the kitchen.

"She called you—"

"Crap. My phone was in the car. Look, we can stand here arguing or I can take Megan to school."

"She's eating right now—"

"Yeah, I see that."

"I'll send her out when she's done."

"Jesus, Joanne. Let me come in and sit with her. Please."

Joanne thought for a moment. "We're giving her good energy right now."

"You're what?"

"She'll be out in a few minutes." Joanne started to close the door.

"Wait!" Ward said, stepping partway in. "You heard what happened over at Scott Randolph's?"

"I'm an emergency veterinary volunteer with the fire department," she said. "I received a call but I wasn't needed."

"I was there last night after it happened," Ward said. "I went back this morning to see if I could help find the bastards who did this. That's why I was late."

"Did you do that for us, John, or for yourself?"

"I just wanted to help," Ward said.

"Help your daughter first," Joanne said. "Prioritize."

She went to shut the door and Ward stepped back. The click sounded loud and final. He had to stop himself from slamming the frame with the heel of his hand. *Good energy.* What was this, freakin' Tibet? Ward turned and kicked the air and walked back to the car and leaned against the hood with his arms tightly crossed. He felt like driving off, like running from the whole poisonous relationship. But he couldn't leave Megan behind, however much Joanne tried to make every conflict seem like abandonment.

Megan came out less than two minutes after her mother left. She was carrying a Green Earth backpack and eating a piece of whole wheat toast with a spread that looked like jam but was probably kelp. He smiled at her; she smiled crookedly back but quickly averted her eyes. He opened the car door for her. Joanne was not watching, as far as he could tell.

"Sorry I'm late," he said.

"Mom explained. She said you're trying to help Mr. Randolph."

"I want to help find the people who hurt him," Ward told her.

"Are you allowed to?" she asked as he settled into the driver's seat.

"I met the police chief last night," he answered. "She—" He was going to say *offered me a job* but he didn't want to get Megan's hopes up. She wouldn't understand the context.

"She what?"

"Wanted my professional opinion so I gave it to her," he said.

"You man, you." She grinned.

He laughed. "Yeah, that's your dad."

"Do you know the way to my school?"

"Haven't the faintest idea," he said as he backed from the driveway.

She smiled back and directed him through town to Basalt Middle School. She declined his offer to take the breakfast he'd bought for her lunch, saying she had her own.

It was a quick trip and a quick good-bye. If Megan was upset with how the morning went, she hadn't shown it much. It seemed—and he hoped he wasn't reading anything into their brief exchange—that his daughter understood him. Ward watched her go, returned her wave when she turned back, then drove off. He was still angry at Joanne for stirring things up when she should have been settling them, but he wasn't as mad as he was before.

Ward ate the pancakes he'd bought, using his fingers as he drove through town. He used the GPS to find the hospital and was there in fifteen minutes. Visiting hours were not until ten, but Police Chief Brennan arrived and took Ward in with her.

"Thanks," he said as they walked down the long corridor. "I guess you don't work undercover after all."

It took her a moment to get what he meant. "Oh, the uniform?" she said. "Yeah, well, I'm on duty now."

"I found blood up by the curb on Ridge Road," he said.

She nodded. "I saw that too last night," she said.

"When?"

"I went back after I dropped Scott off. Also found the partial of a Timberland white sole work boot, size nine I imagine."

Ward grinned. "Nice."

"What?"

"I took a picture of that myself," Ward said. "I was going to take it to a shoe store this morning."

"We try to do our jobs here," she said. "Problem is, about half the county wears those boots. Got 'em myself."

"Did you also notice the blood?"

"Got the lab guy out of bed to take samples. It's Scott Randolph's," she told him. "Got those results before I came down."

Ward was feeling a little stupid; he *had* assumed they wouldn't go right to the curb and check for evidence where the attackers might have parked. What made it worse was that Brennan knew exactly what he'd thought.

The small yellow room got the morning sun and the blinds were angled to throw it in slats across the bed and walls. Randolph looked like he'd gone ten rounds with a heavyweight. His neck was bandaged and his eyes were swollen with a single bruise that stretched across the bridge of his nose; his jaw was also banged up.

"Doc says I hit the ground face-first," the farmer said.

"That was my diagnosis last night," the chief replied. "Mud splatters tell tales." They walked to the right side of the bed. "Everything still works, though?"

"So far."

"That's what matters most," Brennan said.

Randolph nodded. He looked at Ward. "Thanks for coming, John."

"Of course."

Brennan thought for a moment then said, "I just wanted to go over what you said last night. You said you didn't see or hear anything that happened?"

"Only headlights on the wall, my pigs squealing, and me going outside. Nothing till I came to."

"Which we put at about ninety minutes later, according to what Doc O'Hara says about the death of the pigs—"

"The slaughter," Randolph said. "My pigs were slaughtered."

She dipped her head in acquiescence. "Slaughtered. That means the butchers worked fast and knew the lay of the land."

"You mean they knew my property?"

"They knew where to go, where you slept, and how to get up there unseen," she said. "We talked to some of the people on Ridge Road this morning. No one noticed any lights. Is there anyone who was so familiar with your place they could approach in the dark and do this by flashlight?"

"Chief, you know how many people have worked for me over the years," Randolph said. "There's no secret what I have and where it is." He grew solemn. "What I had," he said quietly.

"Other than the encounter with those off-roaders, has anything happened out of the ordinary?"

"What, like UFOs? Crop circles?"

She didn't answer. Even Ward knew he was venting.

"Chief, nothing different has happened for as long as I've been up there," Randolph said.

"What about up at your hunting cabin? Anybody see you dressing a deer? Animal rights activists, anything like that?"

He shook his head. "Not that I know of."

"Has anyone offered to buy your place?" the police chief asked.

"Like I told John, I hear from folks at the bank that it gets run up the flagpole every couple of months but I don't pay it no attention." He regarded her through his swollen eyes. "Look, we know who did this—"

"We don't," she insisted.

"Then we know who *probably* did this," Randolph

said. "Why don't you just question those bloody Muslim kids?"

"Because I have absolutely no evidence," she replied. "I'm not allowed to go on hunches, Scott. I need proof. I need the weapon with which you were assaulted. I need a tag from one of the bikes."

"They probably cart 'em around in a van or truck."

"That's just about everyone who owns an ATV or dirt bike," she said. "I'm not permitted to interrogate someone just because you don't like him."

"How are we going to find anything out if we can't ask questions, let alone knock heads together?" Randolph asked.

She laid a hand on Randolph's shoulder. "*We* aren't going to worry about it. My department is. I've got the lab guys going up to your place later, just to make sure we didn't miss anything. But this isn't a big town, Scott. Someone will say something, boast about what they did up there, and someone will hear it."

"Bare feet and hot coals'll work a lot faster," Randolph said.

"And no court in the United States will admit as evidence what we might discover," she replied.

Randolph shook his head. "I've got no livelihood, I'm takin' my meals through a straw, and I can't help find the a-holes who put me here. I didn't feel this helpless when we had that wildfire in eighty-eight." He turned a bloated eye toward Ward. Suddenly, the eye narrowed slightly. "You know what? I didn't whine then, now that I think of it. To hell with me. How's your daughter? Things goin' okay for you?"

"We're working on it," Ward said. He was proud and impressed at the way Randolph had just bootstrapped himself.

"Good man."

"She read about your exploits?" the chief asked.

"Seems like half the countryside read about it," Ward said.

The chief's hand was still on Randolph's shoulder. She gave it a gentle squeeze. "Look, you need to rest and I need to get to work. Promise me you won't push to get yourself out of here?"

"Chief, *that* I cannot promise. I vaguely remember saying something about wanting to be upright last night and I meant it."

"Okay, but I've left instructions that no one takes you home except me. And if I don't think you're ready, you'll be thumbing a ride in this pretty paper gown."

"That won't stop me."

"Maybe not, so how about this." Her eyes grew hard. "Someone means you harm. If you're here, we can look after you. You go back, feeling less than one hundred percent, and you're putting yourself at risk. Don't be the first Randolph who couldn't tell the difference between brave and stupid."

Randolph was silent for a moment. Then he looked at them, his eyes moist. "I was thinkin' last night, before this went down, that it's good to know folks have my back. Thanks."

Brennan and Ward left without a word. They continued to the parking lot in silence and stopped beside Ward's car.

"Scott's stubborn as a rash but he's good people," Brennan said as she slipped on her sunglasses.

"I really like him," Ward said. He couldn't remember the last time he'd said that about anyone.

"So what are you thinking of doing now?"

"About?"

The police chief gave him a give-me-a-break look.

Ward reached through the open window for the bag with the coffee, now cold. He pried back the plastic lid. "You're convinced I'm going to do something."

"As sure as I know what year it is."

He sipped the coffee.

"Okay, I'll go first," she said. "I've got nothing on this. The lab couldn't tell me much about the weapon used to kill the pigs, other than that it was a butcher knife. The incision on the throat was not designed for a pig."

"Meaning?"

"The butchers could have gotten in and out faster with simple venipuncture of the jugular," she said. "A few quick pokes below the ear, let it bleed out, on to the next. That kind of information is available online. You don't have to wrestle with each pig, the way these guys did judging from the impressions in the pens. No, the throat-cuttings were patterned after human beheadings. Have you seen any of those videos from the Middle East?"

Ward confessed that he had seen several of the many dozen that had appeared online: The videos were included in the NYPD's mandatory anti-terror training. The instructors wanted officers to understand the kind of monsters they were facing.

The victim was typically thrown on his side with the killer kneeling behind his shoulders, literally sawing his throat with a blade while another man held his head down. Ward would never forget the sheets of blood, the dying man's screams, then the awful gurgling as his severed windpipe tried to suck air through the wound, drawing only blood. It took about six or seven seconds for the victim to go limp but it seemed hellishly longer.

"The pigs were slaughtered the same way," Brennan said. "The cut went through the trachea nearly severing the head—far more than was needed to kill it."

"Someone train them, you think? Or did they watch the videos too?"

"Not sure," she admitted.

"But they were definitely sending a message," Ward said, "letting us know what kind of culture they come from, telling us they're not afraid of this level of violence, and warning us that next time it could be people."

"Some of that, anyway," she said.

"But not leaving any actionable evidence," Ward said. "You say the pigs were held down. Was there—"

"Good get," Brennan said. "Yes, we found smudged glove prints on one pig's head as it was pressed into the ground and held there. The fibers didn't tell us anything other than that they were smallish hands. No palm prints."

He took another long sip. It was funny how the taste of cold coffee brought him back to his rookie year and long stakeouts.

"First thing we've got to do is eliminate a frame-up," Ward said.

"Am I missing something?" she asked.

"Pigs, pork—forbidden to Muslims. Somebody looking to frame them for a crime might go for something obvious like that."

"It's a thought," she admitted.

"I met some Utes up in the field earlier. They said they were there to pray for the spirits of the pigs. True?"

"I'd believe that," Brennan said. "They're proud of their past but they don't have their hands out, like so many others. In a lot of ways, Randolph is more like their ancestors than he is like everyone else here. He lives off the land, respects it, doesn't go in for a lot of modern conveniences. He still had an outhouse until about fifteen years ago."

"So who would be on the short list of potential framers?"

"That's just it," she said. "There's a bunch of people here who hate how the Muslims have come in and started buying up the town. There's been a lot of grumbling over at Papa Vito's but there hasn't been any violence against them since that started. Hell, their money saved a bunch of folks from going under. There was some uneasy joking about, 'Hey, it's just our gas money coming back to us.' But nobody has taken it to the next level. There hasn't been so much as a 'towel-head go home' on the community center wall."

Ward drank more coffee. "So did you walk me to my car to chat or is there some other reason?"

"You mean to make sure you got out of town?"

He shrugged.

"I am not so stupid to put ego and bad press ahead of the safety of my town and fellow citizens, Detective Ward—"

"John," he said.

"John."

"What exactly does that mean?" he asked. "You don't seriously mean to hire me."

"Not at this point, but if you're planning on staying in Basalt for a while I can't tell you who you can or can't watch or talk to."

He finished the coffee and looked around.

"John, my folks had one of those fake copies of the Bill of Rights framed on our living room wall, you know the kind that cost a quarter and were artificially aged?"

"Yup. I had the Gettysburg Address."

"Well, I know what that document says. I also know, the First Amendment notwithstanding, that I don't have the right to shout *Fire* in a crowded theater. The Bill of Rights should come with a user's guide and it should have a section called, 'What to Do When a Different Set of Laws Comes to Town.'"

"Meaning what? Muslim Sharia law? We have separation of church and state—"

"Actually, we don't, John, which is the trouble," Brennan said. "We have separation of church *within* state. People haven't grasped the fact that the Bill of Rights gives legal protection to what is effectively a fifth column."

He looked at her with surprise. "You've given this some thought."

"I've got to be one way with folks like Scott to keep them from going off half-cocked, but I'm not naive," she said. "I'm going to say it to you because you've seen it, but I'll deny I said it if it comes up again. Our nation is facing a stealth jihad. That's how I came to read about your experience in New York. Yes, it made some national news outlets but I saw how you were railroaded with the unwitting help of minority police and liberal media. America won't need its throat cut: our hearts are bleeding all over the pavement. It's got to stop." She reached into her shirt pocket, took out a business card, and wrote something on the back. "This is my cell number," she said, handing him the card. "In case you need it."

"You're serious about this," he said. "I mean, my staying."

She said, "Yeah, I'm serious. John, I'm scared for the country."

Ward slipped the card in his wallet. He only just became aware of the sounds of traffic on East Valley Road and nearby Highway 82. He had been riveted, surprised, and unexpectedly heartened by their discussion. He extended his hand. She clasped it tightly.

"Chief, it's been great talking to you," Ward said. "I have some business with Mr. Dickson at the bank. I was thinking about setting up an account for Megan. Any thoughts about him?"

"He had some tough times before the influx of short sales," she said.

"Any chatter about that?"

"He started taking a much harder line on foreclosures," she said. "People looked at him like a collaborator."

"Yeah, I picked up on that when I popped by yesterday. No threats?"

She shook her head then took his hand. She locked her other hand on his before releasing it. There was gratitude in her smile. "I need to get you a hat," she said.

He shot her a quizzical look.

She pointed at the Prius. "White hat to go with the white horse."

When she was gone, he reached through the window of the Prius, grabbed the bag of half-eaten breakfast and stuffed it in a trash can beside a street lamp.

Damn, but she was right. He hadn't felt this clean, this right, this unencumbered in a long, long time. There was no district attorney, no straitjacketing regulations, no sense that lurking behind every good and honest action was a punk attorney looking to stick a pitchfork in his backside.

No.

It was different.

It was the West.

CHAPTER TWELVE

During anti-terror training, Ward learned that one of hallmarks of a terrorist was an air of euphoria that increased in the days and hours leading to an attack. That feeling lessened without disappearing entirely as the hours became minutes and the execution of the mission became all-encompassing. The rapture came from knowing something of which the people around you were oblivious, something that would have a tremendous impact on their lives or even end those lives. That excitement was enhanced by the fact that the terrorist was immune to laws and restrictions. The combination of power and certainty was godlike.

To a smaller degree, Ward felt that exhilaration now. If he were still a cop working in New York where everyone was always on high-alert, where laws and protocol had to be strictly obeyed, he could never attempt what he was planning. He felt liberated in a way he never had.

Ward used his cell to place a call from the parking lot of the Fryingpan Savings and Loan before entering the bank. Earl Dickson was on the phone when Ward arrived. He sat on the sofa to wait for the manager. He acknowledged an elderly woman seated beside him, the only other patron waiting for an officer. She was solving a Word Search puzzle in a magazine.

"The bank doesn't seem as crowded as it was yesterday morning," Ward remarked pleasantly.

"You're not a local," she said.

"No."

"Monday is Take Your Home and Business Day," the white-haired lady explained, with the slight edge of someone describing wallpaper they didn't like. "At least, that's what everyone calls it. The opening of the business week is when the checks are due. Though most people come here with pleas. They'd come with lawyers, but who can afford them?"

"Do the pleas ever work?"

She shook her head gravely. "I'm here to see my banker, Ms. Wood, and open an account for my granddaughter. It used to be so crowded here in the mornings. So crowded. Everyone chatty." The head continued to shake as she went back to her puzzle.

Ward was about to ask what she thought of the new faces in town when he saw Dickson hang up. He excused himself—he actually used the word "ma'am," unaware that it had ever been a part of his vocabulary—and strode to the desk. Dickson had already turned his attention to his computer monitor.

"Mr. Dickson?" Ward said to the man's back.

The manager's thick neck turned. He looked up at the newcomer. There was a slight, formal smile, a touch of inquiry in his eyes, but his demeanor was otherwise flat and uninterested.

"My name is John Ward. I'm the former husband of Joanne McCrea. Your daughter used to babysit—"

"Yes, Mr. Ward. Angie mentioned she saw you. How are you?"

"Not bad."

Dickson swiveled his chair around and gestured to the thinly cushioned plastic seat beside the desk. Before sitting, Ward absently angled the chair so that he could see the front door.

"How may the bank be of service?" Dickson asked.

"Well, I find myself temporarily unemployed and was thinking about opening some kind of investment account. Let my money work for me."

"We read about what happened," Dickson said. "Very sorry."

"Thanks." Ward watched Dickson carefully. "I've been told that the Midwest Revitalization Initiative has been making some forward looking deals and I was also told you might be able to hook me up."

The banker asked defensively. "Who told you that?"

"Actually, I overheard it at Papa Vito's."

"Happy-hour gossip. I've handled some local transactions for them but I am not their agent."

"I see. Do you think it's a good investment?"

"I don't know, Mr. Ward."

"Who would I talk to, then?"

"They have offices in Chicago—"

"Locally, I mean."

"There is no local office."

"But you—"

"Everything I did for them was conducted online," Dickson said with mounting impatience.

"Oh? I understood that they have agents in town."

The banker's expression no longer held even the hint of welcome. "I'm sorry, you really shouldn't listen to men well into their beer. Was there anything else?"

"Yes," Ward said. "I don't believe you."

Dickson shocked to full alert. It took a moment for the electric jolt to fade, then he leaned forward. "Mr. Ward, that kind of bullying may work on the streets of New York. Or in your case, it may not. Either way, it does not intimidate me."

"I'm not trying to intimidate you, Mr. Dickson. I'm trying to help you, to help the town where my daughter lives. I think the MRI *does* have people here and I think they're up to no good."

"I'm not interested in your suspicions—"

"I don't believe that, either. I think they scare the pants off you. Why? Are you into something you shouldn't be?"

"That's enough!" Dickson barked. He rose stiffly. "If you've no business here, please leave."

The staff was looking over. "Okay, Mr. Dickson." Ward stood slowly. He had been watching the door. "By the way, it looks like you've got a visitor."

A swarthy man had arrived less than a minute

before and was standing just outside, talking on the phone.

Ward watched Dickson's face as he turned. The bank manager's cheeks flushed and his eyes snapped back toward the detective. "What have you done?"

"I called the Al Huda Center and told them you have a new investment to discuss," Ward said. He put his face close to that of the banker. "Hog futures. You tell them there's no way in hell they're getting the Randolph farm. You also tell them they're going to replace every last pig they killed, with interest."

"I don't want to get involved in this."

"I don't care," Ward said. "Just deliver the message."

"Why don't you tell them yourself?"

"I'm betting that slob outside knows you," Ward said. "He'll see you're afraid. He'll listen."

Dickson was looking around as though searching a sandbag to throw in the breach. "I'm telling you, you've got the wrong idea."

"I don't think so," Ward replied. "An innocent man would've treated me as a crank caller. That guy outside—he's pissed."

Dickson shook his head. "You're making a terrible mistake, Mr. Ward. Another one. You have family."

"Oh, so we're going the ugly route? You've got family too, which is why it'd be best if this ended here and now. It's up to you."

"You don't understand," Dickson hissed.

"I think I do. We've both got daughters we love,

and they've got yours working at the Fawaz Dry
Cleaner to keep *you* in line. I've mucked that up,
which is all the more reason to talk to the law while
you still can."

Dickson's face was pale. "Get out."

"Mr. Dickson, call me the worst father in the
world but I can't live with the idea of handing my
daughter a broken America, one where women
have no rights and liberty is just a street name. I'm
betting that you and the other townspeople will
stand shoulder to shoulder and stop this before it's
too late."

The banker did not reply. Ward waited. The
man didn't even move. Ward sighed and wrote his
cell number on a foreclosure notice. He pushed
the document in front of the bank manager.

"If you change your mind, call. I'd also like to
know what your friendly neighborhood Muslim outreach liaison has to say, if you care to share that."

He left Dickson standing stiffly behind his desk,
the two men uncertain what would happen next
but only one of them eager for it. Ward passed the
darker-skinned man on his way out. He was about
five-eleven in a well-tailored beige suit and neat
beard stubble, cleared away under the chin. Except
for the facial hair, he reminded Ward of the
muscle he saw in mob stakeouts. The man's fingers
were thick as carrots, his eyes dark, his mouth an
unforgiving line. There was nothing in the man's
body or posture that said "compromise."

Ward passed without exchanging a glance,
though he did look at the man's feet. They were
large—larger than the mush-prints he had seen at

the farm. Ward suspected that this man had nothing to do with the attack. He didn't look the hell-raising sort. This mule was probably just what he seemed to be: the dumb eyes and ears of whoever was unwilling to leave the Al Huda Center, albeit one who could take care of himself if he had to. Defense only. His brain probably wasn't built for tactics.

Ward was sure his picture was being taken by the cell phone. It would be sent to whoever did do the actual ass-kicking. That was fine. He'd be happy to have the bad guys come to him. He only needed to make sure Megan was out of the line of fire. He was betting these guys didn't want to kill anyone yet: if they had, Scott Randolph would be in a box instead of the hospital. Still, now that he'd declared himself, Ward couldn't afford to put anything past them. He would pick up Megan after school, take her home, and tell Joanne to keep her there except for classes or any other activity where she was in a crowd. Joanne wouldn't like it and Megan might be frightened, but it had to be.

Ward couldn't wait for that conversation. But he believed what he told Dickson. His brother had died for that ideal. This was not a poker game with a fold option.

The detective got in his car, checked the rearview mirror, saw the man taking a picture of the Prius. He wasn't even being subtle about it. Ward wasn't surprised. Part of their job was to try and make people paranoid. That was why they call it *terror*. Ward considered going over and calling him out but decided against it. He had a feeling where this was going and wanted to let it play out.

Ward pulled from the spot and headed toward the inn. As he drove up the road he found himself smiling. He had faced down a Russian gunrunner. With guns. Let this guy and his handlers think that Ward could be frightened. The greatest strength of a man, of a people, is when the enemy underestimates them. Ward realized that what he was doing here, what Randolph and Chief Brennan and he were *all* doing, was erasing the destructive hyphenates. They weren't a New York–American or Basalt-American. They weren't a Farmer-American or Cop-American. They weren't a Male-American or Female-American.

They were, simply, American.

CHAPTER THIRTEEN

Immediately after Ward drove off, Earl Dickson went to a back room where the safe deposit boxes were kept. He moved in an unhurried fashion, forcing himself to smile at the tellers as he went behind the counter, affecting composure he did not feel. He said something to no one in particular about that being the "crazy cop from New York" as he entered the room and shut the door, pushed the "in use" button, and with shaking fingers speed-dialed Aseel Gahrah on his cell phone.

The smooth, familiar voice answered at once. "Good morning, Mr. Dickson."

"Scott Randolph's farm!" Dickson said through his teeth. "Did you do that?"

There was a long, unsettling silence. "Why don't you call me when you're feeling better?"

"We need to talk about this *now!*" Dickson insisted. "I heard about it on the radio. I had a sick feeling in my gut but I didn't want to believe you had anything to do with it."

"Do you know this man who came to see you?"

"No, not really."

"Who is he?"

"John Ward," Dickson said. "He's the New York cop who was in the news for harassing a street vendor."

"So Hamza thought when he observed him," Gahrah said. "Another Muslim-hating, unemployed American. Why is he here?"

"He came to visit his daughter."

"Why did he see you?"

"He said he wanted to invest in MRI," Dickson said. "When he brought up pigs I told him to leave."

"Did he really want to invest with us?"

"I don't know."

"I'm told he was at the Randolph place last night. Did you ask if *he* did it?"

Dickson frowned. "How do you know he was there?"

Gahrah did not reply. The banker leaned back hard against a row of boxes. Despite the air conditioning he was perspiring.

"Listen, Aseel," Dickson went on. "This whole thing was supposed to be a peaceful process, everything off the radar."

"Nothing has changed. There is one trouble-maker—"

"*Plus* what happened on the Randolph farm," Dickson said. "Never mind the pigs—they assaulted someone, put him in the hospital!"

"That need not concern you," Gahrah said.

"It need not but it does," Dickson snapped. "Look

I don't know why Ward is snooping around but I don't like it."

"Don't worry about it," Gahrah said. "Your job is to continue making acquisitions and relocating funds."

"'Relocating funds,'" Dickson laughed humorously. "My God, you make it sound clean."

"If the purpose is pure the methods do not matter," Gahrah said.

Dickson was still leaning against the boxes. He shut his eyes. He wished he could undo all of this, had never gotten involved with these people. He told himself he didn't have a choice. It was either that or the bank went under, and with it, himself. His family. His self-respect. He would have been just another of the unemployed locals—Earl Dickson, the man who pulled himself up from poor Auraria on the South Platte, went from a teller in Denver to a bank founder by the time he was thirty-four. Not a prodigious achievement, but he felt darn good about it until the economic collapse in 2008. And with that went his professional and personal wealth. The bank was crippled with toxic loans and tight money. Government loans were slow in coming and he refused to go back to poverty.

That was when the MRI got in touch with him. They had been looking for a stand-alone bank, one without a diverse board of directors. He was it, and he grasped at the lifeline. He had survived, just barely, but then the big money had not even started coming in yet—the major construction funds for more faith-based buildings, the accounts for new residents, the expanding acquisitions. There wasn't enough money to send Angie to school but at least the Muslims gave her a job for the semester she would be missing.

A job. His gut knotted again. *An unwitting accomplice,* he later learned. And now a possible hostage.

Dickson tried to stand but couldn't. The fact that Angie was involved made him sick.

"I suggest you put water on your face," Gahrah said. "Perhaps take a drive to clear your head and then go back to work. Nothing has changed, nothing is different. Hamza will take care of Mr. Ward. He will not bother you again."

"More violence," Dickson said.

"Only if it is necessary," Gahrah said. "We did not ask him to become involved at the Randolph farm or your bank. Whatever happens he has brought it on himself. I believe he left you a contact number?"

Hamza had good eyes. "It's on my desk," Dickson told him.

"Excellent. Get it for me. It is my hope that no violence will be required. I am sure this unemployed police detective will be reasonable. Perhaps we will discover that all he is after is a bridge loan."

"I don't think so," Dickson said.

"As I said, you needn't worry about it," Gahrah told him.

The connection went dead. Dickson folded away the phone, pushed back his hair, and mopped his face with his handkerchief. *Prioritize,* he told himself. He had to put his family first. Gahrah was right about one thing: no one asked Ward to get involved. He brought this on himself.

The banker went back to his desk, once again smiling benignly at his employees, once again the man he wanted others to think he was.

CHAPTER FOURTEEN

Ward was just entering his room at the inn when his phone rang.

"That didn't take long," he muttered.

The Muslims had shown that they weren't afraid to use violence. But they wouldn't want to use too much of it. The more clues that were out there the less likely they were to keep getting away with it. The more indignation that was out there, the less Chief Brennan would be able to work on this quietly. So it did not surprise Ward that the caller ID on his cell phone was from the Al Huda Center.

"This is John Ward," he answered.

"Mr. Ward, my name is Aseel Gahrah. I am the director of the Al Huda Center. I believe you know of it?"

"Couldn't miss it as I drove into town."

"It *is* a good location," the man replied. "I understand you are interested in an investment opportunity."

"Always."

"Would it be convenient for you to stop by this morning?"

"I can be there in about an hour," Ward said.

"Very well," the caller said. "I will see you at eleven."

The caller hung up. It was exactly what Ward had expected. They were going to try to bribe him.

He freshened up and checked his other phone messages. There was one from the Internal Affairs attorney who wanted to have a chat with him about "the incident" and another from Joel Duryea, one of the younger men in his unit. Ward had no interest in talking to the lawyer but he called Duryea back.

"Good to hear from you," Ward said. "How goes it?"

"Same old. How are you, boss?"

"Not as bad as I expected," Ward told him. "Though maybe I'm fooling myself and it hasn't really hit me yet."

"Well, we're hoping it won't," Duryea said. "We've put up flyers in the park and also at the Hilton and the Ritz Carlton asking for anyone who might have been taking pictures down there to give us a shout. The guys pitched in for reward money."

That caught Ward by surprise. It was a few seconds before he could breathe, let alone speak. "Jeez, Joel."

"Don't say it," the kid replied. "We want you back and this is the best shot we've got."

"But tourists don't usually come back for a second day down there."

"True, but the media picked up on it. People

who *were* in the park are hearing about it and calling. We're just hoping we get something we can use to show that the judge and the DA that you didn't abuse the SOB."

"You guys are amazing," he said. The lump was still lodged squarely in his throat.

They chatted briefly about the other men and then Duryea had to go. Ward was glad. The call made him miss the badge and the fellowship so bad it hurt.

Tears pressed forcefully behind Ward's eyes as he drove up to Ridge Road. He knew the feeling of brotherhood would take a hammering when he talked to Joanne. But it would never truly be gone. Cops, soldiers, firefighters all put the strength of teamwork in a special place to draw on when there was no one else around to get your back.

Joanne answered the door, surprised to see her former husband.

"Is everything okay? Megan—?"

"She's fine, fine," Ward assured her. "I just need to talk to you."

"About?"

"Randolph," he lied.

Joanne took him out back where Hunter sat on the patio with his easel and paints. Joanne's laptop was on a metal table. She handled the orders for their art prints. They sat in metal chairs with foamy cushions. As they sat, leaves crackled where they had dropped from the surrounding trees.

"Do you mind if Hunter is here?" she asked belatedly.

Ward shrugged. "This affects him too."

"I thought you said it's about Randolph."

"Yes, that whole thing," Ward admitted.

Until now Joanne had merely been guarded. Now she was concerned bordering on ready-to-blow. "What is it, John? What's going on?"

"I think I found the guys who attacked him," Ward told her. "I've discussed this with the police chief. She can't approach them. I can."

Joanne slapped her knee and shot to her feet. "I told you he'd do that. I *told* you!"

"Jo, I can't just let this sit—"

"*Don't talk to me!*" she shouted. Hunter had put down his brush and come over to hold her. She squirmed away and yelled to no one in particular, "He can't let this sit. Of course not! He can't let *anything* sit, except me and our daughter night after night." Then her eyes found him like lasers. "*Goddamn you*, John!"

Hunter said, "John, I think you'd better leave."

"Yeah." Ward rose.

"You're endangering your daughter's life!" she screamed. "Just how reckless and irresponsible and *stupid* can you be?"

"I seem to have surpassed myself the past few days—"

She slapped him, hard. He knew he deserved it.

"Get out!" she yelled at John. She was sobbing now. "Get the hell out of my house!"

"I'll go, but we need to make sure Megan isn't left alone for the next few days."

"*This isn't happening!*" she cried.

"We can do that," Hunter replied, struggling to keep her calm with his voice, his hands open ready to grab her if she became violent. Ward was guessing he had never seen Joanne this out-of-control.

"You selfish bastard!" Joanne snarled at Ward. "*Christ*, what is *wrong* with you?"

"I don't think anything will happen to her," Ward went on, addressing Hunter for the first time. The painter was a bit of a buttercup but at least his ears were still functioning. "I just want to take some precautions."

Hunter nodded. "Will she be all right at school?"

Ward nodded.

"All right," Hunter said. "I'll pick her up afterwards, stay with her at soccer. But you say you don't think she's really in danger?"

"I'm on my way to talk to these clowns now, make sure they stay focused on me." He looked at Joanne. "Nothing's going to happen to Megan. This will all be over soon."

"Go and don't ever come back!" Joanne said like a lioness flashing teeth. "I swear, I'll get a court order to stop you from ever seeing Megan again. *You put her in danger!* What kind of a father are you?"

Ward left without looking back. He realized that a lot of what he just saw and heard from Joanne had been suppressed for years. He went to the car and as he drove away his mind couldn't help finishing the conversation.

"I'm the kind of father who cares about his daughter's community—"

"More than you care about her—?"

"Caring about her neighbor is caring about her. That

was how it was in our apartment building when I was growing up. Families keeping an eye on other families."

"Those days are gone. You can't bring them back—"

"I have to try! Without the America my parents left me, what kind of future will Megan have?"

"She'll be alive!"

Living isn't the same as being alive, Ward thought. For him, the last few days were evidence of that.

As he headed toward the Al Huda Center, Ward tried to forget the philosophy and concentrate on tactics.

For good or bad he was in this now, up to his neck.

And he was about to go deeper.

CHAPTER FIFTEEN

Ward had taken a flyer from the inn, tucked innocuously among all the fishing, boating, hiking, and skiing brochures. He read it before he went inside. There was a picture of the center on the front and the benevolent-looking director, in a suit and tie, on the back. Inside were statements about the open door policy toward the community, which were invited to use the Ping-Pong table, library, chess boards, and prayer space. Somehow, he didn't think they posed a threat to Papa Vito's and their pool tables. In fact, he couldn't think of anything designed to be less appealing to the locals.

The reason for that was obvious.

The center was probably sold to the city council as having something for everyone when, in fact, it was designed to be unappealing to local tastes. The 5,000 square-foot facility had been designed for a boom that was obviously expected in the Muslim population.

The reception area was like a doctor's office.

There was a woman behind a window, and nothing visible through the frosted glass double doors on the left side of the lobby. The only differences were the pictures on the wall: poster-size photographs of street scenes in some Arabian market.

The receptionist was not especially pretty and not particularly young. The wedding ring made her the wife of the director, Ward guessed. The top of her head was wrapped in a black scarf.

"Good morning," she said. Her voice was not unpleasant but it lacked warmth. She pressed a button on the telephone before he could introduce himself. "Mr. Ward is here."

"How'd you know it was me?" he smiled.

She smiled back. That was all she did. That, too, was cold.

The glass doors clicked open—they obviously felt the need for an electronic lock—and the man from the brochure stood framed within the doorway. He wore a tea-colored Damascan jubbah, a slender overcoat that reached to his feet. His round face sat on the upraised collar. The jacket was smooth, his skin unwrinkled, his beard neat. It struck Ward as a somewhat studied effort to project serenity. *Peace* was an aura, not a declaration.

"Welcome, Mr. Ward," Gahrah said with a slight bow. He stepped back from the door and invited Ward in.

Ward acknowledged him with a nod and Gahrah led him to a windowless conference room directly across from the door. There was a small, oval glass table with six chairs. In the center, on a tray, was a pitcher of water and six glasses. A telephone sat on one side of the table nearest the door.

"No tour?" Ward asked. "Your brochure promised—"

"I will be pleased to show you our facility after we've discussed your business needs," Gahrah said sweetly. The director shut the door and took a seat by the phone. Ward sat as well.

"Okay," Ward said. "Let's talk."

"How much were you interested in investing?" Gahrah asked.

"Just enough to buy a pig farm."

Gahrah smiled. "What do you know about pigs?"

"The porcine kind? Not a thing."

"Then may I ask what your interest is in the farm?"

"Sure. I don't like what happened."

"I'm certain no one does," Gahrah replied, still smiling.

"Really? I guess—well, let me just lay it out."

"Please."

"I think this center was involved somehow in what happened."

"Your tone and inference do not befit one who is a guest in another's community."

"Which community is that, Mr. Gahrah? Basalt or the Muslim community?"

"I am a proud member of both," the director replied. "Nonetheless, I am curious. You think we were involved. In what way?"

"You wanted the property."

"Is that it? That's the entirety of your evidence?"

"So far."

"Mr. Ward, it is hardly a secret that we wished to *buy* it."

"But Scott Randolph would never sell, so you decided to lean on him."

"Oh, really—"

"Right, you'd never do something like that," Ward said. "My question is why? Why do you want it *that* bad?"

Gahrah's smile glistened with cool confidence. "Your question relates to private and proprietary business of the MRI, which I am not at liberty to discuss."

"Of course not. Hide behind fiduciary double-talk. It won't do you any good."

"As for your accusations—including that last one—they are insulting and defy reason," Gahrah said.

"I don't think so," Ward told him. "If this didn't stink, you wouldn't have sent that ox to spy on me at the bank."

"Your phone message concerned me."

"Why?"

Gahrah folded his hands on the table. "Mr. Ward, I am a realistic man. I know there is resentment of my people within the community, and wild charges such as these are an outgrowth of that feeling. I am also a cautious man. You cannot blame me for that. Not here. Not with people like you wanting to harm us."

"Not *wanting* to, Mr. Gahrah. Being *forced* to. I don't know why, but Earl Dickson was crapping his pants. And I don't think it had anything to do with foreclosures or deposits. He was scared."

"Once again, Mr. Ward, you blame us with absolutely no evidence to back your assertion."

"And once again, what you're saying doesn't change the strong feeling I have that something's seriously wrong in this town—and you're at the center of it." Ward rose. "Okay, Mr. Gahrah. If that's all you've got to say, I'm leaving."

"Basalt?"

The question created the definite impression of a threat. That neither surprised nor impressed Ward. He turned to go.

"You know, Mr. Ward, there is a better way to do this."

Ward looked back. "To do what?"

"Clear the bad air between us."

"Does it involve your visiting the police chief and signing a confession?" the detective asked.

"It involves some sort of cooperation," the director told him. "A form of accommodation, if you will."

Now we get to it, Ward thought. "A bribe, you mean."

"Not at all," Gahrah said. "As I said, we've done nothing wrong. Call it a stipend. We at the center sometimes feel endangered. And—I believe you could use a job? You could consult with us on matters of security."

At some point in a face-off with the law every thug or pimp, pusher or mobster, reached this point—usually at the time Ward turned his back. Typically they were payoffs in fat wads or thickly stuffed envelopes, withdrawn from blazers or overcoat pockets and thrust at him. In the past, without exception, he had pushed through the cash to arrest the person behind it.

This was different and his hesitation scared him.

Hold on there, Boss Tweed. Are you actually considering *this?*

Ward's own desperately rotten situation and lack of bargaining power hadn't fully hit him till he was looking into the eyes of temptation. The truth was he couldn't arrest Gahrah even if the conference table were piled high with pigs' feet. And the man was right. Ward was a detective without a beat, a father without an income, a man with zero savings. If, for the sake of argument, he were to take the money, what would happen? Megan would be safe. More than safe; he could actually continue to provide for her. Joanne might stop hating him if he proved that he could put their daughter's welfare above his sense of duty or pride or whatever the hell was driving him. He would also have legitimate employment as far as anyone knew. And a couple of months as security guard for a Muslim community center? That would look damn good on his résumé. It would help to neutralize what had happened in the park. Private companies wouldn't run from him, frightened by the hounds of political correctness.

What other opportunity could solve all his problems in one stroke? What was there in his life to counterbalance Gahrah's offer?

Ward saw a flicker of eagerness flash across Gahrah's face, like sunlight on a still lake.

"Work with me," the director said. "We do not have to be enemies. You do not have to embrace my faith. All I ask is the right to pursue my religious interests and to look after the needs of my community."

The sun was still shining on that serene lake, and Ward saw the eddy that nearly snared him. Gahrah, the inveterate marketplace haggler, regarded the detective as simply a commodity. The look on his face suggested that there was nothing to decide except Ward's price.

But there *was* something else. Something priceless. *Doing the right thing.*

"Thanks, but right now all I need is the door and some air," Ward told him. As he turned to go he saw it. The sun clouding over.

Here comes the next step—the one that always follows the failed bribe.

"Do not be rash, Mr. Ward. You have a family in Basalt."

Ward stepped toward Gahrah. "That's right, I do," he said. He bent low over the seated man. As he stared into the dark eyes and swarthy face, Ward found himself feeling things no civilized man should feel toward any human being. But there it was, directed toward Gahrah and the people he represented with their contempt for the diverse society whose protection they exploited. "You want to know my definition of rash? Some jerk who says what you just said. If you or any one of your goons commit violence against my family, I swear before God they will end up like Mr. Randolph's pigs."

"Strong words from a broken man," Gahrah said.

Ward smiled. "You were willing to pay pretty good money for this broken man." The smile faded. "Anything bad goes down, you'll pay first."

With that, Ward turned and left. It was difficult not to put his foot through the glass door, rip the framed pictures from the wall, toss the chairs around the lobby.

Difficult, but not impossible. Because in the end, he refused to let himself become what he had beheld.

Chapter Sixteen

Grand gestures were a bitch.

Ward realized the problem his had created for him even as he crossed the parking lot. All the Muslims needed to do was create the appearance of a threat to provoke him into overreacting. They could wait in a car and watch the house or school, follow him to the inn, do something he would see. That could very well force Ward's hand even if there were nothing legally actionable. *He* would end up being the lawbreaker. Or else they would apply pressure until Joanne or his daughter broke. The girls would complain to him and the result would be the same. He would have to act.

The Muslims weren't stupid or careless. Planning these kinds of actions were what radicals did, 24/7. Gahrah had shown himself to be the kind of guy who went from the playbook. Ward was the guy who had gone loopy.

Virtue might be its own reward but it defies the laws of self-preservation, he told himself. And the pay stunk.

Ward decided to go back to the inn and do a little research on the MRI. Something actionable might turn up. As he approached the bank he noticed the Fawaz Dry Cleaner van in the parking lot. Angie visiting her father. He slowed and glanced in as he drove by, saw her sitting at his desk with a small bundle of laundry.

"What kind of linen does a bank use?" he wondered.

Maybe she was bringing him a bundle for home. But then why drop it here? Ward pulled into the lot and tucked the Prius into a corner spot, watching. The bank manager tore back the paper, slipped in two fingers, withdrew a shirt partway and gently rubbed the collar between thumb and index finger. Dickson nodded.

"Starch is satisfactory," Ward guessed.

He replaced the wrapper and put the package under the desk. Nothing seemed suspicious other than the fact that his daughter was delivering her father's shirts to the bank. Maybe he spilled coffee after Ward's unsettling visit, needed a new one. Maybe she just wanted to visit and this was a good excuse.

Or maybe something else was going on. Why check the collar in public unless you wanted to show the people around you—and perhaps the security cameras—that the delivery, though odd, was perfectly innocent. Angie had told Ward that the Muslims hired her because she knew the town. That was reasonable, and maybe she believed that. But what if it were something more?

He decided to wait for Angie.

The young woman emerged a minute later. He

wouldn't approach her where her father could see. If she were making deliveries he would follow her to the next stop.

He pulled out after her. As he did, a slumbering sense came to life and told him this was all too neat. He leaves the Al Huda Center in time to see a suspect receive a mysterious package from his daughter. Ward surmised that he was supposed to bust in, seize the package, and discover there were only shirts. The police chief would then have no choice but to put him on his horse and shoo him from town. That was the kind of setup a novice would concoct—and fall for. These jokers were still new at this. Ward hadn't bitten. Would they have a Plan B, and if so, what was it?

The Muscle, he decided.

Ward glanced in his rearview mirror. He saw what looked like a familiar face several car lengths behind his. He couldn't be sure because of the distance but he'd bet his life on it. In fact, he might well be. Muscle usually didn't have an "off" switch. The lug would have been watching to see how things played out, to take pictures. And if Ward followed Angie he would be there too.

There was no real finesse or skill to the plan, but there didn't have to be. The object was to show Ward that they were not going to be intimidated, let him wonder if they were willing to trade one Ward family member for one Muslim. In terrorist circles that was considered a good deal. They were telling him this wouldn't be easy and there was definitely danger.

The question was, what would surprise *them*?

Angie's number was still on Ward's cell phone from the last time he was out here. He called.

"Hey, Mr. Ward. How's it going?"

"Not bad. Say, do you make pickups?"

"Of course!"

"I see. In New York they have all kinds of restrictions."

"Not here."

"Great. Can you stop by the inn? I've got a bunch of stuff that needs cleaning."

"I'm right down the street, at my dad's bank," she said. "I can be there in two minutes."

"I'm heading back there myself but it'll take me a little longer—can you wait?"

"No problem," she said. "I'll meet you in the lobby."

He'd wait before asking if the stop at the bank were unscheduled.

There was a right turn coming up and Ward took it. As he expected, the other car went right by. Ward had slowed so he could check out the driver: it was Muscle, all right, driving the blue Ram. The big man looked down the street at him but didn't turn. When he had passed, Ward made a U-turn and edged to the end of the street. He stopped as the inn came into view. Angie had already pulled in. The Ram followed her. If the big man had her itinerary, he would know the inn wasn't on it. If he didn't have her itinerary he probably knew this was Ward's hotel and he'd want to know why she was stopping there—especially if Ward was not. Ward made a call and then waited at the corner for nearly two minutes before going back onto the road and continuing to his destination. He drove slowly, turning into the parking lot, choosing a spot carefully then sitting there with the engine running while pretending to check something on the GPS screen. He kept an eye on the road and on the Muscle, who was still in his car, watching and waiting—as was Angie.

Less than a minute after Ward pulled in, Chief Brennan's patrol car came racing down the street. As it neared the inn, the Muslim apparently realized it wasn't going to pass by. He went to pull out but Ward had picked a spot that allowed him to pull out and block the exit before the man could reach it. Ward saw Muscle's face which looked confused as hell. The man wrestled with his only option, which was to jump the curb; he clearly thought better of it. Ward saw his big shoulders remain defiantly taut as he glared at the detective in the rearview mirror.

The hotel staff and Angie had gathered at the door of the inn as Brennan rolled in. They watched as the police chief and Ward got out of their cars. Brennan went to the Ram and asked for the driver's license and registration. He handed her an Iranian card from his wallet and a folded paper from the glove compartment. When she took them back to her patrol car Ward sidled over to the driver's side window. The man attempted to roll it up. Ward put his hand on top of the glass and pushed in. There was an ugly cracking sound at the base.

"Muscle, you think this is the first time I've done this?" Ward asked.

The man said nothing.

"You've probably figured out by now that I called the police chief and reported that you were stalking me," Ward went on. "In New York, what you did at the bank and now is a Class B misdemeanor. They've probably got something similar here. Now, if I tell the chief I think you were stalking the girl too, it probably gets bumped up to a Class A. Not likely to result in jail time, but do you really want to clean public toilets for thirty days? Besides, you don't want it on your record, especially if you plan on staying in a foreign country.

"So here's how this is going down," Ward said. "I tell her I won't press charges and that'll be that. But there will be a record of this incident. If you do it again I'll see you get charged with a Class D felony which is for repeat offenders. Any questions?"

The man said something in what sounded like Arabic.

"Yeah, yeah, you don't speak English," Ward said. "Well, you'll have plenty of time to learn it in prison if I see you on my ass again. Got *that*?"

He took a step back from the car as Brennan returned. She said the man's name, Hamza Zarif, when she addressed him and told him that his resident status can be revoked at the discretion of a judge if he is found guilty of stalking. She asked if he understood; if not, he could come to the station and a translator would be found.

He nodded once.

"So you understand me?" Brennan repeated.

He nodded again.

Ward stepped over and told the police chief

there was no reason to take it to that level; they'd reached an agreement and it wouldn't happen again. When Brennan asked if this was the case, the man nodded. She returned the documents and let him go. He drove off, the window rattling comically as he went.

"I believe the technical term for what you did is called 'escalation,'" the police chief told Ward. She didn't seem angry but her mind was clearly processing what-comes-next. Ward knew the look. It was a slightly off-target look, with a crinkle around the eyes. It haunted the features of every beat cop who routinely dealt with gang members or ethnic unrest.

"I made the only move I had," he said. "I met with the director of the Al Huda Center. He tried to bribe me, implied he'd go after Joanne and Megan."

"Did you think about taking it? The bribe?"

Her directness shouldn't have surprised him. "Yeah," he admitted. "I thought about the problems it would solve. But I also thought about the ones it would create."

"Pretty scary how strange you get when you're down."

"It's unfamiliar territory," he said.

"I've been there," she confessed. "Well, not exactly. When I have to bust friends for vagrancy I think about how I'd like to buy a beachfront shack and sell clams. Only no one's made me that offer." She thought for a moment. "You got someone looking after your girl?"

Ward nodded.

"I'll send a car up every couple of hours, just so we have a presence there," Brennan said, thinking aloud.

"Thanks."

"You need a firearm? We've got some throw-aways."

"Probably not a good idea," he said.

"If you're saying you might use it, I don't have a problem with that."

Ward was beginning to think he was in love. The NYPD came down hard on the practice of carrying an unmarked gun to plant on someone who was shot and killed by accident. He was glad the American West had not been tainted by that kind of delicacy.

"No, I'm good for now," he said. "Thanks for your help—and the offer."

"No problem. Stay in touch," Brennan said as she got back into her car.

Ward turned toward the inn as she drove off, saw that Angie was the only one still standing in the doorway. He had one pair of underwear and, if he took them off now, a pair of socks and a shirt for her to clean. The young woman might suspect she'd been used as bait, especially if she knew whose nose Ward had just tweaked. Her worried expression suggested that she had a good idea what had gone down. What that didn't tell him was how *much* she might know.

He resolved to find out.

CHAPTER SEVENTEEN

Ward walked Angie to a pair of wing chairs that sat catty-cornered on the far side of the lobby.

"What was all that about?" she asked. Anxiety played a little around her smile. Ward didn't make much of that; he saw a lot of that around Basalt.

"Do you know him?"

"I've seen him around," she replied.

She was probably telling the truth. It didn't have the slight hesitation of a lie.

"I saw him around too, watching the bank this morning and then following me," Ward said. "I decided to be safe and call the police chief."

"It seemed like you knew her," Angie said. "Chief Brennan."

"I know her a little bit," Ward said truthfully. "You heard what happened to Mr. Randolph?"

She nodded.

"I was there right after it happened," Ward told her. "That's how I met her."

"You were there?"

"Yeah. Heard the sirens," Ward said. "Instinct."

"That was probably pretty awful."

Ward nodded. "Is there anybody you know who might do something like that?"

The young woman's face scrunched thoughtfully. She shook her head.

"What were people saying at work?"

"Nothing."

"Really? Not even, 'Hey, did you hear what happened?'"

"No. But I'm not around the store a lot." Her face relaxed, but only for a moment. "Do you think something's going on?"

"What do you mean?"

"There's just been this strange vibe today. Mr. Fawaz was kind of short and his wife was quiet. Plus my dad seemed pretty agitated."

"How so?" Ward was glad she brought it up. He'd been trying to figure out a way to get there.

"He called and told me he needed one of his shirts," Angie said. "He never does that. Mr. Fawaz suggested that I just bring him all the shirts we had."

"Why did your father need a shirt?" Ward tried to make it sound conversational rather than interrogatory. He hoped he pulled it off. He hadn't grilled a lot of Midwestern girls.

"Dad said he was sweating a lot today. That was, like, TMI, and I didn't ask anything else."

I'll bet he was, Ward thought.

"So, am I going to get great service on my clothes?" he asked.

"The Fawazes are real good, yeah."

"Do you take all your family's dry cleaning to the shop?"

"We take all our cleaning there, period," she said. "We get freebies. Part of my compensation."

"Nice. How often do you do that?"

"Every day," she replied. "Between my parents and my two young brothers, we go through a lot of laundry."

And then the detective knew for sure what was happening: something was being transferred via laundry. Gahrah *thought* Ward had known this earlier, or at least suspected. That was why he had sent the bogus package to the bank.

"Do you have an empty laundry bag in the car?" Ward asked.

She nodded.

"Would you mind getting it? I'll meet you back here."

Angie left and Ward hurried to the gift shop. He purchased a pair of denim *Basalt Rocks* button-down shirts from the rack, along with a couple of T-shirts and also deodorant—which he happened to need. He borrowed scissors to clip the tags from the clothing items then ducked into a recess in the hallway, by the janitorial closet. He put one of the button-down shirts on and crumpled the other and the shirt he was wearing into a fat, wrinkled ball. Then he rubbed the T-shirts under his arms to make sure they had a worn-in smell. He returned to the lobby. Angie was standing there with the bag, suddenly looking very young and very alone. As he stuffed the items in the canvas sack she entered their description into a small handheld device. He followed the young woman to the van as she printed a receipt. He knew the rest of this operation wasn't going to go well. The trick, he'd learned over the years, was to look at the darkness as temporary, the light inevitable.

"How fast can you get these done?" he asked.

"This afternoon, if you pay for Super Rush."

"Let's do that," he said. "Do you bring your own clothes home on your daily run or after work?"

"At night," she replied. "I've got one last run at five and then I take the van home. That's my other perk."

"Do your brothers ever help?" he asked as he knotted the bag. Once again he was striving to make it sound like idle chat.

"How do you mean?"

"By putting away the laundry?"

"Duh! Why would they? They're boys—"

"So they leave it all to you?" He doubted that but he had to ask.

"No. My mom. She doesn't mind *that* part of it."

So Mrs. Dickson knew too.

Angie was suddenly confused. "Mr. Ward, is something wrong?"

"That's what we're trying to find out."

"We?"

Ward calmed her with a look. He had learned that on the beat when he would have to talk to a woman whose purse had been snatched or who was the victim of a push-in—shoved into the lobby of her apartment building while she turned the key, and then robbed or worse. Men just got angry, wanted to lash out; women were always struggling to

regain their mental footing in the face of something
obscenely disorienting.

"I'll explain in a second, Angie. I need you to
answer one more question. Just one. Can you drop
my clothes here on the way home?"

"I guess so," she said. "Mr. Ward, is my dad in
some kind of trouble?"

"I don't know," he answered honestly. "If he is,
I'm on his side and so is Police Chief Brennan.
We're going to help him."

"Oh, God—"

"Listen to me, Angie—"

"Dad!"

"*It's going to be okay,*" Ward told her, "but he's got
to be willing to help us. That's the only way he can
help himself."

"From *what*?"

Ward took one of her small hands in his, relatively sure that no one was watching them now.
This was the part when he went from being a
comforter to being a major league son of a bitch.
Back in the city, his accomplices, the ones who
wore wires or testified against capos or pimps, were
usually deep in the swamp and wanted out. The
only mud this girl had on her was stuff splashed by
her father.

"Your dad *may* be involved in something that's
getting away from him," Ward said. "I want to
throw him a lifeline. But for me to be able to do
that, it's important that you stay calm and focused.
You can't tell him what we talked about or even
that I asked you to drop off my clothes."

"Because—?"

"Men like that lunk of a guy I sandbagged, Hamza, are going to be watching him—and you."

"Jesus." Breath just seemed to go out of her. It took a moment for Angie to find it again, to get back into the rhythm of breathing.

"Angie, it'll be okay as long as they think everything's normal, that it's business as usual," Ward assured her. He held her hand more firmly. It had been soft and lifeless but it responded to his touch. "If they believe that, then we can do what you just saw: box them in and take them out."

"I always wondered—I always felt—" Angie stopped, her voice cracking and eyes tearing. She inhaled and rallied. "I was always *afraid* that something was happening here. Don't ask me what—I don't know. It was just my folks, people at work acting a little different, a little suspicious."

"That's what we're going to fix, me and the police chief and Scott Randolph, and the other folks who care about this town," Ward assured her.

He gave her hand a final squeeze, sought her eyes, and lifted her face up with his fixed gaze. He smiled and she forced a smile in return.

"You gonna be okay?" he asked.

She nodded then got into the van and wiped her eyes with a tissue. She looked out at him before shutting the door. "I don't want anything to happen to my mom or dad."

"That's the goal," he said, wishing he could give her a more concrete assurance.

"I'll do whatever I have to," she assured him.

"Thanks, but I think we're good now," he smiled. "You have my number. Call if you need anything."

She said she would.

As Ward watched her drive off, he found it endearing that she had not asked why a cop from New York was involved in this. In her mind he was a lawman and that was that. He wondered if that trusting mind-set was a result of the Patriot Act and the whole concept of Homeland Security, a generation growing up with the idea that peacekeeping no longer needed to respect boundaries or jurisdictions or even privacy. It was no wonder: those like himself and the police chief afforded the only protection from greedy, anti-traditional social hyphenates and the blind, accommodating zealotry of political over-correctness. Hopefully, fear and an unraveling of the social order would cause defections from both of those groups—people like his liberal ex-wife and groups pushing for same-sex marriage or socialized medicine while civilization itself was being torn apart by monsters.

Every tribe has an ancient blood feud until the nation is attacked by outsiders, he reflected.

Ward waited as Angie vanished into the foothills. His eyes were on the road, watching the cars. He didn't see Hamza, though he hadn't expected to. The Muslims knew her route and could pick up her trail at any time. The clean white van with its black lettering wasn't exactly inconspicuous. They probably didn't anticipate Ward making another move now, and would certainly ask her questions when she got back to the dry cleaner. The truth was, he didn't have another move to make. Not until Angie came to the inn with his laundry and he could get a look at what might be in the Dickson laundry. If he was correct, there was a careful flow to what they were doing. They couldn't afford to hold off even a day.

He went back inside. The inn rented laptops and he got himself a Dell for two hours to see what he could find out about MRI. He first made sure he knew how to erase his footprints before he started. Then he sat back in the armchair and tucked into the work, hunting and pecking around the keyboard. This might be the only chance he got: it wouldn't be long before they thought of hacking into the Wi-Fi signal here to find out what he might be researching and who he might be contacting.

That was fine with Ward. It was just like any crime scene. The bad guys had a head start. To head them off, he would have to get his facts, spin them around in his head, and hit the ground running.

CHAPTER EIGHTEEN

Angie Dickson wished she did not have to be alone right now. In particular, she wished that John Ward had stayed with her. The few times she had met him in the past, he was like nothing else in her life. He was—*solid* was the word that came to mind.

Ward was right. For a while now her father had not been the strong, attentive, *happy* man she had known growing up. The economic situation had sucked the energy from him, made him seem almost like her grandfather . . . old and stiff, even though he still managed a certain robustness in public. For the last few weeks he had been even worse; when he wasn't anxious or snappy he was just plain depressed. Her mother was flat-out sad, with lines and shadows on her face that had never been there before. She said it was the job, having to go back to work as a travel agent after raising a family, but Angie knew there was more to it than that.

Now John Ward's suspicions had confirmed it. It was nice of him to care. That made her feel safe and scared at the same time.

Angie's stomach gurgled and her hands were shaking as she finished her rounds and returned to the dry cleaning shop. She didn't know how to act normal. She usually just *was* normal.

Angie tried singing to herself. That wasn't something she normally did, unless she had her iPod, which she didn't use during work. Mr. Fawaz didn't think it was professional, even though he wore a beanie and his wife wore a headscarf, which most people in Basalt thought was weird. None of that mattered now. She had come to the office to drop off the cash payments and dirty laundry before picking up the loads to make her final run. Mr. Ward's clothes would get rush treatment so she could put it on the van for the final run. Usually, that gave Angie just enough time to go to Papa Vito's for a Coke and hang-time.

The owner's wife, Mahnoosh Fawaz, was working behind the counter. Angie transferred the bags from the car. They were collected by Tariq, the Fawazes' teenage son. Angie reviewed the receipts with Mrs. Fawaz, calling her attention to new clients as well as special orders. She felt her belly turn to liquid when John Ward came up in both categories. She couldn't help but watch Mrs. Fawaz for some kind of reaction but saw none. Maybe she wasn't in on whatever was going on. Or maybe she was just better at covering it up. These Muslim women were pretty quiet.

"My husband would like to see you in the office," the woman said when Angie had finished.

"Okay, all right," the girl replied. She heard her voice, high and fast, and hoped she sounded carefree and not buzzed.

Mrs. Fawaz's brown eyes seemed a little suspicious as Angie eased around the counter, though the young woman thought that might be her own insecurity talking. She made her way along the half-full racks of shirts, suits, and dresses. Joblessness had cut the demand for clean suits. She didn't understand how the place made money. At least the overhead was pretty low; she had heard her father talking over dinner about how rents had gone down considerably since 2008.

Yousef Fawaz was seated behind his desk in the small office in back. He was on the phone as she arrived but he motioned her in. He was not smiling—typical for him—but he did not seem upset. That was good. Angie didn't get called in here often; when she did it was usually for something like a schedule change or a price increase. She wondered if she was going to be fired; she hoped not. She liked having a little money and there were no jobs to be had. A little piece of her wondered what that would be like, being fired. It had never happened to her when she worked at McDonald's or as a camp counselor. Just thinking about it made her want to cry. Then again, after that afternoon, she was already emotionally rattled.

Fawaz hung up and asked her to sit in the swivel chair that used to be his desk chair before he got one that was better for his back. It creaked loudly and the back gave willingly as she sat, crossed and uncrossed her legs, waited while he made some notes.

"I see you brought in a new customer today," Fawaz said pleasantly as he continued to write.

She thought for a second, momentarily perplexed. "Oh, right. You mean Mr. Ward? I used to babysit his daughter—"

"Mr. John Ward, yes."

She felt a jolt of fear, then—she had just placed the receipts on the counter out front. Mrs. Fawaz had not yet gone through them. Her blouse clung to her sides, damp with perspiration. She knew now how her father felt, why he needed a new shirt.

For the same reason? she couldn't help but wonder. *Because of these people?*

Fawaz sat back, his chair bending noiselessly. Angie remembered when it was delivered. That was one expensive chair, over a thousand dollars. She began to think of things like that: the Berluti shoes he wore, the Chanel eyeglass frames Mrs. Fawaz used for reading, the fine embroidery on her pantsuit.

"May I ask what you talked about with Mr. Ward?"

Angie exhaled. "Gosh." She pretended to think back while really trying to relax. "Megan, mostly. That's his daughter."

"Mostly. Not entirely?"

"Let me think. He asked how my dad was."

"Even though he had just been to see him?"

"Oh, had he?" She choked on the last word. She wanted to cry.

"Angie, it is important that we know what he is

doing," Fawaz said. He sounded earnest, concerned. "Perhaps you are aware what your friend Mr. Ward did in New York?"

"It was something about a guy selling things on the street," she said. "One of my—our—customers mentioned it."

"John Ward accosted a Muslim," Fawaz informed her. "He was accused of a hate crime and suspended without pay from the police force."

"Wow. That's serious."

"Yes," Fawaz agreed.

"Was the man breaking the law?" She couldn't picture John Ward pushing someone around without reason.

"We will never know because the gentleman was not accorded due process. We believe that Mr. Ward has a great deal of anger toward my faith," he touched a hand to his chest, above his heart. "We have hired someone to keep an eye on him, very legally of course, and—well, you saw what happened. Mr. Zarif was harassed by Mr. Ward and by the chief of police. It is an ugly thing, and a very difficult time to be a Muslim. Do you understand?"

"I do." She didn't. Her family was Episcopalian yet her father was a wreck. Mr. Fawaz was Muslim and he was calm as her brother's pet turtle.

"Did he ask anything of you?" Fawaz went on.

"To drop off his laundry on the way home."

"Nothing more?"

She shook her head.

Fawaz considered this. "All right, Angie. Thank you for your help."

"So I can go?"

"Of course," he said. "Only—when you leave later, two young men will be riding in the back of the van. Because of his hatred, Mr. Ward believes that we were somehow involved with the attack on Scott Randolph. We are concerned that Mr. Ward may try to do harm to our property in retaliation."

"I don't believe that!"

"He may have been what the police call 'casing' our holdings—the shop, the van. We cannot take that chance. We cannot put *you* in danger."

"Why don't you just go to the inn where he's staying and tell him all this? It's not like he's going to be in town for very long. Or tell the police chief."

"Those are wonderful ideas, of course, but it's a point of law, really. We cannot go to Mr. Ward directly. That would appear provocative. He could say we threatened him. And the police chief will not act unless there is a misdeed. Do you understand?"

She nodded. Whatever Ward thought was happening, Angie knew she was now in the middle of it.

"Mr. Ward will, we suspect, ask to have a look inside the van," Fawaz continued. "If he makes such a request, you will permit him to enter."

"With the men inside?"

"That is right."

"Whoa! Are they going to hurt him?"

"Not at all. They will protect our property and, if necessary, simply remind Mr. Ward that his attitudes have no place in civilized society."

God, why were things so confusing? Mr. Fawaz sounded like somebody being interviewed on the news, totally reasonable and friendly. Now, thinking back, she had to admit that Mr. Ward *had* seemed a little wound up. And Chief Brennan *could* be a dick. She had seen it herself when she and some of her friends had a party on the river during the summer. One of the girls was underage, but not all of them were. Brennan shouldn't have made *all* of them go to the police station.

But her father was agitated about *something* when she saw him at the bank. And he wasn't a Muslim afraid of hate crimes.

"The young men who will be riding with you are my son's friends Hassan and Ali," Fawaz told her. "I believe you know them."

"I've met them."

"They have been instructed not to distract you," Fawaz assured her. "They will sit quietly in the back."

"Unless Mr. Ward wants to check out the van," she said.

"Exactly," Fawaz said agreeably. "When you get to your house, the boys will phone and I will come and get them. Hopefully, they will not be needed and that will be the end of this unfortunate matter."

Angie managed a little smile as she got up. It was cheerfulness she did not feel. She didn't know what she should be feeling—other than scared and worried about her father. Her fear increased as she took her break. She sat alone at a table in Papa Vito's, back in a corner by the busted pinball machine. It was quiet at this hour, before dinner. She absently checked e-mails on her phone.

She was starting to feel like a tennis ball, not just batted to and fro but sore. How did all this happen? Not just today, but to the town? Where did the friendliness go, the comfort, the sense of having a home and a plan?

"You shouldn't be having caffeine, girl," she told herself after she went back for her free refill. It was like the Coke was the only stability she had. You drink it, you know what you're getting. Not like her day. . . .

She finished, then went outside and sat on the edge of one of the small tables out front. The sun was just starting to go down; everything was the color of a hot dog bun. She didn't know why she thought that, but it made her chuckle. She watched as the shops across the street grew redder. A chill came almost immediately. When the sun went down, the mountains sent snowy cold to fill the vacuum.

Angie turned to the dry cleaners and noticed Mrs. Fawaz. The woman was looking at her from behind the counter. It was a blank look, but somehow ominous. Angie answered with a strained twist of her lips that didn't even resemble a smile.

Something was definitely wrong here, and was probably going to get worse.

CHAPTER NINETEEN

Yousef Fawaz's manner changed the instant Angie left the office.

His effort to appear unbothered vanished in a flurry of angry gestures. He pushed his chair back, stood, kicked the leg of his desk, thrust up his open hands in anger, rolled his fingers into fists, and rattled them as he paced. After a minute he sucked down a calming breath, picked up his cell phone, and called Gahrah.

"We need to call off today's delivery," Fawaz said. He was still stalking the narrow length of the office, preparing himself for a fight with Gahrah.

"Did she tell you anything?"

"She doesn't *know* anything," Fawaz said. "I am not surprised. Ward had to know I would ask her about what transpired at the inn."

Mrs. Fawaz appeared suddenly in the doorway. "They are clean shirts, probably from the gift shop," she said. "And they are Super Rush."

Her husband acknowledged with a nod. He

returned to the phone conversation."The clothes Ward gave her to clean haven't even been worn. He wanted to make sure he saw her again this afternoon, on her way home."

"So he suspects there is something in the evening delivery," Gahrah said.

"Clearly. That's why we mustn't make an exchange today."

"And give in to his terror tactics?"

"At least deliver the package later, or directly to the bank now, or in the morning," Fawaz said.

"No," Gahrah said. "That will only postpone a showdown. This man will not give up so easily. For all we know the police chief is involved. She may watch us, flag us for some minor or contrived infraction as they did with Hamza. We must deal with him decisively and we must maintain the flow. And it *is* possible we can use this to our advantage."

"How?"

"Tell the girl that if Ward wants to go into the van she is to let him."

"But I've already told her we do not wish him harm—"

"And that is the face we will present to her," Gahrah said. "I will instruct the boys what to tell Ward—that he is risking what is left of his reputation for something that is entirely in his mind."

"I don't know if that will scare him," Fawaz said. "Ward will want to know what they are doing there."

"Protecting our deliveries," Gahrah told him. "For him to push further will make *him* the aggressor, put *him* in jeopardy with the law. That may be enough. When he came to see me this morning, Ward seemed—how to describe it? Not entirely convinced. Not committed. I could see that the money was speaking to him, the way it did with Mr. Dickson, though perhaps not loudly enough. If we add other voices, in a dangerous situation where he must act or withdraw, he will be persuaded to stop."

Fawaz was not entirely convinced. "We tried to go softly with the farmer too, and that did not work."

"The farmer was different," Gahrah pointed out. "The farmer did not have another home to go to. He did not have another livelihood. He had no reason to bend. Ward is different."

What Gahrah said made sense, though it failed to factor in the imponderables of human nature. But the director was in charge. "We will do as you say."

"What time shall I send the boys over?" Gahrah asked.

"At 4:30," Fawaz told him. "The girl leaves here at 4:45. You are sure they will make an effort to talk to Ward?"

"Talk is always preferable," Gahrah said. "I will tell them what to say and I will tell them what they must hear. Why do you ask?"

"We do not want the girl turning against us," Fawaz said.

"Do not worry about that," Gahrah said. "We have leverage with her."

That was true. It was not pleasant to consider, but a war sometimes resulted in collateral damage.

Gahrah praised the prophet and hung up. Fawaz lit a cigarette and sat for a long while after their conversation. He was not schooled in diplomacy. Until six months before he and his wife had been doing this same job in Mashhad, a city of over two million and the home of the Imam Reza shrine. Because of its holy nature, Mashhad is the nation's tourist capital—and the reason Fawaz learned to speak many languages as a boy. Perhaps, had he the opportunity, he might have become a translator at an embassy or for a government minister. But poverty does not allow such opportunities and the family was incredibly poor.

Fawaz's father, a tailor, always said, "It is strange how Iran under the Shah was rich in material things and poor in spiritual matters." When the Ayatollah returned from exile, the reverse was true.

Now, in America, with the help of his childhood friend Aseel Gahrah, Fawaz and his wife were finally able to have both. He did not like all the violence; he liked it even less than Mahnoosh who felt that the infidels were getting no less than they deserved. But it was a means to honor the cause of *jihad* and to serve his own means as well, for in serving his ends he honored the Prophet who said, "*Do not withhold your money, lest Allah withholds from you.*"

Ward would make his own fate, as each of us does.

Grinding out his cigarette, Fawaz went to make room in the van for its passengers.

CHAPTER TWENTY

Ward might not be a working cop anymore, but his access to the FBI's restricted database had not been canceled.

An oversight, I'm sure, he thought. The Feds were too busy watching for hackers to pay attention to legitimate users who didn't belong there.

Ward found nothing surprising online about the Midwest Revitalization Initiative, which was itself surprising. They were organized in Illinois in 2009 with funding from several anonymous sources, none of which was flagged for suspicious dealings with terrorist-linked organizations. From his Terrorist 101 training in New York he knew that anonymity for property purchases was granted only in the case of domestic individuals who were contributing to religious institutions, or those religious institutions themselves. Without a hacker, that was a dead end for now. As for the board of directors, they were all of Middle Eastern descent and none had criminal records.

The group had tried, at first, to buy properties in Skokie, Illinois, but were perennially outbid on properties by the Skokie Investment Corporation. The SIC had links to Israeli banks, which made sense: Skokie had a heavy Jewish population. The community wasn't going to lose a war to the Arabs, not there. Basalt was their next, and so far only other location. Ward understood the symbolism of Skokie. But why here?

The American heartland? That was possible, but it had to be more. Perhaps the proximity to Aspen, playground of the rich and famous. And if what he suspected were true, Aspen might make a lot of sense. A lot of private planes came in and out of that airport. He was willing to bet that a lot of the overseas flights and their big-spending passengers got relatively free passes at customs.

Ward looked up some of the reports about the Muslims in the local paper, then checked the time. He thought about calling Hunter to tell him he would get Megan but decided against it. It was best if he stayed away from them for now. Joanne was kindling and he couldn't seem to help causing sparks.

He had a late lunch—or was it an early dinner?— at the counter of the empty diner and chatted with his waitress. Debbie Wayne was in her early thirties; she did not wear a wedding band and he guessed, correctly, that she was divorced.

"The economy made the problems we were already having even worse," said the attractive redhead.

"What did your husband do?"

"He drove a limo for a car service," she said as

she filled a sugar container that really didn't need filling. "He still does, though bookings and tips aren't what they were. We were planning on starting our own car company but . . ." Her voice trailed off.

"So have the Muslims been a good thing or a bad thing for Basalt?"

She looked at him strangely. "That just went from chitchat to something else."

"Did it?"

"You a P.I. or something?"

"Why, no one else talks about the Muslims?"

She snickered. "That's all anyone talks about. That and how broke we are. I don't know. You just got that look, you know."

"Oh? What's 'that look'?" he asked around a bite of grilled cheese.

"Your eyes don't wander, you dress kind of city, and you actually listen when women talk."

He chuckled. "I'm not a private investigator, though I used to be a cop in New York until I was accused of—"

"*You're* him!" she said, pointing at Ward. "I heard some of the regulars talking about you at breakfast the other day. Then I caught a little of it on the car radio."

"Now I know how Lindsay Lohan feels."

"No, it's a good thing," she insisted. "I don't know if it helps, but the folks that morning were on your side all the way."

"Actually, that means a lot," he said.

"So I was kind of right, about you being a P.I."

"Kind of," he admitted.

"What's your interest in our situation?"

"My daughter lives in Basalt so I was just curious."

"With her mother?"

He nodded.

Debbie refilled his Coke. "Just curious, huh? I think it's a little more than that."

"What do you think it is?"

"Don't know. But working here you develop a good ear for 'lines,' and that sounds like one."

He smiled again. "Maybe a little."

"How'd your daughter end up in Basalt?"

Ward told her. About halfway through he realized this wasn't like talking to Randolph or Chief Brennan. The woman was paying attention to him, not just his story. It felt good and it took Ward's mind off his objective for the first time since he went over the ridge the other night. He asked—hopefully with more subtlety than he had about the Muslims—if she were seeing anyone.

"Not a soul," she replied. She wrote her phone number and, after a moment, added her address on the back of a check. She pushed it across the counter. "I hope you don't think I'm being bold."

"I'm from New York," he reminded her.

Her mouth twisted. "Dating's a problem when you know half the eligible men in town and wish you didn't, and the other half can't even afford pay cable."

"Right now I can't afford *basic* cable," he said.

"But I bet you know who to talk to so you can fix that."

He smiled. "As a matter of fact—"

"God, I want to visit New York. I see it a lot on TV. It looks exciting."

"It *is* that," Ward agreed.

"It'd be nice to get shown around there by someone who knows where things happen."

"Pretty much on every street corner, at some time or another," he said.

"There, see what I mean? I like cities. I want to go to one."

"Hold on," Ward said. "If you've never been to a city, how do you know you'll like them?"

"I watch a lot of CSI shows," she explained. "They're alive, energetic. Not like here. Hey, you can watch with me and tell me what's real and what isn't."

"I could do that."

"Anyway, I'm home nights. I have a second job from six to ten."

"Doing what?"

"I take phone calls," she said.

Ward's throat dried a little. "Oh," he croaked.

She struck a sacred pose, eyes up-turned, hands together. "I am none other than Madam Night Sky on the Native American Psychic Call Line."

It took Ward a moment to process that. He leaned back, chuckling, and nearly fell off the stool.

"Why is that funny?" she asked.

"*That's* not funny," he said. "I am."

"I don't understand."

"I'm from New York," he replied, half apologizing. "My baseline is somewhere between the gutter and the top of the curb."

Now she thought for a moment; when she got

it her cheeks reddened. They both laughed and she leaned forward to give him a playful smack on the head. She smelled of bacon and woman. It was a near-irresistible combination.

"Good God, I could never do that!" she said. "I know girls who do. They've told me some of the things they have to say. I'd just sit there laughing."

"You take this other work seriously?"

"Very!" she said. "I read cards and all. I don't just sit there and make noises while I do the ironing."

A couple entered the shop. The waitress regarded them. "Tourists."

Ward turned. "How can you tell?"

"Apart from the fact that I know all the regulars, they have that 'isn't this charming' look." She stood, smoothed her apron, and winked at Ward. "I've got to work. Anyway, no pressure." She tapped her address. "If you've got the time and energy after looking out for your daughter and the home- land, I'll be there with my Tarot deck."

"Not sure you'll see a whole lot in my future."

"You never know. Maybe you should do what I sometimes tell my clients: don't worry about it. The future's got its own plan."

As Debbie grabbed a couple of menus and headed around the counter, she said, "And to answer your question about the people we were talking about earlier?"

"Yes?"

"Those men are the girls' biggest clients. They

spend money like movie stars. I think they're all a bunch of phonies."

That may have been the wisest statement Ward had heard in the past few days. Maybe longer.

Ward finished his sandwich, drank his Coke, and left a twenty on the counter. After the beating he had taken in New York, and then from Joanne, he found himself thinking very, very fondly of the two women here who had made him feel like himself again. Ward was not a religious man, but as he left the diner to go back to his room, he offered up a silent prayer of thanks.

His eyes scanned the sky as he stepped into the setting sun. He stood for a while and watched the sharp, orange orb descend behind the mountains. It wasn't the same as watching the sun from Manhattan as it dropped behind New Jersey, planes into Newark cutting across it, smoke from industry smearing the view.

Here, it was powerful and pure. It suggested something bigger than him, bigger than jets and smokestacks.

Maybe he had never been as alone as he thought.

CHAPTER TWENTY-ONE

Ward went to the lobby to wait for Angie. He walked around the small, cozy room which had a den in back and a small commercial corridor to the left. It must have been a helluva mansion in the region's heyday.

He still felt bad for the kid and the pressure he'd put on her. But the alternative was to let the Muslims and possibly her father continue to use her, and that was not an option. Taking cash to look the other way while something crooked went on was one thing. Allowing this girl to be involved was very different.

At least you rolled the taste of payola over your tongue to help *Megan*, he thought. It wasn't much of a consolation but it was some.

The van pulled up at ten to five. Ward went out to meet it and saw at once that something was wrong. Her expression was dull and she was not moving like someone who was near the end of the work day and eager to get home. She was going through the motions slowly, looking at the van, the asphalt, the inn, but never at him. When she pulled his bundle from the passenger's seat instead of from the back, that sealed it. He stopped just outside the doorway and let her come to him.

"What's wrong?" he asked quietly.

"Nothing, Mr.—"

"The van's riding a little lower than before, and I don't think it's my shirts," he said. "Who's in the back?"

That caught her entirely off-guard. "Two men," she answered before she thought about whether she should.

"Are they watching you or waiting for me?"

"You," she said.

"Angie, I want you to go to the lobby and wait."

"What are you going to do?"

"Talk to them," he told her.

"Please don't," she implored. Her hands tightened around the bundle.

"It's going to be fine," he assured her. "I'm used to this. Did you happen to notice if they were armed?"

"I didn't. They were already there when I got in."

"Thanks. Now go," he said, shooing her away as he walked around to the back of the van.

She left reluctantly, as though she were a plug holding all hell back. Maybe she was. Her eyes clung to him in the crawling darkness and she finally snapped them away. Ward waited until he saw her go inside then rapped on the van door with a knuckle. He didn't want to yank it open and startle them. Getting shot was the wrong way to find out if they had guns.

"It's John Ward," he said. "I'd like to talk."

The door opened slightly and he heard footsteps move away. Ward pulled the door wider and climbed in. The exterior lights of the inn had been turned on and illuminated about a foot-and-a-half of the interior of the van. Ward crouched just inside the door, saw two men sitting among the laundry bags, parcels, and clothes hanging along the left side. One was on the right, the other in the center, facing him. They were young men, no older than twenty-two or -three. The one in the center wore a hot, unforgiving look. Ward wondered if that was the kid who had played Chicken with him.

"Shut the door," said the angry man.

"I'd like to have some light in here if you don't—"

"Shut it or I'll kick you out," the man said. "You need to listen, not to see."

At least he didn't say he'd shoot me, the detective thought. *Kid's got an attitude and Gahrah probably didn't want him armed.* Ward scuttled forward and let the door swing closed. He sat with his back against it, legs steepled. He had marked where the handle was if he needed to reach it.

"Talk," the young man said from the shadows.

"Sure," Ward said. "But first, I have to tell you—this beats hitting a man from behind and then trashing his farm."

The other young man snickered. "*Khoshet miad?*"

The other replied, "*Vagh'an azash khosham miad.*"

The tone sounded mocking rather than threatening but Ward remained on his guard.

Suddenly, the first young man moved so that he was on his knees, closer to Ward and facing him. Obviously, his idea of "menacing" was to be higher and closer. That worked both ways: it also put the punk within reach.

"We were just saying that we don't like you," the man said through his teeth. His hands were in motion, fingers jabbing. Presumably, rap would survive the *jihad*. "Now I have something to tell *you*. Don't involve your New York nose in our business."

"What business is that?

"*Any* of it!" he said with a sweep of his hand. "Stay out of our way or there will be consequences!"

"There will be consequences for everyone, including you, if this goes on," Ward said. "Talk to me. Maybe we can find a solution."

"We? Who are *you*? A Muslim hater looking for another lamb to slaughter?"

"Forget what you think you know," Ward said. "I'm a guy who's trying to fix a situation that's getting worse."

"Well, *guy*, I am not interested in discussing this with you," the young man said. "Keep out of our business or the next meeting will not be so civil."

"Is that what this is? Civil?"

"It is more than you deserve. Now get out."

Ward wasn't leaving here without moving this in some direction. He had pricked Gahrah this afternoon or these boys wouldn't be here. He couldn't stop pushing now.

In the dim light coming from the windshield, the detective noticed the clothes on the rack. They were hanging in dry cleaning bags. "Hey, are those what you used to wrap your feet at the pig farm?"

The backhand slap was quick and vicious, too fast to avoid. It struck Ward's cheek, hard, and drove him to his side. He reacted as his hand-to-hand combat training sessions had taught him to react. As he was smacked to the left Ward's right arm came up. He used the force of the blow to execute his own stiff-arm strike against the side of the attacker's head. He caught the man against the temple, causing him to yelp. But that was his only victory. Ward barely had enough time to raise his hands before the other man was on him. Ward was struck on the head and chest, the blows firing through his upraised arms. The other man, the one he'd struck, pulled at Ward's shirt to try and tug his face forward, out from behind his forearms so the other man could hit him.

Ward's only objective was to reach the door handle and get out. He needed to get the fight into the open where passersby or security cameras might see. Otherwise he had nothing on them except his word against their own—a pointless exercise. He thrust his right hand out toward the door in a few tentative stabs, always missing it before having to withdraw the arm to protect himself. Finally, he braved a flurry of blows as he used his arms to push off from the floor and get on his knees. His shirt ripped as the men grabbed at him but he was able to twist the handle and throw himself out.

He managed to swing his hands so they were under him as he hit the asphalt. One of the young men, the one who had not spoken, nearly fell out with him but managed to stop himself on the fender. That wasn't good enough for Ward. The detective reached up and grabbed the man's sleeve, yanking him out. Ward rolled out of the way as the young man fell, scrambling to his feet and stepping over him toward the open van. He reached in, tried to grab the instigator, but the guy swatted his arm away.

"Come on, you rat—hiding in the dark!" Ward yelled. "You've got the odds and ten years on me! Are you afraid?"

The kid refused to take the bait. He jumped out, helped his friend up, and they walked away.

Ward was losing his cool. He went to slap at the back of the kid's head but his friend saw the blow coming and pulled him away. Ward smacked air, spun off balance, and the friend snickered.

"Even from behind you cannot take us," his target sneered.

"Yeah, not as sure a thing as attacking when a man is asleep, you damn coward!" Ward snapped.

The young men still weren't biting. They were walking toward the street, toward the Al Huda Center.

So much for pushing. The whole thing had just imploded. Or worse.

Ward's shouts had brought people from the inn and from the car wash next door. There was no way he could afford to be seen going into the van to get the package. Not now. That would put him in jail.

Angie had run outside. "Mr. Ward, are you all right? What happened?"

"You dropped off my laundry."

"What?"

He looked at her, saw upset in her eyes as she looked at his face and his shirt. He spoke quietly so no one else could hear. "You dropped off my laundry inside and you have no idea what happened here."

She nodded as what he was saying had sunk in.

"Are you okay?" Ward asked. "Can you drive?"

She nodded again.

"Then just get in the van and continue your rounds *now*."

Moving like she was underwater, Angie got behind the wheel. "I left your clothes with the desk," she said as an afterthought.

He waved her away as he heard a siren growing louder along Midland Avenue. A few moments later he saw a familiar police car. Even if she were already on patrol, it would have taken longer than this for someone to see them fall from the van, call 9-1-1, and for dispatch to reach her.

Someone else had called.

Ward began to realize that he'd been had.

CHAPTER TWENTY-TWO

Police Chief Brennan did not arrive at the inn by herself. A familiar Ram followed her patrol car in.

Of course, Ward thought. Gahrah would not have sent those kids alone. They weren't muscle. They were messengers with no authority or orders other than the message they were sent to deliver. He would have had Hamza watching and *he* would know what to do if things got out of hand.

Ward ignored the stares of the staff and the few guests who had come out to see what was going on. Brennan did not look happy as she pulled up beside Ward. Hamza was as implacable as before as he stopped beside the police chief.

"Mr. Ward, would you please wait for me in the lobby," she said as she got out of the cruiser.

He knew the drill. She was going to question the witnesses then question Ward. The desk clerk gave Ward a wet cloth, told him his cheek and forehead were bleeding. He hadn't noticed. He thanked the young man, who also handed him his laundry as an afterthought—that was almost funny—then plopped in a chair to wait for the Riot Act.

It didn't take long. Chief Brennan used a small videocamera to record Hamza's statement then entered the lobby and motioned Ward to get up.

"Let's go to the den," she said.

As they left, Ward happened to notice Debbie Wayne watching him from the parking lot. She wore her street clothes and a look of concern. He shot her an "OK" sign as he disappeared into the back room. The room was carpeted with a Persian rug and there were deer heads on the wall, above the fireplace. There was no door so they went to a corner and sat in a pair of facing arm chairs. Ward sat with the bundle of laundry in his lap. In a flash of hope he wondered if Angie had slipped him the bag bound for her home. She hadn't.

Too bad, he thought. *That would have been interesting, especially with Brennan as a witness.*

"I can't even begin to tell you how fouled up this situation is now," Brennan said, leaning close.

"Then don't."

"Sorry, but I have to. They've got you on trespassing and assault—those are a lock—and a possible hate crime."

"That's rich. They were in there waiting for me."

"Sure, but where's your proof? Our friend out there says they were just seeing how they could make the route more efficient."

"Right. They wouldn't know efficiency if it were written in Farsi. And the guy who hit me— I looked into his eyes before I shut the door. That was personal. Definitely the ATV rider I faced down on Randolph's farm."

"Also possible. But they say you're an Islamophobe and given what happened in New York they could make that stick."

"It was bull when I got here and it's bull now."

"And at the risk of sounding like a talking doll I say again: I believe you, but none of that matters. Here's the bottom line. Speaking for the two young men, Mr. Zarif says they are disinclined to press charges on one condition. You have to leave Basalt."

"If that isn't a confession of criminal activity, I don't know what is."

"You keep scoring bull's-eyes on a Kevlar target," the police chief told him. "None of that helps. Not a bit."

"When do they want me gone?"

"Right now."

"Not to Aspen, I'm guessing."

"To New York," she told him.

Ward was starting to boil. "This is a load of crap and you know it. They won't press charges. They can't afford to have this matter under scrutiny."

"Can you afford to take that chance?"

"I don't know." He was thinking back, looking for loopholes. "The way that kid blew up—and for the record, he was the one who struck the first blow—I'm guessing he was also the one who clocked Scott Randolph."

"Okay, he's got a short fuse and I'll surely look into it," she said. "But right now there's only one guy in the hot seat and he doesn't pray to Allah."

"Maybe I should," Ward said. He calmed himself the way he always did, with what he called his hard-times mantra: *a year from now this will be behind me and the bad guys will be in jail.* Besides, fighting the police chief would accomplish nothing except fighting with the police chief. "What I really want to do is tell the Muscle and his fellow thugs to drop dead. Have I got anything else to lose?"

"Can't see what, and that's surely your prerogative," she said. "In which case you'll have . . . I'd say about ninety seconds between the time I tell him you're not leaving and me coming back here to arrest you."

"What's bail on something like this?"

"You're looking at low five figures, would be my guess. But you're a potential flight risk so the judge may up that or make you wear an ankle bracelet or deny it altogether. She takes a pretty hard line on multiple charges. And given the complexion of our community these days, I wouldn't blame her."

Ward felt like one of those two-strike losers he used to bust in his early days on the street. He didn't quite get how he'd screwed the pooch twice in one week. There wasn't a choice to make. Prison here would sink his chances of getting even a lowly security job from someone who had a soft-spot for ruined cops.

"I'll leave," he said, "but you know this is wrong. They're manipulating us."

"I know it. And for the record, I don't look forward to a future of more-of-the-same. They've gotten good at this kind of manipulation. Every time you disagree with them, it's a hate crime." She smiled slightly. "It felt good before, though, cold-cocking the big lug. Thank you for that."

"You're welcome. Did they specify where I have to go? How far?"

"Unless the plane to New York makes a pit stop, that's your destination. I said I'd take you myself."

The monkeys were running the zoo. Ward couldn't get his mind around the idea that America had gone from being the land of the free to the home of the frightened. Where were *his* rights in all of this? When did the mainstream become toxic and those who support the mainstream become unpatriotic?

It was a half-hour ride to the airport. He still had enough time to do one thing. It was risky, but they had left him no choice.

"Do you think Muscle would mind if I had a few minutes alone to call my daughter?" Ward asked.

"I can make that happen, as long as you promise you won't try and go out the window," she said. "I've never had a fugitive and I'll be real disappointed if you're my first."

"I won't go anywhere without you," he promised.

She chewed her cheek while she looked at him. "Okay. Five minutes," she said, turning and walking toward the entrance.

"Thanks."

She paused and pointed at the bundle of clothing. "And you might want to change your shirt. You look like you bodysurfed the sidewalk."

"I did."

When the police chief had left—she had not gone far, was chatting with the man at the desk—Ward took out his cell phone. It had survived the fight and he quickly scanned the directory. He was about to play his one option.

He called Angie Dickson.

Chapter Twenty-three

As she made her way toward the deliveries on Homestead Drive, Angie couldn't stop thinking about John Ward.

It wasn't just about what had happened to him but how he made her feel—safe. It wasn't just that he looked after her, the way he chased her from the scene of the fight. It was his manner. Unlike her father, who was uncharacteristically wary, jittery, and gloomy this past year, John Ward was consistent, confident, and level. She knew Joanne pretty well but now she wondered how well she really knew her. Megan's mother seemed so put together, but she didn't understand how anyone could be unhappy with John Ward.

She hoped that nothing was going to happen to him. She didn't know what she could have done any differently, not without getting into trouble—

Her phone sang Lady Gaga. Ward's name came

up. She felt a rush of excitement and hoped, prayed it was good news. She pulled over.

"Mr. Ward, how are you?"

"Fine, but the police chief wants me to go back to New York. That means these guys are going to continue getting away with assaulting people and destroying property. Unless you're willing to do something for me, something that's a little risky."

"Risky how?"

"I don't know, Angie. I wish I did. I *do* know that if we do nothing, the risks could be serious for your dad. I hate to drop that on you but—"

"It's all right. I'm in."

"Good girl," he said. "First, check your rearview mirror. Is anyone following you?"

She glanced back, saw well along the straight, darkening road. "Not that I can see."

"Fine," he said. "I'm going to ask you a big favor. You can tell me no and I'll understand. I need you to look in the bag of laundry you're taking home."

"Now?"

"I've got about three minutes before Chief Brennan comes to get me."

That overrode any concerns or reservations the young woman might have had. Holding the phone to her ear with a shoulder, she twisted from the seat and went through the van into the back. She pushed away bundles until she reached the ones that were going to her house. She pulled them out. There were three in all.

"I assume you want my dad's?" she asked.

"Please."

"Opening now," she told him.

"Can you do it in such a way that it can be re-sealed?"

"I'll try," she said.

It was dark in the back of the van, her body blocking most of the light from the front window. She turned around, placed the parcel before her. It was wrapped in brown paper and tied with twine. She slipped the rope off by working it back and forth. Then she carefully pulled one taped end open and sat the parcel on its side. She saw her father's white shirts stacked endwise, folded neatly. She slid her hand between two of them in the center.

There was a bundle of paper inside. And another beside it. And more between two other shirts. She slipped one of the little packages out, working it back and forth until it came free. It was a business envelope. She slid a finger carefully under the pre-pasted flap. It came up easily. She looked inside.

"Holy crap," she said.

"What is it?"

"Money," she told Ward. "Cash. Like, a lot of it."

"Denominations?"

"Hundreds."

"Are the serial numbers consecutive?"

She flipped through them. "No."

"New or old bills?"

"Old."

"Not counterfeit," he said. "How many bundles are there?"

She poked through the shirts. "Feels like ten."

"And how many bills would you say are in each stack?"

"I don't know—I'd guess twenty-five?"

"Laundering twenty-five thousand a day," Ward said. "A quarter million every ten days. Can you take a picture with your cell phone?"

She hesitated. "Is someone going to use this against my dad?"

"God, Angie—I hope this can *save* him," Ward said. "Your dad's going to be in serious trouble when he's found out, and he will be. If we can use the picture to get him to cooperate, that may be his only way out."

"I have to trust you," she said, more for herself than for him.

Angie held the money in front of her, took a picture, then took additional photos of the shirts, holding them apart as wide as she could with one hand so the camera could see the ends of the envelopes tucked inside.

"Done," she said.

"Can you send the photos to me?" Ward asked.

"I will when I get back up front. First I want to close up this package."

"Okay, but I don't have a lot of time."

"I understand," she said.

Angie was about to put the cell phone down and get to work when she heard the sound of a car. She froze as it passed, honking, the driver complaining loudly about something as he went around the van.

"Jesus," she sighed.

"What?"

"A car went by, almost gave me a heart attack,"

she said. "I shouldn't have pulled over here. It's, like, not very wide."

She set the cell phone on the floor of the van as she carefully replaced the money—checking first to see which way the others were facing so she didn't slip it in the wrong way. Then she ran her fingers along the sides of the shirts to fluff them, covering the indentations her fingers had made. She carefully folded the paper back over, had a tougher time getting the cord to go back around it, but finally put everything together. If she stumbled when she went in the house and dropped it, that would explain the wrinkles in the paper. She scooped up her cell phone.

"Going back to the front now—"

There was another sound, louder than the car. She jumped into the driver's seat to move the car as an ATV pulled up beside her.

The driver throttled down. It was Javad, Mrs. Fawaz's cousin. He motioned for her to roll down the window.

"Hello, Angie," he said.

"Hey."

"Mr. Fawaz got a call from Mrs. McCrea wanting to know, 'Where is my dress?' He asked me to come and see if you got a flat or something."

"Oh, no, no," Angie said. "Some, uh—some bundles fell over. I stopped to fix them."

"While you were talking on the phone?"

"A friend," she explained, then said into the phone, "I'll call you later," and snapped it shut. "Hey, I can multi-task," she added.

"You know, Mr. Fawaz doesn't like when you drive and talk like that."

"I wasn't! I called while I was fixing the bundles."

The young man looked at her darkly. She didn't wait for him to say anything else. She just started the van and drove off. Angie watched in her rearview mirror. He didn't leave. He had pulled over and flipped out his phone.

Probably calling Mr. Fawaz to tell him I'm on my way, she thought.

She hoped.

The McCreas were the next stop. She decided not to call Mr. Ward until she had made the drop that had caused that little commotion. Ringing the bell, Angie handed the dress to their teenage son Cabot.

"Tell your mom I'm sorry," Angie said.

"For what?"

"For being late," the girl replied.

He shrugged. "No foul," he said, his words like an electric wire held to her spine. "She's not home from work yet."

CHAPTER TWENTY-FOUR

Ward jogged over to Brennan and pulled her aside.

"You've got to find Angie Dickson," he told her.

"What are you talking about?" The police chief took his arm and walked him back toward the den. "What have you done *now?*"

"She opened a dry cleaning parcel that was going to her house," Ward explained. "She found twenty-five thousand bucks inside."

"A payoff? From Fawaz?"

"I don't think so," Ward said. "This has the ear-marks of a scheduled drop. Money laundering, more likely."

Brennan was incredulous. "Earl—his own daughter a mule?"

"Hell, I'm not sure he's thought it through. Any of it. From the Muslims' point of view, though, she makes a perfect hostage."

"If everything goes as planned, she never finds

out," Brennan said. "If Dickson gets cold feet, she suffers frostbite."

"Exactly."

"You said I have to *find* her?"

"Angie was on her route, hung up before she could send me photos of the cash—I think someone may have been checking up on her."

"You called her."

"Yeah."

Brennan made a sour face, but only for a moment. "Where was she when you spoke with her?"

"I don't know. She was making her rounds and pulled over."

"That could be anywhere." Brennan considered the situation. "Even if they suspect her they probably won't act now. They'll talk to her father first."

"You must deal with a different breed of smuggler than I do," Ward said. "How do you know they won't take her back to the shop and interrogate her with a leather strap?"

Brennan recoiled. "Where do you live, in the Roaring Twenties? The lifestyle is different out here, even for criminals."

"Tell that to Scott Randolph."

"Mr. Ward, our perps knocked Scott Randolph out and killed some pigs as a last, desperate move. From the bulletins I read, you've got homeless people in New York who do worse with a brick, on a whim."

The police chief had a point. Ward was just panicking over the box he'd persuaded Pandora to open. Yes, her father was in danger. But that wasn't the only thing that prompted him to use her. He *wanted* these guys. He didn't feel too good about moving her more directly into the kill zone.

"No, she'll get home just fine," Brennan said. "And before you go off on 'What did I get her into?—'"

"Too late."

"—It was her father who got her into this. You opened the girl's eyes. I'm not condoning how you did it, or the fact that you pulled a fast one on me, but if we can procure the evidence you say she has and convince Earl Dickson to cooperate, you may be responsible for sparing him a life term."

"Cell phone photos won't be enough," Ward said.

"I know. We'll need the cash. But he can get us that."

"True. And there's the larger issue of where it's coming from and what it's being used for, though I think that's obvious."

"Oh?" Brennan said. "Enlighten me."

"I've been researching Gahrah's Chicago group MRI," Ward said. "The corporation buys property, a lot of it here. A single-enterprise firm that makes a lot of foreclosure purchases which are then being sold to individuals and institutions more or less at cost has to buy that property with loans or profits from another sector. This company *has* no other ties, at least none that I can find."

"Couldn't it come from mosques? They're tax exempt. If they can shoot money to terrorists, they can surely buy a few houses in town."

"They're tax exempt, but they know they're being watched—closely," Ward said. "That's one reason we've cut off a lot of sleeper cell funding. If a government-affiliated mosque in Iran wants to get money to terrorists, it's got to go to Yemen or Iraq and from there to here. Slipping it into the country and getting it to terrorists has a lot of moving parts. They have to make sure all of them work; all we need to do is tag one of them to stop it."

"I see. But I still don't get the MRI–Earl Dickson connection."

"They're getting him cash somehow, he's putting it in accounts, they're transforming that into property, and instead of funding terror directly they are establishing beachheads from which terror can be launched and directed."

"Holy crap. And you're saying one of the ground zeroes—*the* ground zero—is right here in Basalt."

"Which explains your cautious criminals," Ward said. "As long as computer programs are watching them they've got it covered. No red flags get raised. As soon as real live eyeballs get involved, looking for the cash, they have problems."

"Then why risk the Randolph attack?"

"They want that property. A lot. I'm guessing it's got to do with psyops."

"You lost me."

"It's the high ground, the highest in the region," Ward pointed out. "It's got a view of the entire town. More important, the entire town can see *it*, especially if you build something big and Muslimy up there."

"A mosque."

"Not just a mosque, or even just a mosque on

the high ground," he said. "It would be a mosque on the ruins of a pig farm, an animal expressly forbidden by the Koran."

Brennan's expression showed that she understood just how much bigger this situation had become.

"I've got to admit, it's clever."

"Deviously," Ward agreed. "That's what some of these guys do for a living, think of ways to muck us up."

"But there's nothing we can use to call in state or federal authorities," she said.

"I've got colleagues in Homeland Security, but no one who'd lift a pinky to help me while I'm toxic," Ward said. "We need to nail down that money trail."

She nodded. "And I've still got to get you to the airport."

Ward looked as though she'd hit him with a sock full of quarters. "You're not serious."

"I am," the police chief said. "I've got to take you there. Maybe not to stay, but we've got to go."

The detective considered that. She was right. "Fair enough. Let's grab my stuff," he told her.

"You've got a plan?"

"Getting one," he said.

They walked to his room; from the corner of his eye Ward saw Hamza standing just outside the inn, watching. They reached the room and Ward left the door open as he packed his few belongings.

"They know my Prius," he said. "I have to drive that and you'll take your car. I'll turn the rental in, you'll see me to the gate. We have to assume someone will be watching me that far. I don't board but change my clothes in the bathroom in case someone's still there. Standard undercover procedure. I rent a car from a different company and come back when it's dark. When I need to, I'll sleep in the car in some out-of-the-way spot. I've done it before."

"And probably enjoyed it," Brennan guessed.

He grinned. "I love it."

"Then what?" she asked.

"Well, before that I'm going to camp outside Angie's home tonight, make sure they're not watching her," he said. "Someone may go to see her father—it would help to know who on the totem is talking to him, whether it's through a messenger or the community center director himself."

"Right. They may feel safe again, get a little bold with you out of town."

"Exactly," Ward said. "I'll call you at sunup. Hopefully, Angie will have sent those photos. If not, one of us will have to convince her to do so. We need to get a serial number and see if we can trace the cash."

"You can do that?"

"Since 9/11, banks are required to scan and track at least three notes of every big-bill packet they make. If that comes up empty, we'll have to get a warrant to search the van and get one of the bundles themselves."

"Poor kid," Brennan said.

"Yeah, but we're pushing her through this so she'll come out the other side. Right now, with her dad as the only buffer, she's in serious danger."

The police chief was getting a little restless. "We'd better go before—what'd you call him?"

It took a second for Ward to come back. "Who? Oh, Muscle."

"I like that," she said. "We'd better go before Muscle gets antsy and figures out that we're plotting against his boss."

Ward shouldered his bag and followed her out. The desk clerk handed him his receipt as he passed, the onlookers who had stayed around continued to observe—except Debbie, who had her calls to make. He was glad. He felt embarrassed, her seeing him like that. Muscle was still standing there, watching him.

"You follow. I'm going to give you the flashing lights on the way out of town," Brennan said. "It'll show these guys I'm taking this seriously."

"Good call," Ward said. It would also have a psychological impact that went beyond the constabulary display. The detective picked that up from the look of satisfaction that redefined Muscle's expression as they drove past him.

You think this is over? Ward thought as he headed toward the highway. *So did Pharaoh when he banished Moses, you son of a bitch.*

Hoping that God didn't smite him for that, Ward figured he couldn't do any more damage by noting that, thanks to the patrol car in front of him, traffic parted for them all the way to Aspen.

CHAPTER TWENTY-FIVE

When Angie got home she did not send the photographs. She didn't know why, other than that she just didn't. Outwardly she had a sleepwalker's glaze; inwardly she was in turmoil. She sat through dinner with the family—a Dickson custom, now without exception since it was the only time both parents were around—all the while avoiding eye contact with her father. He, too, seemed distracted and appeared not to have noticed her own evasion.

It was around eight o'clock, when her father was having his nightly cigar on the enclosed patio, that Angie finally went to him. It was chilly, but there was a space heater. She switched it on. Her father was still wearing his work clothes, as he always did until he went to bed. Casual was not his style. He once told her that a banker was like a cop, never really off duty. He said that when banks were closed in Basalt they were open in Tokyo. That always made her father seem super-powerful to her, like he was plugged in to the world.

The analogy with a cop seemed more than a little freaky today. Angie tried not to think about it.

Right now Earl Dickson seemed unplugged. He sat in one of the two big wicker chairs, his head sunk in the pillow hanging from the cobra back. His hands were flopped on his knees, one of them full of cigar that was heavy with ash. Angie pulled the matching chair over, held the ashtray under the cigar and tapped. The ash fell in a solid lump.

He smiled thinly at her. "Thanks, Ang."

"You're welcome." She sat back, her phone in her hand, her hand damp with sweat. "Are you okay?"

Her father didn't answer. He was staring through the screen, past the trees at the road. It didn't look to her as if he was seeing any of it.

"Dad?"

He turned to her. His face looked pale in the ruddy glow of the heater, his expression waxy and lifeless. "I'm sorry. What were you saying?" This time he didn't have a smile for his daughter.

"I asked if you were okay. You seem a little—I dunno. Spaced out."

"I'm fine," he assured her. They were words without conviction. Earl Dickson went back to staring out the window.

"Can I talk to you about something?"

"Sure, Precious."

Saliva pooled in Angie's throat. She had always been open with her father, but that's when she was the subject.

"I have a problem," she said.

He remembered the cigar and put it in his mouth. He looked at her as he puffed mechanically, waiting.

He lifted his other hand, offered it to her. "Talk to me," he said.

For a moment, at least, Dad was back. She grasped his hand gratefully.

"Something happened while I was driving home," she began. "I was about to make a drop-off at the McCreas and I had to brake to avoid a cat. Some of the stuff in the back of the van fell."

His grip tightened.

"Ow," she said.

His hold relaxed at once, like a tendon had been cut. But his eyes were no longer soft. "What fell?" he demanded.

"Y'know, maybe this isn't such a great time to talk," Angie decided. She started to rise.

Her father held her. "I asked you a question. What fell?"

His voice was a monotone. It frightened her.

"Bundles. I had to stop and pick them up and so I was late making my rounds. I didn't want you to hear that from Mr. Fawaz that, like I was being lazy or something."

"Why would Mr. Fawaz call *me*?"

"Well, I figured he banks there . . . he might mention it."

She gave her hand a tug and he released it, but he did not take his eyes from his daughter. She looked away. Her phone pinged. She ignored it.

"You did that during dinner," he said accusingly.

"What?"

"Barely looked at me. Why?"

"I was thinking of things, of nearly killing the cat—"

"Was there a cat, Ang?"

She hesitated. That was as good as a confession.

"What *happened*?" he demanded again.

"I found the money," the young woman said softly. She took the ensuing silence to mean he wasn't sure what she meant. That was what she prayed. "The money in your laundry," she added for clarification.

Her father was silent a moment more and then he tossed his cigar to the floor, grabbed her shoulders, swung her toward him and dug in his fingers so hard he felt bone.

"*Dad*—"

"*Why* did you do that?" he hissed.

"*You're hurting me!*"

"Answer me!" he yelled.

She sobbed more from the verbal assault than the physical one. "A guy said you were in trouble—"

"What guy? The cop? Ward? He approached you?"

She nodded miserably.

"Who else? Did anyone else talk to you?"

"Mrs. Fawaz's cousin saw me stopped, asked if everything was all right. He didn't see the money, though—"

"Jesus!" Dickson released her with a shove. "Christ Jesus Almighty!"

Angie sat there crying, dimly aware of her mother appearing in the doorway. The older woman took a moment to figure out what had happened, then rushed to insert herself between her husband and her daughter. The short, petite woman squatted, looking at Angie, caressing her damp face.

"Are you all right?"

Angie nodded.

Mrs. Dickson started to rise, taking her daughter's elbow and urging her to her feet. "I think you should go to your room."

"No—I'm afraid," she said. "I'm afraid for dad!"

Mrs. Dickson turned toward her husband. "Earl. Talk to her."

"I knew this would happen," Dickson snarled, staring outside, oblivious to the presence of either woman. "I *knew* it."

"Is it true?" Angie wept to her mother. "Is Daddy in danger?"

"I—I don't know," she said.

"Like hell you don't. Now we're *all* in danger," Dickson said despairingly, his voice drained of fire.

"We're not," her mother told her. "Let me talk to your father."

"We are in trouble, I know," Angie said. She stood and looked down at her father. "Mr. Ward says he can help you. I believe him. Please, we need someone to get us out of this."

Dickson remained silent and staring.

"Go," her mother said to her. "We'll talk later."

She started to leave and her father grabbed her wrist, startling her. "I'm told Mr. Ward has gone back to New York. He can't do any more damage. But you *can* make this worse if you tell anyone else, even your brothers. You've got to promise to say nothing."

Angie looked from her father to her mother.

She got no help there. Mrs. Dickson looked as dismayed as her daughter felt. Sniffing up a new round of tears, the young woman nodded then left the patio and ran to her room.

Closing the door, Angie sat on the floor by the foot of her bed and hugged her knees to her chin.

What have you done? she asked herself.

Her phone rang again. It was John Ward. She answered.

"Angie, I just wanted to make sure you're all right—"

"Don't bother me anymore," she said. She was angry, now. Angry at everyone, but mostly at herself and John Ward.

"Why? What happened?" he asked.

"My dad went off on me—he said I would screw things up even worse if I did anything else."

"That's not true," Ward said. "You need to listen—"

"I don't need to do anything!" she said. "You're gone and I just want my life to get back to the way it was!"

"Angie, I'm not gone," Ward said.

"What are you talking about? My dad said—"

"I'm not going anywhere until we fix this," he said. "Just tell me—do you still have the photos?"

The young woman's mouth twisted angrily. "Jesus! Is that all you care about, the damn Muslims!"

"No, Angie. What I care about is you and your family—"

"Yeah, right. Screw you."

"Angie—"

She held the phone in front of her, opened the

file, and deleted the pictures. "I don't have the photos anymore," the young woman told him. "Now I want you to leave me alone, leave *us* alone!"

"What did you do?" Ward asked.

"I got rid of them."

There was a long silence. The dead air felt good. Angie had regained a little composure, a little control.

"All right," Ward said. "Look, I'm sorry I upset you. If you or your family needs anything, call me anywhere, at any time."

"I told you what I need," she said. "Good-bye, Mr. Ward."

Angie snapped the phone shut.

She couldn't believe what she had done. She'd hurt her father, a man who had always been so kind to her, based on the say-so of some crazy Islam-hating loser from New York. There was probably a good reason her father was doing whatever this was. He was a smart man, a successful man.

You should have trusted him, she reprimanded herself.

She thought for a second, then flipped her phone open. She scrolled down her phone list, found a number, and placed a call she hoped would set everything right.

CHAPTER TWENTY-SIX

John Ward sat in the newly rented red Volvo, watching the Dickson home from three houses down the street. It was as close as he could get without sitting under a street lamp. And he still had a good view of anyone who came or went along the street, or of anyone who left the home. Unless Angie herself went out, he would stay put. She was the one he'd put in danger. She was the one he'd watch.

He didn't know if anyone had been watching him at the airport. He presumed he was followed, but, the ban on profiling be damned, it was not a place where a swarthy kid or a woman in a scarf wanted to hang around just *looking* at something.

Ward was too busy mentally hammering himself to worry about who-saw-what. He had managed to piss off the only person he had who was nominally inside, and as a result she had deleted a lead. He was not sure how else he could have played this; Angie was scared going in and, quite naturally, she ended up choosing personal security in her house and circling the wagons with her family rather than trust a man she didn't know, someone who could not even leave town honestly.

Still, he felt an obligation to keep an eye on her, at least for tonight. He still didn't have a bead on how worried or reactionary Gahrah and his people might be. They were still relatively new at the idea of empire building. Reading online archives of the local newspaper had told him there was a reclusive imam attached to the community center, a seventy-six-year-old named Bagher Kharrazi. The Internet had virtually nothing on the man, not even a photograph, but Ward had to imagine he was given this post for a reason. The Muslims did not need financial help, they had plenty of that through the MRI office in Chicago. But it would stand to reason the cleric had at least some experience in the tactics of stealth *jihad,* the undermining of a non-Islamic system from within.

His phone vibrated around nine p.m. It was Joanne.

"Hey," he said. She'd probably heard he was leaving. This would probably make him wish he had.

"Where are you?" she asked.

"Long story."

"Can't you answer a simple goddamn question?"

Ward sighed. "I'm in Basalt but everyone thinks I've gone back to New York."

"*Still* the undercover cop."

"I guess."

"Your daughter heard from a classmate that you were given a police escort to the airport."

"I did, but that was just for show."

"For *show.* What are you, a freaking *Lipizzaner?*"

"Cute."

"I'm not trying to be funny! Is Megan still in danger?"

"That's a little strong," Ward said. "As long as the bad guys don't know I'm here, she's safe and all you need to do is make sure she's not alone or doesn't take any Korans from strangers."

"This *is* a joke to you!"

"No, Joanne. I'm just trying to nip your fuse."

"Big fat flop, John."

"Well it used to work, when you didn't have me in your sights."

"It worked when I was twenty-four years old and you were my husband and you had some common sense," she said sharply. "Not when I'm thirty-five and you're an ex who has morphed into some kind of loose-cannon vigilante!"

"I'm not a loose cannon," he said. Even as he defended himself, he knew it was pointless. "And for the third or fourth time, I'm looking out for *your* home, not mine."

"I'm sure you believe that," she replied icily. "I know you, John, and what you're looking out for is your shattered ego. Dammit, I'm not going to call again. Just let me know when this is over so I can take my daughter off the leash you put her on."

"*Our* daughter," he said.

She hung up.

And you thought this relationship couldn't possibly get any worse.

Ward tucked the phone in his shirt pocket. He should have realized that when Joanne moved to Basalt as quickly as she did, all that remained behind was her husband. Their unfinished business went with her, packed in a trunk and ready for easy access whenever he showed up.

The detective sat in the dark, in the cool night, missing the Prius. This seat was not as comfortable, and he could have kept the heater on without making any noise or smoke. He wished he had had one of those when he was doing all those stakeouts at Queens warehouses and Bronx factories and JFK cargo terminals.

Alone with his thoughts for the first time in days, he asked, *Is that part of your life really over?* It seemed impossible. But he also didn't see a road back, especially if an enterprising New York reporter ever came to Basalt to see what he did on his little vacation. *Maybe I can become a spokesman for Angry Unemployed White Judeo-Christian Men,* he thought. There was a time when the implication of that label alone would have horrified him as a human being and as a member of society. Now it screamed of self-preservation, a necessary evil against the tide of special ethnic and religious interests. *Though I can't say AUWJCM is a particularly appealing acronym,* he decided.

Ward waited until midnight. The lights had been out in the Dickson house for nearly an hour and there were no signs of activity in the street. The detective hoped that he had overestimated the danger and that they were safe.

That left Ward with his next big problem: where

he was going to spend the night. In his car, of course, but he needed to put it somewhere out-of-the-way, a place none of the Muslims would pass it while he slept.

A church parking lot?

And that was when it hit him. *Debbie.*

It was late, but the way Debbie had talked about the men in town he wasn't likely to interrupt anything, and he was betting her job as a telephone fortune-teller kept her up at least this late. A lot of her business, like a lot of his, probably depended on the crazies who came out at night.

He reached into his shirt pocket for her number, realized he had changed shirts, turned to grab his carry-on bag, then froze. The shirt the paper had been in was torn during the fight in the fan. The pocket had been ripped away.

Something crept into his brain, slowly and terribly.

No. No way.

He thought back. He would never remember the telephone number but he tried to see the check, to picture the address she'd written. Experts had taught visualization as a matter of course in the NYPD so that officers could remember license plates, if not the numbers, and makes of car that they had only seen in passing. Everyone bookmarks each moment in some way. They had to imagine themselves back there, think of what impressed them about that instant, then walk from that dogear to the thing they needed to recall. He "saw" the back of the check, her bold printing with a black pen, the kind of printing a short order cook could see without pulling it from the carousel or counter. There was something related to New York in her address—

Park Avenue. No—Park . . . not Place, not Road . . . Circle. Park Circle.

Ward was punching the street into the GPS even as he remembered the number, thirty-three, because it was between her age and his.

He hoped he was just being ridiculously cautious. But his driving didn't reflect that as he tore down the street toward Homestead Drive.

CHAPTER TWENTY-SEVEN

Hassan Shatri felt a kind of rage that had been unknown to him—until he met John Ward.

The nineteen-year-old had experienced suspicion and even prejudice growing up in Chicago. But there was a Muslim community and it offered support and a sense of security. Here, in the Christian world, he was not learned enough to be a prophet in the desert. But in Basalt he felt repressed enough to be a slave in revolt, especially where that smug and arrogant New York cop was concerned. Shatri had run up against his kind in Chicago. There, he had to take it: each cop had a precinct to back him up. Here, the guy didn't even carry any legal weight with the local police department. And they were cowards, anyway. Rather than fight their own battles and investigate their own cases, Angie Dickson said the police chief conspired to let Ward come back to town.

That would prove to be his biggest mistake. Shatri smiled.

As Ward had thrown himself from the van earlier that evening, his pocket had ripped in Shatri's fist. The young Muslim found the dinner check in his hand, along with the outer fabric of Ward's pocket. He suggested to his uncle that it might be of use to them. They had gone there and waited. Shatri and his three friends parked their minivan toward the end of Park Circle and, pulling on ski masks, walked back several hundred meters to number thirty-three. The lights were still on in an upstairs room. There was only one car in the driveway of the small home and it was not a rental. Wherever Ward was—Hamza had suggested he was probably watching the Dickson home—he wasn't here. But he would be soon, Debbie herself would see to that. Because the heart of *jihad* was not just to win. It was to subjugate. As the imam had told them many times, defiance is crushed by putting bystanders in jeopardy.

"*There is no such creature as an 'innocent,'*" he had told them during his weekend sermon just days before. "*They are complicit by their silence and no less deserving of destruction. Their pain discourages resistance. The man who would willingly accept torture will not watch as his daughter's eyes are cut out.*"

That dogma fit with Shatri's own fierce desire to punish Ward.

The men crouched behind shrubs on the lawn, hidden from the house, from the street, and from the driveway. They studied the grounds. There was no evidence of a dog. Light from an adjoining home revealed no run, no fence, no bowl outside. The men circled the house once and selected the back door. It was easy to slip the catch from the lock using a pocket knife and they entered the kitchen. The glow of the clocks on the microwave and oven was not enough to illuminate the room, so Shatri took out a small penlight. The floor was linoleum and it might make popping sounds. He looked to the side, saw another exit, one that opened onto a carpeted living room. They went that way, making their way to the staircase. He killed the light. The bedroom door was open. The woman was talking quietly on the telephone. She seemed to be giving someone advice. The four men ascended slowly but without exceptional caution; there was no way down, now that they were on the stairs. And she wouldn't be able to scream for more than a moment before one of them silenced her.

Shatri reached the landing. The door was just to his left. The woman was still talking. He waited and motioned the others to do the same. He did not want to frighten her and have whoever she was talking to phone the police.

He heard her wish the caller a long and prosperous life; it was an odd salutation, almost Islamic. He heard the bed squeak and she muttered something about the caller needing a therapist and not a tarot reading, her voice coming nearer. He swung in just before Debbie reached the door and they stood face-to-face for a moment at the foot of the queen-sized bed. She was wearing pink satin pajamas and a stunned expression.

Shatri moved first, putting one hand behind her head and the other on her mouth and pressing hard. Her cries were muffled by his palm. He walked her backwards, forcefully, out of the doorway so the other men could enter. The second man in edged between them and the wall, pinning her arms behind her.

"Gag her," Shatri said over his shoulder. "She's biting."

The third man came up with a handkerchief, went to push it in her mouth when Shatri moved his hand. She wanted to scream but pressed her lips together and wiggled her head from side to side in an effort to thwart the man. He pinched her nose shut, forcing her mouth open to breathe. He pushed the handkerchief in and Shatri clapped his hand over that.

The men carried the kicking, wriggling woman to the bed. Stripping the pillows, the fourth man tied one around each wrist, and each of those to a bedpost. One of them held her legs down while another looked around for more bindings.

"Use her pajamas," Shatri ordered.

Hearing that, Debbie screamed louder into the handkerchief and began to pull against the headboard with coordinated jerks, then with random, depleted effort. All the while, two men coldly, methodically pulled off her bottoms. One ripped them in the center and used the halves to bind her kicking legs to the bed. She flopped up and down, side to side, then fell back sobbing and exhausted.

The four men looked down at her. She was panting hard, sucking air through her nose, her eyes wide. Shatri stood by the headboard and looked down at her. She looked up at him, tears falling from the corners of her eyes.

"You are afraid because you know you have sinned."

She moved her head vigorously from side to side. He bent down and held her cheeks firmly between his thumb and index finger, stopping her. She could not see his features so he would have to convince her by the strength of his words.

"You must do as I tell you, do you understand?" She did not react. He released her face. There was a deck of tarot cards and a lighted candle on the night table. Beside the candle was a box of wooden matches. He struck one and dropped it on the woman's bare belly. She writhed pitifully and screamed into the gag. He lit and dropped a second match before the first had gone out and then a third. Before he could strike the fourth she was nodding vigorously.

He set the matches aside and continued to look down at her. Shatri felt a strong desire to hurt the woman not just because she was a sinner but because her injury would devastate Ward. He found himself wrestling with that thought as the others stood there waiting for instructions. His breath quickened as the idea took root, as he anticipated the satisfaction it would give him. He touched her far cheek with his fingertips. The woman recoiled. He slapped her hard, then again, harder. Then he again touched her with his fingertips. She trembled but did not pull away. He traced a line down her throat, felt her pulse throbbing hard against her flesh. He stopped at the collar of her pajama top.

Her fear was intoxicating. He used both hands to rip the top button away. She was breathing so fast one of the others commented that she was like a dog. Shatri ignored the comment. He moved along the hem and pulled apart the second button. He could see the edge of her bare breasts rising and falling against the fabric. He tore away the remaining buttons, threw the flaps to the side, then straightened and glared down at her.

They had been with women before; they were still young American men and they had grown up in Chicago. But since meeting the imam, Shatri had come to mistrust and then detest women. The Koran said, "Believers, you have an enemy in your spouses." They were all wanton sinners by whom men were corrupted. They were a means to children and grandchildren, no more.

For Shatri, there was nothing sexual about this woman, about her helplessness. He was an extension of the imam, the sword of the prophet.

"Your dress was immodest to start," Shatri told the woman, his anger rising. "I have merely completed what you began." He picked up the deck of tarot cards. "As for these? The Koran says that devils mislead men. These images are all aspects of the devil. What does that make you?"

The woman shook her head as she grunted something in denial.

"You are a sinner," Shatri said. He threw the cards at her and slapped her again. "You will lead no more men—"

Suddenly, one of the men hushed the others.

"What is it?" Shatri demanded.

"I thought I heard a car."

They all listened. Shatri heard what sounded

like a car door closing. He told one man to kill the light, motioned another to the window. The man looked out, craned to one side, shook his head then shrugged.

"I can only see the side of the yard."

"Headlights?"

"Nothing."

Shatri thought for a moment. "Perhaps it will not be necessary to have the woman call him after all."

The young man turned the bedroom light back on and switched on the clock radio. He told one man to stay upstairs with the woman while he took the other two downstairs. He unlocked the front door and quietly told the others what to do. A street lamp lit the green carpet with green squares here and there. Shatri waited in the nearest long shadow, just beyond the door. There was fire in his belly and strength in his heart. The young man felt an urgency in his limbs that he had not experienced before, all of it fueled by the words of his uncle still fresh in his ears.

"Unless you can tear the eyes from all who might see you, and deafen all who might hear you, the wisest course is to withdraw."

Even Gahrah could not condemn what Shatri had in mind, any more than he could the actions at the farm the night before.

Allah was good.

CHAPTER TWENTY-EIGHT

Ward sped through the dark, unfamiliar streets as the GPS directed him to his destination. He parked beside a Camry in the short driveway and was somewhat relieved to see a light on upstairs. It was past her call-time; she must be reading. The light didn't have that ever-changing rainbow glow of TV. He got out, went to the front door, opened the squeaky screen door, was about to knock, hesitated.

The guys who had sucker-punched Scott Randolph had drawn the farmer out with "normalcy."

Ward decided to do a circuit of the house. He quietly closed the screen door and went to his left, past the two-car garage. He picked his way in the dark, careful not to trip over a garden hose coiled on the ground and just avoiding a collision with garbage pails. He reached the small backyard, saw the second-floor bedroom light more clearly, stood and watched for movement. There was none. He lowered his gaze to the back door. He went over, could see nothing in the dark. If anyone had broken in, this is where they would have done it. He opened the screen door, held it open with his foot, and reached for where the knob should be. He bumped it with his hand, felt the door give inward.

It was not locked, not even properly shut. The door swung into the darkness.

Ward took out his cell phone. He had to go in but wanted to make sure backup was on the way. He turned it on and scrolled down to the police chief's number. He pushed the button and heard footsteps inside, looked up. In the dark he still managed to see a black hole moving toward him. It took a moment for him to realize it was a mask, though instinct had kicked in before his mind ID'ed the object. His body moved back as gloved hands reached through the doorway. They clutched at him, trying to grab his shirt at the shoulders. Attack patterns are like fingerprints, and he recognized the force and feel of the fingers, the smell of their owner. It was the kid he pulled from the back of the van. Ward dropped the phone so he'd have both hands free. His immediate goal was to generate enough offense to keep the guy in the doorway, preventing anyone else who might be inside from reaching him. While he did this Ward listened, trying to determine how many other men were inside. Hopefully, anyone else was upstairs watching Debbie and this kid was just a lookout.

The attacker had the advantage of seeing Ward silhouetted against the light of the house behind him. Effectively blind, Ward hunkered down into a low boxing stance, his weight forward, shoulders hunched, to protect his chest and simultaneously deliver gut punches when he wasn't protecting his head. The detective didn't hear any footsteps, any voices coming from inside—

Ward saw the shape to his right an instant before it wrapped him in a bear hug and propelled him to the ground. He landed hard on his side with the attacker on top of him. Before he could lift his arms a heel came down on his forehead.

Of course they're not inside, his brain told him. *You're in the door so they went out the front.*

A kick to the his left temple caused Ward's arms to lose strength in a wave from the shoulders to the elbows. They dropped to his sides, his head rolled to the right, and amber circles swam in what was formerly dark, dark night. Any resistance the detective had was purely intellectual.

A voice asked, "Did he call the police?"

Ward heard heavy breathing move around his head. "It looks like he did."

"Is the phone *off*?"

"Yes. I didn't hear him say anything."

"Then they won't know where he is," the other speaker said. "We have time. Move the vehicle and stay near it. We'll meet you on Elk Run south of here. They won't be coming that way." Ward heard the voice come closer as he felt hands on his shoulder. "Help me bring him inside."

Ward felt himself being lifted. His fingers clutched at the grass, tried to resist. He must have fought them harder than he knew since a fist crossed his jaw and added clusters of white pinpricks to the display behind his lids. He relaxed, allowed himself to be borne through the door and up the stairs. His closed lids registered brightness without and he forced an eye open a sliver. His vision was blurry but he knew where he was. There was a bed and someone tied to it. He could just see the side of a leg, an outstretched arm. They flopped him in a chair and he tried to resist; someone punched him in the jaw once, twice, three times, all on the same side. His head throbbed painfully from chin to skull. The still cognizant detective part of him noted that he was hit by a strong left. The other guy in the van had been a lefty.

"Open his eyes," someone said.

Rough, gloved fingers pressed down on his lids and forced them up. It hurt to blink. Ward had a better view of the bed but wished he hadn't. He saw Debbie bound there, looking at him with the widest, most horrified eyes he had ever seen. She appeared to be naked save for her open pajama top. Beside her stood a man in black. That was all he could see. Someone had shut the light; the only illumination came from a single candle on the night table.

He heard something slice the air followed by a terrible, muffled cry. The figure in black had moved; he moved again and there was another slash and then a second muted scream. Silhouetted against the glow of the candle Ward could see that the man was whipping Debbie with what looked like a belt. He lashed her over and over, across the thighs, the belly, the chest, the face, then back down again.

Sharia "justice," Ward noted in the small corner of his brain that could still be dispassionate.

The man worked methodically, like someone who had witnessed this kind of punishment before. Ward knew it from his rookie days when he'd seen a blackjack at work. You don't hit the same spot twice in a row or the new pain overwrites the old. You hit different places so that each wound can cycle through to maximum effect.

The woman's cries were constant and her body twitched and jumped and writhed with every blow. Ward looked the man over, tried to find something distinctive he could identify in a lineup. It was difficult enough to stay focused, let alone pick out details in the dark. What could he do, ask the suspects to swing a whip so he can ID the technique?

Ward's head lolled against the armchair as the belt struck for the last time. He could only hear hoarse, nasal gasps from Debbie Wayne. The last few blows themselves had caused her to jump—she was no longer moving of her own volition.

The man who had beaten her came over to Ward. He looped the belt behind his neck, pulled him forward to the floor, onto his face. Then he kicked Ward in the side, in the head, in the hip. The detective found himself wishing the guy would spit on him; at least then they'd have his DNA. But either he was too smart or too spent for that. With a final kick to the cheek, he and the others left the room.

Ward's ears were ringing and he could no longer hear Debbie. He had to get over to her, to a phone.

His ribs were broken; he found out that much as he tried to roll onto his side. A sharp intake of air caused them to stab him a second time and he dropped back onto his chest. He was going to have to claw his way across the carpet to the bed. He was glad for the thick pile: he would grab two fistfuls then use his elbows to drag his battered body forward. It took a while but he finally reached the side of the bed where he was able to reach up and wrap his fingers around what turned out to be the bindings on Debbie's right leg. With one hand on those and another pressed to the floor he was able to get on his knees. He moved slowly, accommodating the busted ribs, found it painful to put weight on his right hip; there was a lot of pain but it did not feel broken.

The men had extinguished the candle at some point, which was just as well. Ward did not have to see Debbie's body to know what they had done to it. The sheet was thick with her blood. He used the side of the bed to support himself as he sidled toward the nightstand on his knees. There was no landline but he felt around and found her cell phone.

He did not know the police chief's number but 9-1-1 would suffice. He pressed it and gave his name and the address and then dropped in a limp twisting motion to the floor.

CHAPTER TWENTY-NINE

Ward became dimly, slowly aware of sounds and images. He was not firmly in command of his senses until he opened his eyes and saw white walls and felt an ache deep in his ribs each time he breathed and a duller pain inside his elbow. Then he knew where he was.

He did not try to rise. His bandaged chest warned against that. The IV drip in his arm would not permit it. Ward lay on his back, moved his legs and hands slightly, making sure that everything still worked. He heard voices in the hallway, turned slightly to his left to see that the door of the private room was shut. He swallowed a few times and managed to utter a weak sound.

"*Hey . . .*" he rasped.

No one came. He moved his eyes as far as they would go on either side, saw the call button hanging from a line on his right. Ward cautiously raised his hand back over his head to grab it. His shoulder didn't hurt much, his arm not at all.

A male nurse and the police chief arrived together. Brennan shut the door and stood beside it, facing the bed, while the nurse took Ward's blood pressure, slipped a thermometer in his ear, and checked the vital signs monitor.

"I'm Howard," the young man said with a pleasant smile.

"Hi . . . Howard," Ward said. His mouth was sand-dry.

Howard hushed him. "Respiration and heart normal. Temp—99.6, which is good. That means your body is healing. Excellent. Your blood pressure is actually a little below normal, but that's natural for as long as you've been sleeping."

"How long has that been?" Ward asked as his mind became more focused.

Howard give him a drink, water from a cup with a straw. "You've been here fourteen hours."

"And what am I 'healing' from?" he asked when he'd finished drinking.

Brennan stepped forward as Howard checked the IV drip.

"You collected three broken ribs and a variety of minor cuts and contusions," she said. "Randolph still has you beat."

Ward thought back to the house . . . the masked men. . . .

"Debbie!" he said suddenly.

"Ms. Wayne's in the next room," Brennan told him "She lost about two pints of blood and took over forty stitches here and there, most of it on her face and torso. She should be all right, though. At least, physically."

"Should?" Ward asked.

"They've got to watch for infection. And she may need a little reconstructive surgery on her chest."

Ward stared back at the scene in his mind. He filled with hate. He was sure his blood pressure was rising.

"Would you please excuse us?" the police chief asked the nurse. "If you're done, of course."

"Finished," the young man said. "I'll be with Ms. Wayne." He gave Ward a gentle pat on the shoulder and left.

"We borrowed him from pediatrics," the police chief said. "Ms. Wayne needs constant attention for the first forty-eight hours."

"I'm going to kill them."

Brennan pulled over a plastic chair. "What happened?"

"Oh, God. Debbie—she gave me her number earlier in the day. It was in the shirt pocket that those two punks ripped."

"I wondered how they found her."

"Have you got anything on them? Any evidence at the house—?"

"I wish I could tell you we went right out and nailed the folks who did this, but the place was pretty clean," Brennan said. "Ms. Wayne couldn't tell us much, other than that they wore gloves and ski masks. The welts on her skin show the impression of a belt buckle, but it's one of her own. We didn't find any bodily fluids, no spit, no perspiration other than her own, blood was hers, and she wasn't sexually molested."

"The vehicle?"

"No one saw anything, not at that hour. Some stuff was stolen . . . her wallet, jewelry, a laptop—"

"To make it look like a robbery," Ward said. "One which I had the misfortune of interrupting—right?"

"That's how the morning paper reported it," the police chief said.

"*They* did it, the Muslims," Ward said bitterly. "They figured I'd show up there sooner or later, since I had nowhere else to go. Even if I didn't go to her house, hurting her would send a message."

"Likely, but none of it remotely enough for an arrest."

"No," Ward agreed. "And if you interrogate them—"

"Harassment. I can't do that without some kind of lead, which is what I was hoping you could give me. Their voices?"

"Can I lie?"

She made a face.

"They were muffled by the ski masks," Ward said.

"Were they the same kind of masks you saw on the off-roaders?"

Ward exhaled. "I don't know. I was looking into a headlight up on the plateau. And when I wasn't, it was too dark to see anything."

"What about height? Build?"

"Nothing useful. The only light was a candle that the guy was blocking, and I spent most of the time on my belly, checking out the carpet. Is there anything that matches the attack on Randolph?"

She shook her head again. "The tire tracks on Ridge Road were inconclusive, those plastic bag footprints in the mud have no analogue here, and Scott didn't even get a glimpse of them."

"The fact that they whipped her won't convince anyone they were raised on the Koran," Ward said. He was staring at the white ceiling. All he could see was the arm coming back at her again and again, mechanically, making her shriek into her gag with every descent. "I'm going to get them. I don't know how, but I will."

"I didn't hear that," Brennan said.

"Want me to say it a little louder?"

"Only if you want me to get it exactly right at your murder trial," she said.

The police chief was right, of course. Ward loved that lady. She was thoughtful and consistent, not like the other women in his life. "It had to be Angie," Ward said, thinking aloud. "I didn't see Muscle, I didn't see any other vehicles. She was the only one who could have tipped them off."

"She knew you were here?"

"I wanted to make sure she was okay, so I called."

The police chief gave him a look. "Was that the real reason?"

"Not entirely."

"Uh-huh. And she refused to help you."

"She hung up on me," he told her. "Or was that Joanne? I forget."

"You *do* have a delicate touch," the police chief said.

"I don't get a lot of practice in crack dens and gun parlors," Ward said. There was nothing of an apology in his statement.

"Fair enough."

"They both hung up on me," he said, thinking back.

"I've found—and this is just me—that things work better, at least out here, when you knock instead of kicking in the door."

"A guy with a hostage or a bomb doesn't always give you that luxury," Ward said.

"Hey, we've got crazies out here too," the police chief said. "I once had a kid who took an old stick of TNT, sweating nitro, and hung it by the fuse from the inside doorknob of the Jolly Burger office. We didn't know at first that it was there. If my team and I had busted in, as the former police chief recommended, two hostages would have died and you and I would never have met."

"What did you do?"

"Found out what he liked to drink, slipped someone into the restaurant, spiked the root beer, then just waited him out."

"That kind of tactic is tough when you've got nine kinds of media watching you," Ward said.

"Only if you care."

Ward laughed, instantly regretted it as spikes of pain shot from navel to armpit. He sucked air through tightly drawn lips.

"Yeah, that's gonna hurt for a while," Brennan said. "What gets me is you probably feel you deserve it—"

"Damn right."

"Why? Because you fell for the same ploy that got Scott Randolph?"

"Not entirely," he said. "I was actually calling you when they made their move. I'm angry that I didn't pull out of the kill zone the instant I realized there was one." The pain subsided and he relaxed. "Has Debbie been awake at all?"

"She drifts in and out. They've got her doped up for the pain, so mostly, she's out." The police chief moved closer. She swung an old wooden chair from the wall to the bedside and sat. "I want those sumbitches too. I agree that it's probably the kids from the community center. Hell, they're the only ones around here smart enough not to get caught. But they need to be drawn out, the way you almost did inside the van."

"If I hadn't blown that—"

"This would still have happened, maybe worse," Brennan said. "Stop beating yourself over the head, it isn't helping."

Ward shut up.

"Before we can hope to get back on this horse, you need to heal some and things need to settle a bit," she said. "The oddballs always stand out when the world is otherwise normal. That's the whole idea behind airport security, right?"

Ward nodded.

"So here's a thought. I was kickin' this around with Scott a bit. He's getting out today and is going to open up his cabin in the mountains."

"He told me about that. His hunting place."

"Right. You can both stay there. No one will bother

you. Christ, no one can *get* to you without creating a ruckus of rock and brush. Can you ride?"

"A horse?"

She made a face. "No, one of those *Avatar* birds. Yeah, a horse."

"No."

"You'll have to learn. It'll be too difficult a climb in your condition."

"Learn where?"

"Yakima Corrigan's."

"Where?"

"'*Who*.' Yak owns a stable on the north side of town," Brennan said. "That's where Scott gets his rides. Anyway, you can fake it up the mountain with their help, spend a few days at the cabin recovering. When you're ready, we'll talk again."

"You ready to go off-the-books?" he asked.

"I don't see that we have a choice," she said. "Playing by the rules leaves us on defense and we can't afford that." She regarded him for a moment. "Do we have a deal?"

"A deal?"

"You got my concession, now you give me yours."

"Meaning?"

"I may not need the radiation suits Homeland Security bought for us, but I do read the white papers and alerts. No Wasp tactics."

The police chief was referring to the strategy of sending a single operative into enemy territory to cause havoc; it was named for the disruption a single insect could cause at a picnic or in a room. In the case of anti-terror warfare, a Wasp could be an ethnic ally who infiltrated a house of worship or training camp, or it could be an outsider who sabotaged hardware, software, or ordnance. In al-Qaida strongholds, the CIA was especially fond of contaminating explosives rather than attempting to apprehend bombers. Electronic surveillance was used to collect intel from a given site; a premature detonation got rid of the personnel and robbed radicals of the media platform afforded by foredoomed extradition efforts.

"Don't worry, chief," Ward said. "My head's cooling. It's the hive I want, not the drones. I want it bad."

Brennan nodded once, put the chair back, then looked down at the detective.

"Heal," she said. "When you're better, we'll get 'em."

"What are you going to tell Gahrah if he asks why I was back in Basalt?"

She thought for a moment then replied, "I'll tell him your hate crime back east put you on a no-fly list. Let's see him complain about *that*."

CHAPTER THIRTY

The prayer space was thick with purpose, and the purpose was more than prayer.

The early morning ritual had been completed, the devotees praising God and ritualistically asking for their faith to be increased, their sins forgiven. The fourteen men who worked in and around the community center left, save for Gahrah and the imam. The director of the Al Huda Center rose and helped the elderly cleric to his feet.

"I must speak with you, *abuya,*" Gahrah said. He used the word for "father" to show personal rather than clerical deference.

"I know your concerns." The imam's dark eyes fixed on those of the younger man. "You fear for the young men."

"Very much so," Gahrah admitted.

"Why do you assume responsibilities that are not your own?" the imam asked. "Can you protect them better than God?"

"Imam, of course I make no such claim—"

"They are soldiers in a war, with a clear and important role to play."

"A dangerous role," Gahrah said. "One I fear we make more dangerous by impatience."

The imam bowed his forehead in agreement. "We have always been a patient people yet these are changing times. Events must not move ahead without us. The citizens of this town must fear that which has come among them. How is that to be done by other means?"

"We had a plan," Gahrah reminded him. "They must fear without being able to attach blame."

"*Dawah*," the imam said with contempt. "A *jihad* conducted with stealth. Have we become women that we must conceal our true meaning?"

"Imam—"

"Believers have fear of God and *only* God, not of the infidel," the cleric continued. "Do you no longer believe, Aseel?"

"I believe with every breath."

"Then you know that He will resurrect the dead when the earth has been cleansed. God has willed it and it is our sacred duty to prepare the way."

The cleric clasped Gahrah's hands within his own then turned to go. Gahrah continued to hold one of his hands gently.

"Imam, *please* hear me," the younger man said.

The imam regarded the locked hands then looked up, his eyes unforgiving. Gahrah released his grip. The imam stood there, waiting.

"We came here to make a beginning," Gahrah said, choosing his words carefully, running passages of the Koran through his mind in an effort not to contradict the word of God. "We had a plan and it has been unfolding."

"The man from New York was unexpected," the imam said.

"Yet the end is certain because God has willed it," Gahrah said. "Might we, in our haste to deal with this insect, take the wrong path? If by our new efforts the locals discover what we are really doing—"

"Then they will die in a holocaust of fire sooner rather than later," the imam said. "There is no wrong path in the war we fight."

"Then why not just send the young men out with bombs and guns today?" Gahrah could not keep the desperation from his voice.

The cleric was unshaken. "Yes, that is one means, an honorable way, and it may come to that. But for now I am content with the skirmishes that frighten them without costing us resources."

"But it frightens them to *action*! You've seen that."

"Their action is to attack us blindly, for they *are* blind," the imam replied. "Let them become a mob. Let them attack. The American president himself will speak against them. Our sacrifice will be their defeat."

There was no convincing the imam. Like many other clerics he had embraced the strategy that had worked in New York at the Ground Zero Mosque and other locations. The rage of the citizenry became the story, not the territorial gains of Islam.

"The fire of anger creates smoke, and that is our greatest shield," the imam said, his comforting manner returning. "When the enemy is distracted, like a dog by his basest drives, one is free to act in the open."

Gahrah had not yet reached the level of faith or absoluteness that the imam had achieved; he was still, at heart, a businessman. That was why he had embraced this mission, this role, to own and control town after town, city after city, state upon state until the nation was theirs. It was a goal to play out over a generation or more, financed by petrodollars, smuggled by increasingly diverse means as loyalists or greedy infidels controlled more and more of the airports and harbors. The project had been precipitated by the start of the Great Recession in 2008; cash had proved a great inducement to those who had no political or theological agenda other than to stave off poverty.

The architects of the master plan in Riyadh had conceived of something that was simple and infallible. Gahrah was not an ideologue; he had committed himself because it would be the greatest financial takeover in world history. Only recklessness could cause them to fail, and that was what the imam espoused.

He does not have the time that I have, Gahrah reminded himself as the elderly man left the prayer space. *He does not relish each property we collect, each street we control. Before he goes to Paradise he wants to see the end of America well-begun.*

That was why he and the boys, working with

Tehran, had conceived another plan, one that would run simultaneously with the Saudi operation. One that would shake the nation to a degree unprecedented in its history.

Gahrah still did not agree but it was not his call. The young men were with their cleric. They had suffered bias in Chicago and were nurtured to be zealots. All he could do was manage the original operation. To which end it was clear that Angie Dickson apparently knew something about it now, and that could be dangerous. If her father became frightened for her, that would be more dangerous still.

Perhaps the imam was right, Gahrah thought. Perhaps the cleric knew, intuitively, how people must be manipulated and controlled. They needed the absolute cooperation of Earl Dickson, and the promise of financial salvation or the threat of prison might not be enough to retain that.

Reluctantly, he went to his office and called Hamza.

CHAPTER THIRTY-ONE

Earl Dickson was having a very bad day.

It began with barely concealed tears from his daughter at the breakfast table. His wife had to leave for the travel agency and, after sending the boys to school, Dickson tried to talk to Angie. They were sitting across from each other, breakfast done. Dickson felt a gulf that was far greater than the table.

"I'm sorry about last night," he said.

"It's all right, Dad," she said. Her voice was a soft monotone.

"No. It isn't—"

"I surprised you," Angie said. "I didn't mean to."

"I know. This situation is just a lot more complicated than whatever you may have seen, whatever Mr. Ward may have told you."

Angie looked at him. "What *is* the situation?"

"There are certain—" he started, then stopped. He regrouped, took time to create a proper lie, one she might buy. "You know how the people in this town feel about the Muslims."

She nodded.

"As you might imagine, some of those Muslims are afraid to come to the bank. So we transact business this way. It's easier."

"Hiding cash in bundles of our laundry?" she said.

He could see she didn't believe the words. He had to sell with just his own conviction. "That's right. Unorthodox, I know, but we didn't want people to know about the money because many of them are hurting and would love to get their hands on it. You know that robberies are up at convenience stores, gas stations, even banks—"

"Is that why Mr. Fawaz had those two men ride in the van?"

Dickson hadn't heard about that. He tasted his grapefruit juice coming back. He couldn't think of a quick enough cover-up. "What men?"

"Two of his relatives. They rode with me and had a fight with Mr. Ward. A real one, not just yelling. When it was over, all he was worried about was how *I* was. I was scared. I *am* scared, and he's a cop. That's why I told him what I saw."

"The money."

She nodded.

Dickson was so angry at the world that he wanted to swipe everything off the table and scream until he was spent.

"What—what was his reaction?"

"He didn't seem too surprised. He wanted me to take pictures, and I did—but then I deleted them."

Thank God in Heaven, Dickson thought.

"I deleted them because I was afraid they would hurt you. I found out that Mr. Ward hates Muslims, like you were just saying, and that what I was doing was helping him to do that."

"So he never even saw the pictures," Dickson pressed.

She shook her head.

"Thank you," Dickson said, relieved.

"I also told them about him."

God, make this stop! Dickson thought. "You told Mr. Fawaz about Mr. Ward's suspicions?"

"More than that," she said, her eyes guilty. "I told him that Mr. Ward didn't go back to New York like he was supposed to."

"How did you know that?"

"Because he called me last night. I told him I never wanted to hear from him again. Then I called Mr. Fawaz."

"Does Fawaz know *you* know about the money?"

"No," Angie said. "I just wanted him to know we were not helping Mr. Ward. I thought Mr. Fawaz might be able to talk to Chief Brennan, let her know that he came back."

The juice refused to go back down. Dickson did not like where this was going. "How did Mr. Fawaz take that?"

"He seemed a little surprised, but grateful."

"Did he ask why Ward called you?"

She shrugged. "I guess he knows I was their babysitter," Angie said. "I listed Mrs. Ward as a reference on my job application."

"Honey, that's got nothing to do with the money."

"I know, but I don't have an answer!" she said.

"Mr. Fawaz asked and I told him the same thing, *I don't know.* I told him that Mr. Ward just asked me to keep an eye out for anything suspicious."

"The money wasn't mentioned?"

Angie shook her head.

Ward was probably just fishing, then. Still, Dickson did not feel better. He wished he could take Angie to work with him, like he did when she was a little girl, so he could keep both eyes on her.

"Do you feel up to going to work today?" he asked.

"Yeah, sure," she said.

"You were pretty upset last night," he pressed. "Maybe you need a rest."

"I felt a lot better after I straightened things out with Mr. Fawaz," she said. She managed a smile. "I'll be okay."

Dickson wished Fawaz was as trusting, as naive as his daughter. He also wished he could roll back time.

What have you gotten her into?

"All right," he smiled. "Just take it easy today, okay?"

"Sure, Dad."

It was with a feeling of great unease that the banker kissed his daughter on the forehead and sent her off to work. She felt as cold, as bloodless as she looked. Dickson finished getting ready. He was in a trance, going through the motions. He dimly remembered a time when he enjoyed going to work.

As Dickson was about to pull from the driveway, his cell beeped. It was Gahrah.

"There has been a serious breach," the Muslim said without preamble.

"I know," Dickson replied. "I'll fix it."

"It's gone beyond that," Gahrah replied.

"Mr. Gahrah, listen to me—" Dickson said.

"You will hire a new security guard," Gahrah went on. "Hamza Zarif will begin working for you today."

"With so many qualified local men unemployed? How will I explain that to my staff?"

"You will tell them that I am your largest depositor and I wish someone to watch out for *my* interests," the Muslim replied. "No one would question an oil company or car factory that came to Basalt and made a similar request."

"That's different and you know it."

"That's true. My stockholders are not bound by the SEC," he said. "Moreover, Mr. Dickson, I promise you this. If John Ward comes back to the bank, or if anyone else tries to examine our business or discuss it with you, life as you know it will change. It will change most terribly."

"Look, I can't control where he goes—"

Gahrah hung up before Dickson could finish. The banker's hand remained at his ear, still clutching the phone. His other hand was on the wheel. Both were trembling. He didn't realize how tightly he was squeezing them until perspiration rolled over his thumb.

The world seemed unreal, like a vision. He didn't remember driving to the bank, or walking in, or even noticing Hamza until the Muslim approached his desk with a completed employment application. The big man wore a brown business suit and an ungainly smile; the expression was clearly unfamiliar to him. If it was meant to disarm anyone who saw him inside the bank for the first time, the effect was quite the opposite.

Dickson made a show of looking over the application.

"What are you really going to be doing?" he asked.

"Guarding the bank."

"No, really," Dickson said angrily. "Intimidating cops, watching me, or both?

The man did not reply.

"What am I supposed to tell the police chief when she comes in?" Dickson wasn't asking Hamza, he was thinking out loud. "That I was impressed with how well you handled yourself trailing John Ward, that the bank has a new policy of minority hiring, of outreach to the Muslim community?"

Hamza's smile turned smug. "Minority? Just wait a few months."

Dickson felt as though ice water had been poured down his back. He lay the paper on the table.

How did this happen? he wondered. *Not just to me, to all of us? To the country . . . to the world?*

His worldview had instantly broadened. What had other nations done when faced with this same problem? How did they survive, and at what cost? What was he going to do? What was the nation going to do?

Hamza did not appear to be thinking any grand thoughts. He simply assumed that his application had been accepted and went to stand in front of a potted fern a few feet from Dickson's desk. As he crossed the carpeted lobby he was openly followed by one, then another set of eyes. The chill that had afflicted Dickson rolled through the bank like a cold mist, and everyone knew from the Muslim's posture and the manager's broken expression that it was no longer just a strip mall and a few foreclosures that had come under the control of something from the outside.

Something malignant.

CHAPTER THIRTY-TWO

Vito Antonini knew there was no hiding his heritage.

He was Italian, first generation, raised by Simona and Massimiliano Fabrelli of Newark, New Jersey. He grew up in an Italian neighborhood, hung out with Italian kids, became a foot soldier for a powerful capo, and after his best friend was killed in a small war that broke out between Newark and Trenton interests, he got out. He did this the only way a mobster gets out except in a pine box: by wearing a wire and then diving head first into the witness protection program.

But as his handlers knew, nothing screams "WitSec" like an Italian with a name like Bob Smith or Frank Jones. So he chose a surname from a Denver book—just so there would be others in the state, folks to whom he could claim kinship—and added it to his father's middle name.

That was thirty years ago.

Vito was sixty now. He lived with his wife in the house they had purchased in 1982 and ran the business he had opened that same year. He didn't walk with the same shouldery swagger as then, the eyes weren't as sharp and the knuckles were arthritic. But Papa Vito's had changed too, for the better. It was more than just a pizza parlor. It was an informal town hall, a place for the jobless to commiserate and network, a bank where everyone's credit was good. For six months, ever since the Muslims had started buying up Basalt, there was also a cardboard cut-out below the Coors sign over the bar, a familiar silhouette with the words *Alamo* written in red marker. Antonini owned this corner of the strip mall and had refused lucrative offers to sell—all of them from guys with surnames as revealing as Fabrelli. Names like Al-Jubeir and Alireza and bin Hamad.

Business had always been good, especially for the customers who could play pool a little better than their buddies. Business still was good, though from the 11 A.M. opening to the 1 A.M. closing the place was crowded less with diners as with men who had nowhere else to go. They were truck drivers and tour guides, farm hands and public works employees, forestry specialists and construction workers. They were jobless in record numbers without prospects for future employment. They were kids who couldn't afford to go to college and couldn't find enough lawns to mow or trash to haul. Ironically, a lot of the public work was being done by community service cons who used to be grocery store clerks and depart-

ment store checkout personnel who got caught with
not-so-nimble fingers in the till.

The pizza parlor crowd reminded Antonini of
how the older goombahs used to describe the docks,
when stevedores would show up at dawn hoping for
day-work. There, at least, ships were coming and
going and the prospects for work were no worse than
fair. Here, the only real traffic coming in and out of
Basalt were Muslims.

Half the drivers and carpenters refused to work
for them. They did not blame the newcomers for
what had happened to the town, to the economy.
But they did feel they were exploiting the situation,
grabbing cheap properties and paying off-the-book
low hourly wages. One barely employed accountant
said that if a government institution tried tactics
like that they'd be hauled before a congressional
committee before the week was out. Another man,
Ethan Ford, who owned a concrete company that
hadn't poured a driveway or a foundation in months,
put a finer point on it. He said it was like being an
illegal immigrant in their own land.

The grumbling ebbed and flowed, not hate but
frustration, not bias but disbelief that any group
was permitted to push so hard without push back.
And Papa Vito's was one of the few places where all
of it could be voiced safely, among brethren.

It was shortly after noon, when paying customers
fractionally outnumbered the people with nowhere
else to go, when pizza outsold pitchers of beer, that
Scott Randolph came in with John Ward.

The door opened and the two men were black

shapes against the bright noonday sun. They were not quite human forms, both of them slightly bent; Randolph was leaning forward as his neck healed and Ward favored the left side, the one with fewer broken ribs. But they walked in gamely and there were heartfelt cries of welcome and a few raised mugs as the men entered. The cheers were mostly for Randolph, who all the men knew. Chairs were freed up around the long Formica-topped table. As they made their way through the crowd, Randolph introduced his companion to the locals. Some of them knew him from the news, others from local gossip, still others just because they didn't know him and figured out who he must be.

Antonini came over with a pitcher of beer.

"On the house," he announced with the kind of flourish that was another reason he never could have passed for anyone but a Sicilian.

Both men thanked him, though Ward did not touch the glass that was poured for him. He laughed inwardly at that bit of restraint; he never drank at all when he was working, unless he was in a bar and it would blow his cover. He did not have the badge any longer but his mind was still deep in the game. This was a case and he *was* working it.

Everyone knew what had happened to Randolph and he had to assure them that he was okay, and that insurance would cover the loss of his pigs once the investigation was completed. But few knew what had been done to Ward. They also had not heard about Debbie. Not a lot of men had reason to eat at the inn but a few of them had dated her.

"If this was Jersey, those punks'd be in the Hudson," Antonini said as he drifted toward the phone to take an order.

"We got a river," someone offered.

"I got cement," Ethan Ford added.

"Yeah, then we'll bring our dirty clothes to Fawaz and let him wash away the evidence," said another.

"Yeah, like that Roald Dahl story where a woman killed her husband with a leg of lamb then served it to the constable who was investigating," said Boyd Guinness, an unemployed librarian.

No one let that literary reference kill the buzz. They went on, wondering if it would be an honor or sacrilege to wrap the bodies in prayer mats.

Ward's PC gag-reflex was still functioning from years on the NYPD. He had rarely allowed himself to think thoughts like that, let alone say them—even off-duty, among friends. You never knew when someone from Internal Affairs was listening.

This was liberating. People who couldn't vent, who had to watch every word for any minor offense, were people who became National Socialists when a Hitler came to power, pouring years of spleen and repression against a single target.

"So what do we do?" a man asked from somewhere in the crowd.

"Nothing," Ward said.

His single, soft-spoken word quieted the restaurant. *That* was a buzz kill.

"Uh-uh," said a voice in the crowd. "We've gotten good at that, spent too much time *doin'* it."

"Yeah, and we don't like it," yelled another from a corner. "Brennan doesn't have enough of a force to run an investigation."

"I know Officer Joel Hawks," someone muttered. "The police chief doesn't have *anyone* except him and a few traffic cops."

"Hey, the chief is okay," Randolph said.

"She's more than okay," Ward added petulantly. "She's working this as best she can."

"Then why hasn't she busted those kids down the street?" someone asked. "Everyone knows they're behind this. You can see it in their damn eyes—in their swagger."

"Because she can't *prove* it," Ward said.

"That's why God invented rope," someone pointed out.

The room got very quiet again. Obviously, that someone had carried things a little *too* far and these people knew it.

"*That's* no answer," Randolph said quietly. "These guys need to hang themselves. He thrust a thumb at the *Alamo* sign. "Besides, you just whack at the guys who come through the gate, you'll wear yourself out. You need to knock them off at the source."

"So we hang the imam," a man said.

"Any of you guys ever hear the word 'martyr'?" Ward asked.

That shut them up again. He knew it was only

one or two men making those remarks, but their comments made him angry.

"For those of you don't know me, *I* got shafted by the system," Ward said. "But I still believe in it, because I believe in us and I believe in this country. If we go ahead and uproot what makes us strong—our sense of fair play—then we become *exactly* what we're fighting. Stopping these guys takes the law and *that* requires evidence. We're going to get it, but not with cement boots and Muslims wrapped in rugs."

There was a general murmuring but no further discussion. The men returned to the chat and drinking in which they'd previously been engaged.

Randolph leaned toward him. "You really believe that?"

"Trying real hard to," Ward admitted.

"Me too," the farmer said with a grin.

Ward and Randolph huddled around their small corner of the long table. Ward leaned as much weight as he could on his right forearm. The crowd gave them their privacy.

"I tell ya, these used to be some of the kindest and most generous folks on the planet," Randolph said.

"We've all had the crap brutalized out of us," Ward said.

"Some of us more than others," Randolph noted.

"But it's tough, man."

"What is?"

Ward looked out at the townspeople. "Practicing what I just preached. Remember that gunrunner in New York I told you about, the one who went free when I couldn't finish testifying?"

Randolph nodded.

"I needed to build a case against him, piece by piece over seven months. Even as we did it, everyone on my team knew the world would've been better off if we'd just taken him out and some of them argued we should just do it. We could have pulled it off, too, made it look like one of his own sales had gone wrong. Funny thing is, if I'd done that I'd have probably gotten the same reprimand, been in the same damn place, as I am for having roughed up that Muslim crook."

"Except that you would've known the difference."

"Yeah," Ward said.

The men were quiet for a long moment. "You want to go see your daughter before we head up?" Randolph asked.

Ward shook his head. "I'm going to leave them be." The detective rotated his left arm. "Let's hit the road. I need to get my body working again. And apparently, I need to learn how to ride a horse."

"That you do," Randolph said, patting his forearm. "I'll get some pies to go. Do you care what's on 'em?"

Ward shook his head and the pig farmer headed off. Ward noticed the lighted menu behind the counter and wondered, in passing, if he would order sausage or ham.

There was a lot of moral ambiguity circling inside his head like flies, tough to pin down and more pesky than intrusive. However, Ward was certain of one thing: this approach was right. However much he wanted to lash out for what was done to him and especially to Debbie, who was blameless other than to have given him her number, patience was the correct response.

Even, as these men had demonstrated, if it was not the easiest.

CHAPTER THIRTY-THREE

Seeing the Rocky Mountains from the foothills did not prepare John Ward for being among them. And nothing had prepared him for riding a horse.

Their first stop was Dunson Ranch. Matt Dunson was in the stables where he kept his dozen horses. Ten were recreational, one was a stud, and one was a ribboned participant in the Indian Relay competitions.

"That's more a celebration of the riders and their courage," the white-mustachioed Dunson explained as he limped to the stall on the end to admire the Appaloosa. "It's bareback riding around a track. The rider demonstrates his skill by leaping from horse to horse during the race, against competitors. It takes a lot of training just to keep the horses from startling each other."

"I don't think we'll be doing any of that," Randolph laughed.

"I wouldn't let you," Dunson explained. He pointed to his hip. "Caught between two horses seven years ago during a relay, mashed my hip. And *I* knew what I was doing."

"Doc Stone wants him to get the hip replaced," Randolph chuckled, "but Matt likes people asking about it. When they're too polite, like you, he tells 'em anyway." He turned around, showed Dunson his bandaged neck. "I caught a tire iron across the vertebra. John had a boot in his ribs. You know what the difference is?"

Dunson frowned, shook his head.

"At least the horses didn't mean it," Randolph said.

"No," Dunson agreed, his voice grave. "You can't hate a horse."

Ward stood a little apart from the two, leaning against a wooden upright to take the weight off his side. He was taking it in, quiet admiration in his expression. He appreciated the NYPD Mounted Officers who managed to keep their steeds under control in traffic and during protests. But this, out here, was an entirely different way of thinking, of living. Forty-second Street might well be the crossroads of the world but it clearly wasn't the world. That was easy to forget back there.

"You ever ridden?" Dunson asked Ward.

"Had a hobby horse when I was five."

Dunson's mouth disappeared into his moustache. "Well, the good news is you won't have developed any bad habits. A first time rider is like a first time parachute jumper. You're careful because what you know is squat."

"In my case, not even that," Ward confessed.

"Good. It gets dangerous when you get cocky."

Dunson motioned over his teenage son Garth and wife Tessa, who were shoeing a mare. He introduced them to Ward.

"I read about you on the FAOB," Garth said admiringly as he yanked off his thick glove and shook Ward's hand.

"That's the For Americans Only Blog," Tessa explained as she was introduced. "They write about injustice in the news."

"Was I the perpetrator or victim?" Ward asked.

"I don't know about that, but you're a hero," Garth replied.

"FAOB is not about Constitutional wiggle room," the elder Dunson said. "It's about common sense. The worst attacks against America come under the guise of interpreting what the Founding Fathers meant."

"Like the right to bear arms," Garth Dunson said. "It's okay to attack the Constitution when it suits the left."

"You raised him right," Randolph said, chuckling at his own wordplay.

Dunson and Randolph put the pizza on a picnic table and went into the house for paper plates. Mrs. Dunson, a petite five-footer with chestnut hair and a big smile, led the horse to a small, fenced-in area beside the stables. Ward rested against the fence, figuring he would be there for maybe fifteen minutes as she showed him what to do.

He was wrong.

"The first thing you need to do is make sure your horse is comfortable, which means a quick grooming," she began. "It gets mucky up there and you'll need to brush off any clods of mud or tangled hair that could bother the horse under the saddle."

This reminded Ward of the kind of work his advance teams used to do. Before a stakeout, two men would case the places they were planning to use as a base of operation, make sure the bad guys hadn't gone there first to bug the apartment or hotel or office or slipped a man in as a night watchman or janitor. This wasn't as exciting but the horse seemed to like it, if contented neighing was any indication. During this process the woman cooed and repeated the horse's name, which was Scout.

"Named after Tonto's horse?" Ward asked.

The woman seemed puzzled. "No. His breed used to be popular with U.S. cavalry point riders."

Oh, Ward thought. How dude could he be?

The saddling itself was straightforward enough. Ward did it all while the woman talked him through. He shook out the saddle blanket and, standing on the left side, placed it precisely between withers and rear—careful to slide it so hair didn't clump. He flopped the right stirrup and cinch over the saddle seat so they wouldn't alarm the animal, then raised the saddle high for the same reason. He lowered it carefully onto Scout's back, leaving enough blanket up front so it did not crawl back during the ride.

Ward followed the step-by-step instructions that he doubted he would remember, running the tie strap through the cinch ring and rigging ring, tightening them just-so, making a cinch knot—he did not remember the rest clearly. There was more fastening and tightening and then he was walking the horse in a lazy circle to make sure the animal was relaxed. Ward wondered whose chest felt more constricted as they got accustomed to one another.

The detective left the animal tied to the fence while he had two slices of pizza. Randolph saddled his own horse during that time after which it was time to go. Once again, Ward took his instructions with a firm hope of remembering some of it. He was back on the left side of the horse—an old custom, he discovered, owing to the fact that most people were right-handed and men used to wear a sword—and after turning the stirrup out and putting his left foot into the stirrup he grabbed the back of the saddle with his right hand and swung himself up with a painful arc. The horse bucked a little because, due to his broken ribs, Ward had not distributed his weight evenly and the animal was trying to fix that.

Ward held tight and Mrs. Dunson quickly quieted the animal with her cooing while the detective settled in.

"You okay?" Matt Dunson asked, ambling over with his hands tucked in his deep pockets.

"I'm not sure these khakis are the best riding pants," Ward told him. "I feeling like I should have more padding down there."

"Walk her around again and sit as tall as you can so you're centered. You're putting all the pressure on your most sensitive parts."

Ward made an effort to sit up but the bandages constricted him. He adopted a kind of rolling seat that at least shifted the pressure forward and back.

Randolph rode over after hitching a thick roll to the back of his own horse. The farmer was polite enough not to make a face that would reveal whatever he might be thinking about Ward's horsemanship *or* the delicate reference to his sensitive parts. He handed the detective a windbreaker.

"Slip this on," Randolph said. "It's gonna get chilly before long."

Ward struggled into the jacket while holding the reins. Miraculously, the horse stayed very still.

"You probably didn't realize you were just putting weight in the stirrups," Randolph anticipated his question. "That tends to keep them in place."

"Lesson learned," the detective smiled. Picking up a skill by application was worth all the tutoring in the world.

Ward found that guiding the horse was easier than actually riding it. Scout tended to follow Randolph's horse, a roan named Busey. Ward thought it was strange to name a horse after the actor; he learned that the name came from Bucephalus, the name of Alexander the Great's horse.

The winds grew stronger the higher they rode. It picked up grit and scraped his flesh like those pumice soaps Joanne used to buy. He understood now why cowboys wore scarves. He couldn't remember a stakeout where he had been this uncomfortable. It didn't help that Ward was hurt, but that was only part of what left him feeling unsettled.

Scared? he wondered.

He had never felt so out-of-his-element, so green, so dependent on others. As he and Randolph followed a winding stretch of dirt that appeared to be a trail, Ward realized then that so much of his adult life had been driven along gridlike roads toward hard-hitting goals that could take all the high-caliber energy he threw at them. Of course, there were always markers along the way that told him whether he was going in the right direction. Here, those goals were vague and distant along paths he couldn't begin to anticipate.

A shrink would probably tell you this was all good, he thought.

He doubted this momentary vulnerability would make him a more rounded man, more social or diplomatic. John Ward liked who he was. A lot of people did, even if a couple of do-gooder rookie cops and his former wife didn't. And if he hadn't changed for her, he by God wasn't about to do it for a bunch of Muslims and a horse.

And with that settled, and the horse cooperating, Ward felt a little better about this adventure. All he had to do was all he ever did: customize the skills and instincts he already possessed.

As he thought that, it was those instincts, that awareness of surroundings near and far, that enabled him to hear the sound that was going to change whatever any of them had been planning.

CHAPTER THIRTY-FOUR

Angie Dickson's contentment—thin as it was—was short-lived.

Though brief, the breakfast chat had been the first heartfelt talk she'd enjoyed with her father in over a year. It left her feeling good, like an adult, and it let her reconnect with a man who had been caught up in a problem he never wished to share. Angie felt she may have helped him a little too, letting him talk openly, allowing her to assure him that everything was okay.

She arrived at the dry cleaner's feeling upbeat, even smiling at Mrs. Fawaz. The owner's wife seemed suspicious rather than pleased by Angie's expression.

Angie dropped her family's bundle of laundry in the bin behind the counter then went to the nail where her clipboard always hung, the one with the printout of the morning deliveries. It wasn't there.

"Where's the route?" she asked innocently.

Mr. Fawaz's office was just beyond the nail. He heard her and came out.

"Hassan has it," he said.

Nineteen-year-old Hassan Shatri emerged from the office just behind Fawaz. He came out slowly, holding the clipboard waist-high and looking down at it. The young man's eyes snapped up at her with such disapproval that she actually took an involuntary step back.

"He will be riding with you," Fawaz said.

"What? Why?"

"I have asked him to see if there is a more efficient way we can serve our customers," Fawaz told her.

"I don't understand," she said. "I always take the most direct route."

"Perhaps there are things that can be improved," Fawaz said. "There is no harm in having fresh eyes on the operation."

"No, of course not," Angie said.

Angie's compliance seemed acceptable to Fawaz, if not to Shatri who still regarded her with disapproval. But her good humor had evaporated in that instant, replaced by dread. It wasn't that someone would be watching her; she had nothing to hide and, except for the run-in with Ward—which she assumed was past her—she did her job well. It was the young man's open disapproval that made her uneasy.

"Mr. Fawaz, can I talk to you?"

"Yes—"

"In your office, I mean," she added hastily.

"I'm extremely busy," he said. "I haven't told

you this, but we're planning to open a new store in El Jebel."

"Oh, nice," she said. "When?"

"In three weeks."

"Will you be working there?" she asked Shatri.

"My work is here," he replied.

"Angie, is your question something that can wait?" Fawaz asked.

"Yes, of course," she said, angry at her amiability.

"Oh, there is one more thing," Fawaz said. "You will have additional bundles to deliver to your home."

"Did my dad bring—" she started, then realized what Fawaz meant. More money. She had not yet embraced the idea that this delivery system was not just a convenience, it was part of an operation. The potential scope of it suddenly terrified her, like someone going down the Fryingpan River in an out-of-control raft. John Ward suddenly loomed very strong again, very kind, someone she suddenly, desperately wanted to be around.

"I'm sorry, was there something you wished to know?" Fawaz asked.

"No," she said.

"Did your father bring . . . ?" he coaxed.

"Nothing," she said. "More shirts," she added lamely.

"No," Fawaz said. "He did not."

The young woman's heart was thumping hard, her chest tight. She did not want any part of this, or them. Angie felt terrible for her father, afraid for him, and he *was* her father; but this was his work, not hers.

"Mr. Fawaz, I would . . . I think . . . I'd better give you my notice."

"Your notice? Are you leaving us?"

"I am. Right now, in fact." Angie began to turn away from him. "I don't feel well. I have to go home."

"I think you'll feel better when you begin your route," Fawaz told her.

She caught his eyes before she had finished turning and stopped. They were cold, unyielding.

"If you are unwell, Shatri will drive for a while."

"Mr. Fawaz, I'd really like to go home."

"And I would like you to make your deliveries, please," Fawaz replied.

Angie stared at him. His "please" was the most sinister word she had ever heard. She was close to tears but refused to break down.

"Do you think you can manage this?" he asked.

"All right," she said.

"That's better," Fawaz said, his expression warming a little.

Shatri sidled by in the narrow corridor, brushing her with his hip as he passed. It was a hard, almost threatening bump. He looked at her with open contempt.

"You will continue to work with us for the next two weeks, I hope," Fawaz said. "That is conventional, is it not? Two weeks' notice?"

Angie nodded limply.

"Then it is decided," he said. "You will no doubt

talk the matter over with your father. Perhaps he will have a different opinion? Should you change your mind, I will be happy to continue your employment."

"Thank you," she said, utterly deflated. All Angie wanted to do right now was escape the dimly lit hallway, get out into the sunlight.

Fawaz returned to his office and Angie turned. Shatri was still standing there, his expression unchanged. Beyond him, Mrs. Fawaz and her son Tariq were gathering the bundles for the boy to put in the van.

"Excuse me," Angie said and started around him.

He blocked the way by bending toward the counter. There were two built-in shelves; on the topmost was a cardboard box. In it were black scarves. The dry cleaner did the laundry for the entire Muslim community in Basalt. Shatri drew one of the long, black head coverings from the box.

"Put this on."

She glared at him. Outrage was overcoming her fear. "I am not Muslim."

"You are immodest," he said. "When you ride with me, you will wear it."

Angie did not move. "No," she said.

Shatri stepped toward her and draped it over her head, threw the ends around her throat to cover that as well. He pulled them tight.

"You *will* wear it."

"She needs an undercap," Mrs. Fawaz said.

"This will do for now," Shatri replied as his hands relaxed. "Because of you I am missing important work," he said to her as he folded the ends one around the other. "I will not also have my eye offended."

His fingers felt foreign to Angie, intrusive on the nape of her neck. Now the tears came, though she struggled to remain very still. If the Muslim man had pulled off her blouse she could not have felt more violated. He tugged at the hems with rough little jerks so the garment covered her hair as much as possible. Then he stood back to admire his work with the same cold eye as before. What would people think when she went to their doors, saw her through the window of the van.

"I will see you in the van," Shatri said. Satisfied, he turned away.

"I can't do this," Angie sobbed, still standing where he had left her.

"It is long overdue," Mrs. Fawaz said. "You will become accustomed to it."

"I will not be here that long."

"Whether you are in our employ or not doesn't matter," the woman said as she finished checking off the laundry bundles. "Before you are very much older, this is the way the world will be."

When Angie thought the moment could not have become worse, that remark turned her world on its side. She felt everything she knew, everything that was dear to her falling away. And for the first time in her young life she understood something that other people had been discovering for years.

The meaning of the word "terror."

CHAPTER THIRTY-FIVE

"Do you hear that?" Ward asked.

The sound, though faint, was one the detective had heard before—in the field, in the distance, the day he first went to Randolph's assistance.

"ATVs, probably," Randolph said. "Probably recreational, though it could be rangers. Maybe they increased patrols after the attack."

"Nice. Where were they when you *needed* them?"

Randolph laughed. "Big mountains, my friend, and too few men to cover them. I always felt that was why these guys chose Basalt. Takes too long to get to from the regional outpost. Anyway," he added, "chances are just as good it's something else. A lot of people use the bikes for recreation and transportation. And it may not even be nearby. The mountains scoop up sounds and funnel them all over. Those engines could be anywhere."

"The canyons of Lower Manhattan do that too," Ward replied. "But I know the streets and their personalities." His tone was surprised, not critical.

"It's different here," Randolph replied. "We're not talking straight, level blocks, we're talking winding, uphill miles."

"Sounds like it's above us," he said.

"Sounds like it, but see that dust cloud to the south," he said, pointing to a faint, tawny cloud rising from behind a flat cliff. "See how it trails west to east before the wind takes it north? I'm guessing the noise is coming from the valley beyond."

Ward grinned. Randolph was being polite. He wasn't *guessing*—he knew for sure it was coming from there. He just didn't want to make Ward feel as green as he was.

With a clicking sound in his cheek, Randolph urged his horse forward.

Ward thought they only made that sound in movies. He didn't attempt it. He didn't feel he'd earned the right to play cowboy.

In less than an hour, after following a gently sloping trail, the men were more than 2,000 feet up. Though there was just enough room for them to sit side-by-side, Ward spent most of the ride behind Randolph. The horses found each other somewhat distracting, and his mount seemed to enjoy the relative side-to-side freedom he had ascending alone. Randolph explained that horses feel more competitive when they're beside each other and one will often try to rump-check the other. Whether he was riding on the outside or up against the cliff, being knocked sideways held no appeal to Ward.

Randolph was correct about the jacket. Though the sun was still out the temperature had dropped thirty degrees, to about forty, and the winds blew rather than caressed. They reached the cabin shortly after five p.m., which included a short break for the horses before the final climb. The last 500 feet was at a thirty-degree incline along a runoff-rutted trail. The gullies were deep and often concealed by grass; a misstep here could break a leg. When they set out, Randolph allowed the horse to pick its own way forward as he watched the ground ahead for pitfalls.

The cabin was more or less what Ward had expected, save for the smell. The logs were broadax hewn and supported a steep rafter roof. It was about six or seven hundred square feet, a single large room that sat on a rock-ledge clearing a hundred or so feet back from the cliff. The logs were so tightly fitted that it hadn't been necessary to fill them with plaster. It had been built by Randolph's grandfather who was a part-time trapper, and the remnants of his work were everywhere. Antlers were functionally suspended for hanging pots and coats, and pelts lined the windward wall to retain the heat. The heat was generated by direct baking from the sun from late morning to late afternoon, and a large stone fireplace at night. There was a single bed, but among the items Randolph had brought was a bedroll for himself.

Rows of smaller antlers mounted near the door supported a total of four rifles. As soon as the horses were tied up and the supplies brought inside, Randolph started a fire while Ward had a look at the firearms.

"*These* aren't antiques," he said admiringly.

"No sir," Randolph said. "One on top is a Henry .22 pump, then a Browning lever-action rimfire—"

"BL-22," Ward said. Randolph seemed impressed. "That's one of the rifles I bought from that dirtbag gunrunner."

"What'd you tell him you needed *that* cannon for?"

"Car trunk. Human trafficking—Chinese and Malaysian girls, mostly."

"You had a whole story set up?"

"Had to," Ward said. He tried not to let his gut boil when he thought of Cherkassov.

Randolph sensed his companion was slipping to a bad place. "Ever fire one?"

Ward smiled. "Had to see if it worked. Some guys hold back a piece of the firing mechanism and charge you a few grand extra for that."

Randolph continued the tour. The other two rifles were Anshutz models which Randolph said were his favorites. "I'm a sucker for the old-fashioned bolt-action." He pointed to a small night table near the bed. "I've got a set of .38s too in case a mountain lion or one of the other locals decides to say hello."

"You need *two* for that?" Ward laughed.

"Naw, only for coyotes," he said. "You get a hungry pack deciding your kill is dinner, you want both hands full of firepower."

Ward didn't bother to ask if that ever happened. The detective kept a pair of guns in his apartment too. A man who wasn't prepared wasn't a man, he was a corpse.

The rest of the day was busy. To Ward, healing his wounds did not mean sitting still. He believed in working through pain. Since the injury wasn't going anywhere soon, he had to deal with it. And to deal with it, he had to experience it at its worst. That meant doing everything that Randolph did. Fortunately, the older man subscribed to Ward's philosophy, using work to get through his neck injury. Each man spotted the other as they cut wood for the fire, trapped small game like rabbits and quail, and walked the horses through the relatively level woods that surrounded the cabin on three sides. Ward was tightly bandaged and that proved enough to hold him together.

What struck Ward about being in the mountains was how the sun became their clock. When it went down that first night, the two of them, exhausted from the day's activities and their natural penchant for overexertion, went right to bed. Ward didn't even remember lying on the cot. He was out. They were both up at dawn, not just from the light but from the animals that rose with it. Birds were not something he heard often in New York, except for pigeons, and that was usually in the third person as a pedestrian cursed them out. He couldn't begin to isolate the countless chirping sounds he heard.

Ward was surprised to learn that a lot of them weren't birds at all, but insects—locusts and beetles, mostly. He didn't want to contemplate their size.

The first full day was spent getting the cabin in order which included digging a latrine since the place had no plumbing. Water for drinking and washing came from a pump well in the back which was fed by an underground stream. If that went dry, there was a creek in the woods fed by cool water from the higher elevations.

Ward didn't mind because he knew the stay here was finite. He resolved never to complain about New York tap water again. At least it came to a bathroom that was inside one's home.

But it was the smell inside the cabin that surprised him most of all. Built without modern materials, Randolph's place reeked of the Old West: the musk of the old skins, the nutlike smell of the ancient wood, the ever-present smell of the foliage and the animals—especially the dead ones that had fallen somewhere outside the perimeter. Whatever had not been eaten was left to rot in the sun. Except for those carcasses the smells were not unpleasant, but they were different and unchanging. In New York, smells changed from room to room and certainly from block to block.

This cabin, this small piece of land scratched from the mountainside, may not have been where Ward would have chosen to live. But he had that choice because the thousands of settlers who came before him had made places like this their home. They had fought the weather, the terrain, the others who had lived there before them, others who wanted to live there after them; every conceivable hazard the mind could imagine, those people faced with ax, gun, and courage. They did not have organizations or foreign governments or banks behind them. They had only their resolve and ingenuity. Being out here was like attending a religious service, only the sermon wasn't spoken. It was felt. The efforts of his forebears got into Ward's soul in a way that surprised him. In New York, one heard the stories about immigrants. Their fingerprints, their ghosts were unavoidable in what used to be neighborhoods of Irish or Jews or Chinese or Italians. But there was, at least, some semblance of structure into which they could fit their skills and ancestry.

Out here? You were lucky to find a stream that didn't dry out seasonally. Even rusty tap water was better than that.

It thrilled him, this piece of Americana the size of the Louisiana Purchase. He cherished the living spirit being added to the one he already knew. It formed a more complete picture of America, the place he had instinctively moved to defend.

Now he understood, viscerally, why he had done it and why it was so important. His only regret was that his daughter was not there to experience this with him. Words would not be able to convey the richness of what became a permanent part of him.

And that was just the first day.

The second day was different. The second day the noise returned, the sounds he had been unable to place. Only now they were much closer, though they did not seem to be making their way toward the cabin.

Which is why he and Randolph decided to make their way toward the sounds.

CHAPTER THIRTY-SIX

The only thing Randolph and Ward knew for certain was that the sound came from the southwest.

"That's pretty steep rock there," Randolph told him as they saddled their horses. "Too steep for recreational riding."

"But those are definitely ATVs," Ward said.

"That's what the dirt cloud's tellin' us," Randolph agreed. "Chainsaws'd be darker smoke, not kicked-up dirt. Can't think of what else it could be."

They would find out soon enough. After sliding the two bolt action rifles into saddle scabbards and handing Ward a leather pouch filled with shells, Randolph started them out through the woods. After a few hundred yards the mountain went up again. The men took a trail that had been cut over decades by larger animals like black bear and elk. It was wide but not *that* wide, and once again Ward found himself impressed with the spirit of the people who tried this with carts or wagons. How many dead ends or too-deep gullies, hastily bridged with logs, did they have to endure before getting through?

"The bears and deer didn't always live up this high," Randolph said. "Civilization drove them out of the lower elevations. The elk still have plenty of pine needles and grasses, and the bears do okay with the fish up here, though campers avoid the area. The bears seem to like canned beans more than trout."

"Or maybe *with* trout," Ward suggested.

Randolph chuckled. "True enough. Who knows what's on the mind of a bear?"

"You ever have to shoot one?"

"Have to? No. I did once, as a kid. The whole Davy Crockett rite-of-passage thing—"kilt him a b'ar when he was only three." Except I was twelve. I felt bad afterwards 'cause I learned it was a mother. I left food for the cubs the rest of the winter."

The men rode on, the ride pleasant, the scenery stirring. It was one thing to be among the man-made skyscrapers of New York, which went back a hundred years or so. It was another to be in a place where the "towers" were measured in geologic time.

The temperature stayed the same throughout the morning, in the low forties. The chill of the higher regions compensated for the unimpeded rays of the sun. They were at 3,000 feet; above them, atop another 3,000 feet of sheer, sloping wall, Ward could see snow. It humbled him again to think of a man with a family, and maybe only a mule, perhaps no water, little or no ammunition, coming to this height and—not knowing what or who was on the other side—deciding to go on.

We owe it to them to see this through, wherever it leads, he told himself.

The men went south when they reached the cliff. The path here was nothing more than areas clear of fallen rock; it was a jagged, carefully negotiated passage. Ward found himself surprisingly comfortable in the saddle, the major discomfort coming from his ribs and not from the ride itself.

The sound they followed was naggingly intermittent. At one point it was gone for an hour and the men stopped until they could get a fresh fix on it.

"I'll be danged if I can picture exactly where it is," Randolph said.

"You know the mountains that well?"

"Well enough to know that unless a man's got some screws loose, he wouldn't come up to this part of the peaks for recreational riding. There's a valley ahead with trees sticking from walls that are too steep to ride and a floor that's full of the kind of landslid rocks we've been negotiating. Even an off-road vehicle couldn't navigate that."

"But someone is, and has been for at least two days," Ward pointed out.

"A bunch of someones, at least three from the sound of it. And like I said, I can't figure who or why." Randolph dismounted, knelt, listened. He put an ear to the ground the way the Indians had for centuries.

Ward remained in the saddle. He had an unsettled feeling, something he felt when he was running on instinct without information.

"Yep. It's there," Randolph said, pointing.

The men set off again when the farmer had ascertained that the sound wasn't bouncing from some other direction. That gave him a fairly specific compass reading and it still pointed to the valley.

As they rounded the massive peak, Randolph suggested that they dismount and leave the horses.

"The ground isn't too solid ahead. This is one place you don't want to take a header," he said.

They left the horses tied to a ponderosa pine that looked about a hundred feet tall. Ward had always wondered why people looked up at buildings in New York; now he understood. If it's new to you, it's damned impressive. Randolph took his rifle and Ward did likewise. He assumed it was for wildlife, but then he wasn't so sure. The farmer also took a pair of pocket binoculars from his saddle bag, along with extra shells. A field of mostly flat, red boulders the size of pool tables lay in front of them. Randolph led the way, after first taking off his belt and turning it around. The buckle was polished brass and the sun was ahead of them: he obviously didn't want it to reflect.

The guy's not just taking a look, Ward told himself. *He's reconnoitering*.

Ward pulled out his shirt tails and let them hang over his nickel-plated Brooks Brothers belt. He approached slowly, bending as much as the bandages would permit. There was nothing to hide behind at the ledge. Since Randolph wasn't cinched around the middle he was able to approach at a very low crouch, creating a small, squat profile. Ward simply followed at a distance, waiting for instructions. He figured he could crawl if he had to.

Randolph reached the edge, lay down, and remained very still for what seemed like a minute or more. Without taking his eyes from the valley, he stretched an arm behind him and motioned Ward forward. Ward got on his hands and knees, placed the rifle on the ground in front of him, crawled a little, then reached back for the gun and repeated. He did that a half-dozen times before reaching Randolph's side. All the while the engines were an insistent buzz, like an electric carving knife, strangely more muffled now that they were upon them.

"Quieter, right? Randolph said. He was peering through the binoculars.

"I was just thinking that."

"It's because they're under the canopy of those cottonwoods," Randolph said.

He pointed to a thick clump of trees on the western side of the canyon. Between the thick foliage and the extremely steep stone walls the area was almost entirely in shadow. Randolph looked to the east.

"See the way the ledges cut in and out over there?" the farmer said. "I'll bet the sun doesn't hit the ground there for more than an hour a day."

"I'm missing something," Ward said. "Why is that relevant?"

Randolph continued to study the spot through his glasses. "No old campfires that I can tell."

"Meaning?"

"It gets real cold up here. They toughed it out rather than risk smoke giving them away."

"But we saw the dust cloud they kicked up—"

"That dissipates real fast. Not like a fire that smudges the sky."

"Maybe they built them under the trees," Ward said.

"The way that canopy hangs there they'd damn near suffocate," Randolph said. "Campfire needs an open space or a natural chimney."

"Portable heaters?"

"Possible, though they'd have to transport gallons of kerosene each week and these guys look like they already got a full load."

"What do you mean?" Ward asked, straining to pick out anything useful with his naked eye.

Randolph handed him the binoculars. "See that really tall cottonwood, the one slightly higher than the rest?"

Ward swung the glasses over, focused. "I see it."

"Go east to the rock, then straight down."

Ward did. He watched the spot for several seconds before he saw movement. Someone in a black jacket appeared from the rock before disappearing under the tree.

"A cave," Ward said.

"The mountains are riddled with them. Some are sacred to the Native American population—a lot of 'em served as tombs for chiefs and shamans. They're supposed to be off-limits, but new ones are being discovered all the time."

"Those aren't Native Americans, are they?" Ward thought aloud.

"I'm guessing hell-no," Randolph replied. "Even the kids, the rebellious ones who don't give a spit about their history, treat the caves with respect. They certainly wouldn't go roarin' anywhere near them with dirt bikes."

"But we know people who might," Ward said.

"Yeah. We do. And I'm guessin' they didn't just happen on that cave over the last day or two. There are rutted tracks down there."

Ward checked them out. He was right. The thought was chilling, not because of the fact that the Muslim kids might be hanging out in the caves. It was what they could be doing there that alarmed Ward.

The detective passed the field glasses back to Randolph.

"You don't come up here for recreational riding," Randolph said, picking up the thought where he'd left it earlier. "You come to this spot because no one lives anywhere near here, the sounds are tough to pinpoint, and it'd be real difficult to see anything from the air even if you were looking for it. It's pure luck that we found this. Hell, I wouldn't even have known about it if we hadn't come up here off-season."

"White supremacists have hideaways in remote regions," Ward said ominously. "They stockpile guns and explosives."

"So I've heard tell," Randolph said. "Hey, look at this."

The farmer gave him back the binoculars, directed him to an area where a large boulder was covered with vines.

"See that?"

"What am I looking for?" Ward asked.

"A bike under the vines draped north side of the rock," Randolph said.

"Got it. So?"

"It's not with the others. It's partly covered with branches. Someone's up here permanently."

Ward backed from the ledge and sat. He needed to straighten his back. And think.

"We need to check this out," Randolph told him. "I'll mark myself a trail while it's light and go down after dark—"

"No," Ward said. "We stake it out and go back before dark. That gives us, what, five hours?"

"More like four—sun'll go behind the mountains before it sets below."

"Okay, four hours. We watch to see what they do, what time they leave. Then we go back and check topographical maps. There may be a couple of ways into and out of that cave. We get the lay of the land as much as possible and then we make a plan and see how many other riders we need to execute it. We shouldn't have any trouble getting volunteers."

"What about the police?"

Ward shook his head emphatically. "They'll come out of that cave with, what, a couple of guns? What did they say at Papa Vito's—Hawks and two traffic cops?"

"He was just bein' cute—"

"Still, Brennan doesn't have the manpower she needs to do this right. Besides, what does she charge them with?"

Randolph smiled crookedly. "You're not thinking about hogtieing these punks and putting 'em on trial."

"I am not," Ward admitted.

"But you were against a lynch party—"

"Still am. Maybe they've only got prayer mats and Korans down there. Maybe they're not Muslims at all. But if they *are* armed, if there is something else going on down there—that changes things."

Randolph looked back at the valley. "Some stuff does figure, though. If it's the same guys who hit me, my property gives them better access to this spot. They've probably been coming up that way since I've been gone."

"It also gives them privacy," Ward said. "No neighbors."

"To do what, though?" Randolph asked.

That was the question, Ward thought. Assuming these were the Muslim kids, and assuming they were not out for joyrides, could this be what the NYPD terror briefings had feared? Not only homegrown terror but the birth of an al Qaeda–like movement on American soil. It was one thing to watch for names on no-fly lists or to search the ports with radiation detectors or spot-check vans for explosives. To fight an organization among us was a very different matter. It would require more CIA and FBI eyes to be diverted inward, as the resources of NORAD were after 9/11. The satellite and ground-based radar were no longer looking for Russian planes crossing the DEW line up north. They were looking for domestic commercial flights that diverged even a quarter-mile from established routes. *Fortunately, there are no MiGs coming after us anymore,* Ward thought. But there are still foreign combatants. The war on terror was difficult enough on one front. On two . . .

But that in itself wasn't Ward's only concern. He still hadn't answered the question *Why Basalt?* There were plenty of depressed towns, probably a lot of them bordering isolated regions hard-hit by the recession—lumber towns, steel towns, coal towns. There had to be bankers in those places who would be happy to launder money. Maybe the Muslims were in some of those already.

Is Basalt part of a cross-country route? Or is there something about this city in particular? Ward was guessing the latter. Moreover, the Muslims had pushed to get Randolph out of the way for these last couple of days. Probably, as he suggested, through his property. That told Ward something was imminent.

As they turned from the cliff, Ward knew one thing for certain: because the Muslims took the risk they did at Randolph's place, there might not *be* a couple of days more to figure it out.

Chapter Thirty-seven

The bank day was long and miserable.

Earl Dickson felt the eyes of Hamza on him every moment that he was at his desk. His havens were the lavatory and the vault, and he could only stay in those for a few minutes. Even then, knowing that he had to go back to behaving normally when he didn't feel normal made those moments anything but relaxing. When the financial world had caved in on him a few years before, he had wept in his wife's lap. But he had never in his life felt trapped enough to want to scream.

Until now.

And then there were the other officers and the tellers. The Fryingpan had never needed a security guard before. Was there a threat they should know about? Were *they* being spied on for some reason?

"No," Dickson had assured them individually, even though he himself was anything but a poster child for calm. "The police simply advised us to do this because—well, you know, tough economic times make banks a tempting target and we are close to the highway. On, zip off, and get on again. This makes us much, much safer, I guarantee."

It did, too. One look at Hamza and a potential robber would pick some other target.

Only Dickson didn't feel safe.

Typically, the bank manager sent out for lunch and ate at his desk. Today he went to the one place he knew Hamza wouldn't follow him, Papa Vito's. He didn't care if the big guy sat in the parking lot and watched him. He needed to put a wall or window between himself and the big man.

But Hamza didn't follow. He remained at the bank and ate in his car.

The pizzeria was crowded as always. After ordering his slices and 7UP, Dickson found an empty chair at one of the wooden tables. He pushed away an empty beer pitcher and paper plate and then virtually deflated.

Vito himself brought Dickson's tray, leaning between Dickson and Monty Stringer, an out-of-work landscaper who was watching CNN on the flatscreen over the bar. Dickson suspected it was he who had emptied the pitcher.

"I always see you over there," Vito said, cocking his head of gray hair in the general direction of the bank. "What brings you here?"

"I needed to get out."

"I know the feeling," Vito replied.

"I doubt it," Dickson told him. His eyes were on his dull, distorted reflection in the pitcher. He seemed startled when Vito removed it. "Hold on.

Why did you say that—'I know the feeling'?" Dickson asked upon reflection.

"Let's just say I done some not-so-nice things when I was a young man," Vito replied. "It was very difficult to leave them behind."

"What kind of things did you do?"

Vito shot him a wry look. "Not-so-nice things."

"Illegal?"

Vito's twisted expression answered in the affirmative. Dickson stood and pulled him aside. They stood under the Budweiser clock near the entrance to the restroom. No one else was around.

"Talk to me," the banker said.

"I can't," Vito replied. He looked at Dickson knowingly for a moment then jabbed a stubby index finger at his face. "But I recognize that look. You've done something too. You need to get out of *that*."

Dickson nodded. He was too beaten down to deny it.

"Do you sleep at night?" Vito asked.

"Not so well."

"Is your family hurting?"

Dickson nodded.

"Then you need to make a change," Vito said.

"I realized that today," Dickson said. "I just don't know *how*."

"I'll tell you this much," Vito said. "Nothing comes without a price. You leave a terrible job, then you're unemployed. You end a bad marriage, you may upset the children and you lose half your things."

"It's worse than all that," Dickson said.

"Then the only question you need to ask, and answer, is, 'Will the place I'm going be better than where I am?'"

Dickson considered that. "Is yours?"

Vito smirked. "Some days yes, some days no. But what keeps me awake isn't in here," he touched three steepled fingers to his heart. "*That* pain was going to destroy me. This is part of my atoning."

"What about your family?" Dickson asked soberly. "Were they at risk?"

Vito hesitated then glanced down. "There are some situations—how to say this? You start a family and then you realize they need a different father. To keep the one they have, as he is . . . that's a risk of a certain kind. It was the kind that weighed on me when I closed my eyes and saw their future."

"This change you made wasn't just about you, then."

"No. Where I was—I would have done anything to give my wife, my baby, a different life."

Dickson pursed his lips and nodded. Vito took him by the elbow back to his seat, straightened the chair, and sat him down.

"One trick I learned," Vito said, raising the stubby index finger. "Actually, it was told to me by someone who helped me to get out. This fellow, he said, 'Vito, a year from now this will all be behind you.' I clung to that—and he was right. It's been many years and I do not regret my decision. My family is happier, and because of that I'm happier. My own disappointments?" He shrugged. "What man doesn't have some?"

Dickson thanked him then sat and chewed on

his pizza as he thought about his wife and especially Angie. It had hit him hard this morning over breakfast. His daughter was in a situation not of her making, one that had criminal implications. He had no right to do that to her, regardless of what it cost him.

You sent your thug on the wrong day, Dickson thought as he finished his meal and walked into the sun and stared at the Al Huda Center on the opposite side of the street.

He did not return immediately to the bank. Instead, he turned right and crossed to where the street intersected Two Rivers Road.

CHAPTER THIRTY-EIGHT

Ward felt a little better having stretched the bandages, then rising and walking back and forth across the rock, then down to where they had left the horses. He didn't delude himself into thinking he was healed, but he knew he felt good enough to do whatever he had to do.

Now, all he had to do was convince Randolph. The farmer was over by the horses, preparing them for the return trip.

"I'm staying," Ward announced as he arrived.

"To do what?" Randolph demanded.

"You don't leave a stakeout scene unmanned," Ward said. "You just don't."

"Uh huh. And—you got a radio? You got backup down the block?"

"Will my cell work up here?"

"Probably," Randolph said. "Got about a half-dozen towers disguised as poplars scattered around. But I'm not exactly a quick sprint away."

"That's okay," Ward told him.

"You realize then that you're here for the night. Horses don't do well in the dark. And you'll have to gather grass to feed him—get him to the creek for waterin'."

"I can handle that."

"Take the saddle off—"

"I was paying attention."

Randolph huffed. "You're just sayin' what you think I want to hear."

"I'm saying I'm staying," Ward said.

Randolph shook his head. "You're a grown man. I ain't gonna argue."

"Thanks."

"You're not gonna do anything stupid, reckless, like you did back in New York."

"Hopefully," Ward said. "Go. Move it. You need to get back to town and check those maps."

"I've got a laptop at the cabin."

Ward looked at him with surprise.

"I got WiFi too," Randolph said. "I'm not a caveman. I'll find 'em online in the city archives."

"Okay," Ward said. "Call me when you find out something."

"Your phone is on vibrate?"

"Always," Ward said. "Professional eavesdropper can't afford to have Celine Dion coming from his belt."

"I'll leave that statement be," Randolph said as he mounted. "Awright, John. I'll talk to you later and I'll be back in the morning. Just remember—it gets *real* dark up here. We don't have streetlights and there isn't a decent moon for another week."

"Got it."

Randolph handed him the field glasses. "You'll be needing these to keep watch. But remember something—there's only two ways down there, with a rope or falling. And you ain't got a rope."

"I know."

With a long, lingering look as mistrustful as any Ward had ever witnessed, Randolph swung his mount around and started down the rocky path. Ward did not wait for him to disappear under the tree line before returning to the cliff. He liked and respected Randolph, but he needed to apply himself to this thing without distraction. And not from a distance. There was no way to find out what was going on below if he was up here.

Ward looked out at the sun. He figured it would set behind the tallest peak in about twenty or thirty minutes. That would provide some darkness for what he was contemplating.

After seeing to the needs of the horse—the creek was just fifty yards back and removing the saddle was easier than putting it on—Ward fashioned a shoulder harness from his belt. He looped it over his left arm, tightening it high, and fastened the gun to his back. That would also help to keep him rigid so he didn't re-injure his ribs. He jumped up and down, moved from side to side as much as the bandages would allow. When he was sure the rig would hold, Ward went to the saddle and took a six-inch knife from its scabbard.

"You'd probably think this was nuts if you understood it," he said to Scout.

The horse was too content to acknowledge him.

"It *is* nuts," Ward said as he cut away the stirrups. "But this is war, fella, and war is never sane."

The stirrups were bell-bottom aluminum with leather studs that kept them from rubbing the horse. They should work perfectly for what Ward had in mind. Next, he slipped the reins from the bridle and cut them into two equal strips. Then he sliced two smaller straps from the bridle. Returning to the ledge, he sat and wrapped the leather straps around his hands. He made them tight, like a boxer, but not so tight that they cut off circulation. The difference in his bindings and those of a fighter is that he wrapped the index and middle fingers of both hands as well, tying them together.

Ward had been studying the cliff while Randolph had been watching the valley floor. The problem before him was not the two thousand foot cliff. It was the first five hundred feet or so. The slightly sloping surface was like a waterfall made of rock, a striated plug of stone that reminded him of pictures he'd seen of Devil's Tower in Wyoming. The rock was dark and there were thick, vertical ribs of stone bulging here and there. Since most of the surface *was* rock, there was little risk of stirring dust that would catch the sunlight and be spotted below. Below that, as far as he could see, was a more navigable surface: aspens jutting from a carpet of soil and ground foliage, mostly vines and thick, short grasses littered with what the binoculars told him were probably pine cones. The way the detective figured it, once he reached the tree line he could descend in a zigzag fashion, on his seat, using the trees to break his descent by going from trunk to trunk. The tall old trees seemed deeply rooted in the cliff face and did not appear to be more than twenty feet apart at most. It looked like they could take him skidding into the boles. Even if he couldn't get all the way down, Ward knew he could get a much better view from anywhere other than here. The reasons for doing this were compelling; they had to be. Once he committed to it, there was no scrambling back.

He stuck the field glasses in his right pants pocket, made sure the phone was securely stuffed down in his left pocket, and fastened the knife sheath to a belt loop. He took a final sip of water before laying the canteen over his other shoulder. He sat and put the stirrups over his shoes, securing them with the two smaller bridle strips. Though he may have looked the part of an army ranger, he felt like a crazy New Yorker.

He wasn't sure that was a bad thing. An army ranger would be too smart to try this.

Ward edged to a spot in the cliff just above one of the bulging ribs of rock. It was nearly as wide as he was and should serve his purpose. He got on his knees facing the horse. Scout seemed preternaturally content, which had a calming effect on the detective. He flexed his fingers to make sure they had some play, breathed slowly and steadily the way he did before busting into a crack house.

And then, when the sun was gone, he lowered himself over the side.

CHAPTER THIRTY-NINE

The 7UP Dickson had slugged down felt like it was still bubbling in his gut as he crossed to the community center. He was anxious, no doubt about that. Vito's talk had only given him so much confidence when it came to "doing the right thing." The rest was a combination of desperation, indignation, and anger.

You tried this earlier and it didn't work, Dickson thought. *But things were different, then. You weren't ready to call his bluff.*

Now he was. He looked up a number and programmed it into his cell phone, kept the device in his hand as he entered the center. He noticed, before going inside, that Hamza was in his car at the bank parking lot. The thug was watching him.

Dickson didn't care. With a little luck, he'd be rid of the man before very long.

He walked up to the reception desk and asked to see Gahrah. The receptionist told Dickson he was in a meeting with the imam.

"Where are they?" Dickson asked. "I'll be happy to talk to them both."

That felt good. These people had told him what he could or couldn't do for the last time.

The woman just stared at him for a moment, then punched a number, spoke a few words in Farsi, and told Dickson the director would see him in the office.

The banker knew the way. He turned from her without smiling. He'd had it with being polite. She hadn't earned that courtesy.

The door buzzed open, he went inside, and walked quickly down the corridor. The insurance he needed had a shelf life of maybe five minutes.

Gahrah was just entering through a side door as Dickson came in the front. The director stepped behind the desk and wordlessly held his hand toward a seat.

"No thanks," Dickson said. "This won't take long." He was taller than Gahrah by nearly a head and for the first time he felt it. "Mr. Gahrah—we're done."

"Mr. Dickson," the director said with a trace of impatience, "I thought we put this behind us."

"I guess not. Having your man in the bank has everyone on edge. They're afraid we're going to be robbed and that I'm lying to them. And your boy hanging around—I don't like it."

"I am sorry those things were necessary, but it was your own—"

"Stop! I'm tired of being blamed for things that are just *you* being a control freak, overreaching because you think you have me in a corner. Well

I don't care anymore. If I go down, you go down with me. All of you."

Gahrah eased into his chair. "Are you sure you want to do this?"

"You've left me no choice. I did what I was supposed to, we both benefited, and now I'm finished. That's how business works, Mr. Gahrah. A lot of partnerships simply come to an end."

Gahrah reached for the desk phone without hesitation. He speed-dialed a number and put it on speaker.

"Yes?" said the voice on the other end.

Gahrah said, "Do it."

The director hit the mute button and watched Dickson. He heard someone tell Angie to pull over.

"Who is that?" Dickson asked.

"Hasan Shatri," Gahrah said. "He is making the rounds today with your daughter."

"Why?"

"Learning the route," Gahrah replied. "I had no choice, you see. Your daughter gave her notice today. I believe she was going to discuss it with you this evening."

Dickson felt sick as he heard her ask why she had to pull over. He told her there was something he needed to do. There was silence for a moment, the squeak of a tire against the curb, then Dickson heard scuffling and sharp, muffled sounds. Slaps? He thought he heard Angie say something but he couldn't be sure. There was too much other noise—wire hangers moving on metal bars, boxes falling. Then he heard a sound and knew what it was: his daughter had screamed a short, choked cry.

"What's going on?" Dickson demanded.

"He is putting your daughter on her back," Gahrah said, his voice losing none of its silky poise. "He is wearing his Bluetooth in case you want me to stop this. Of course, if it falls out I won't be able to reach him."

Dickson raised his hand to call the number he'd input, dispatch at the police station. "I'm calling the—"

"Police? They will not get there before he has finished raping her. And yes, he is willing to go to prison for me." Gahrah's voice became uncharacteristically hard. "He will *die* for me. And you will be in the same place because next time it will be your wife or your sons. Perhaps, with the boys, we will use the knife to make sure *they* have no sons." Gahrah sat back, his voice resuming its normal tone. "Or you can stop all of this now."

Dickson heard a few shrieks. From behind his mouth or a gag—he couldn't be sure.

His resolve crumpled to ash. "Stop it! Stop him!"

Gahrah leaned forward casually and killed the mute. "Shatri!" he said. "You may stop!"

The sounds of struggling ceased. There was only sobbing.

Dickson's hand fell to his side. "Tell him to let her out."

"They will finish their route."

"Christ, he just assaulted her!"

"She will consider herself fortunate when she

realizes that you have saved her, that she is safe now. You will reinforce that later at home. And, Mr. Dickson, you will never deliver an ultimatum again."

Dickson was not just beaten, he was without hope. Whatever Vito had been doing he obviously got out, got away, before anything like this could happen. There was nothing a man himself would not endure to spare his family this kind of trauma.

He left the center in a daze and threw up his lunch on the street. He didn't know if anyone had seen him and he didn't care. He was in hell and it was worse damnation to know that he had brought his family with him.

He went to his car and sat there crying until he had nothing left. Then he called the bank and said he was going home for the day.

When he left, Hamza followed.

CHAPTER FORTY

No one became a cop unless they liked danger, at least a little; no one became an undercover cop unless they liked danger a lot.

John Ward had always loved taking risks. As a kid, a playground wasn't just a playground. It was an adventure. He would approach each piece of recreational equipment as a challenge: how to ramp up the thrills. With a swing it was easy: you got a good arc going back and forth then slipped your arms inside the chains that held the seat. Unencumbered, you were free to launch yourself into space. With the slide, it was trying to walk down the slippery, shiny metal surface. Monkey bars were more exciting, he discovered, if you tried to work them sideways, facing sideways like a fly on a wall and using the same-side arm and leg to try and climb. Even a broken wrist and countless bumps on the head didn't stop Ward from always going back and risking more. Though even he had to admit that transforming himself into a mountaineering Frankenstein Monster, a pastiche of West and street, was probably the most reckless expression of that.

Yet in his adult life there had always been a correlation between risk and purpose. One fueled the other and he had never yet found the limit of that synergy, when one would fail to drive the other. That was especially true when pain was factored into the equation. His torso was protected by the thick bandages and flannel shirt, but all that did was prevent further injury. The breaks he had still punched like little awls through leather. But it was okay. Once, in his rookie year, he'd been palm-heeled in the face by a drug dealer in Washington Square Park. The pain of a broken nose, the taste of his own blood on his tongue, made him chase the guy even when his legs told him to stop. Another time he'd been hit by a car while pursuing a perp across Broadway. He kept going, despite a hairline fracture to his hip. It isn't only a matter of using the pain or refusing to succumb to it. He believed the shock to his system helped him get through the moment, like an afterburner.

Purpose and pain. Together, they fueled his determination to reach the tree line.

Using the studded stirrups as brakes, Ward went down the cone of rock on his belly. It struck him as a big, fat firehouse pole that was well off the vertical. It guided him, prevented him from rolling down helplessly. He kept his hands beside his shoulders, the leather helping him to add some drag to his fall. In that way he half-slid, half-pushed himself down the slope. He was even able to find small, nublike handholds here and there that were invisible from above. Those helped to keep him from building up too much speed. The biggest discomfort was the bunching of his shirt, which rode up to his chest within moments and stayed there. He should have thought to tie it down somehow. The good news was the bandages held and prevented him from abrading the flesh of his belly.

The slope became a little less severe the lower he got. Toward the end he felt more like Spider-Man than just a guy sliding down rock. Ward actually had to push himself down the last 200 feet or so as the momentum alone no longer carried him. He made a soft landing on the fringes of the foliage, flopping over onto his back so the vines and thistles didn't rip up his face as he came to rest. Breathing heavily, he lay on his back in the dusky quiet and pulled down his shirt. It had been bunched up there so tight he had to rip it to get it down. As he flattened the frayed edges, his eyes rolled up to the top of the cliff. He couldn't believe he'd attempted the descent, let alone made it. He still had about a thousand feet to go to the floor of the valley but he was eager to see what his journey had given him in terms of reconnaissance. He looked for the nearest tree; there was an aspen seven or eight feet farther down. He sat up, took off the bindings and stirrups, then rose on a pair of very wobbly legs. After a few seconds he dropped back on his seat.

You can't see anything sitting on your butt, he told

himself and got up again. He kept his legs under him long enough to stumble down a grade to the aspen. He hit it with a hard hug but at least he remained standing.

Not only was he closer but he had navigated to the east. That gave him a better, though still not optimal, view of the valley floor. Through the foliage he could see a few feet into what was definitely a cave. Lanterns had been turned on—the glow was too steady to be a fire, and interlopers wouldn't want smoke to rise from the site—and there were probably four people inside, judging by what appeared to be the number of off-road vehicles outside. Even with the binoculars, he couldn't tell much. The ATVs still were not clear enough to see what, if anything, they had been used to carry. He hadn't heard the engines in a while; he suspected that if the men had brought anything up it was offloaded by now.

"All of which still tells you a big fat nothing," Ward muttered. Even if one of the riders showed himself, Ward was still too high to ID him. "And for doing what? Driving around on public land and going into a cave?" He needed to get to the valley floor.

If he moved now, he still had some light to make it down. But he also ran the risk of being seen or heard by the people inside, especially if he accidentally sent some rocks rolling down the slope. It would be safer when they left—save for the one who Ward guessed was a permanent fixture up here. That was what the rifle was for.

Ward started down. He was surprised how far

back he was forced to lean in order to remain upright. The footing was not as inviting as he had imagined, with roots and gopher holes or soft mole furrows buried beneath fallen leaves or concealed by grasses. It wasn't like a pothole in a street or a tree root that split the sidewalk. You could *see* those. Unlike the first portion of the descent, this section required careful navigation. It reminded him why he always preferred the city over the country. It was one of the arguments he and Joanne had at least once a week.

And I was right, dammit, he thought.

The detective wondered where the wildlife was—not that he particularly wanted to run into any of the creatures Randolph had mentioned. A chipmunk or raccoon he could handle. Then he realized there was no water on the slope, except what washed down during rains, which might explain why the undergrowth was so thick. None of the larger herbivores came around to eat it.

His ribs were acting up now too, reminding him they were there, and broken, with little stabbing pains every time he drew a breath. Ward hadn't realized how hard he was breathing until it started to hurt. He didn't slow his pace but found that taking shallow breaths more often mitigated the pain somewhat. It didn't help that he was trying to keep an eye on the cave in the event that someone came out and he had to make a hard stop.

It happened when he was about one hundred feet from the bottom of the slope. Two men emerged from the cave. They stood just outside, smoking cigarettes. Ward had descended west of the cave mouth so he could observe it at an angle; he was well out of their line of vision. It was dark and they did not look up.

And then a third man emerged. He did not look up either. But Ward looked at him. Carefully, through the binoculars.

The drama had come full circle, and the detective tasted something vile in the back of his throat. The man was holding an AK-47 assault rifle, no doubt purchased from someone like the New York gunrunner. They could be purchased legally, but Ward was willing to bet none of these guys wanted their names attached to that gun. The Russian-made weapon could fire 600 rounds with an effective range of roughly 350 to 450 yards on full or semi-automatic settings, respectively. That was a lot of firepower, enough to bring down a herd of deer, the hunters who were stalking them, and any ducks that happened to be flying by. It was not a hunter's weapon.

What made this one especially creepy was the bayonet attachment.

I'm guessing you're the permanent resident, Ward decided. The kid could take out a snooper or innocent hiker up-close or with a short pop at a distance. Chances were good no one would find a body or two up here, especially if they were left near a watering hole where huge chunks would vanish overnight.

Why an AK-47? Ward wondered. Up here, where shots would echo—and where any hunter's rifle would have a distinctive, single burst—a handgun with a silencer made more sense. Then there was the way the kid was examining the gun. Ward was disturbed by the way he turned it over, hefted it, sited it without firing. It suggested that this was the first time he had held one. Since the team had obviously been coming here for a while, that suggested to Ward the gun wasn't necessarily for use in this little stronghold.

Something else was clear now as well. The young men weren't just using this cave as a clubhouse.

Somehow, Ward was going to have to get inside.

CHAPTER FORTY-ONE

For the first few moments—after realizing that there was a real situation at hand—John Ward felt strangely at home. Not relaxed, just on familiar turf. He was doing what he spent most of his professional life doing—watching—and it sat on his shoulders like a seasonal coat taken from storage.

Then the particulars of the job itself took over, as they always did. Ward hugged the tree with his side for about an hour, watching, daring not to move. When the men went back inside he moved lower on the mountainside and found a place behind a boulder where he could sit and watch. He realized, then, that he had left his snacks in the saddlebag.

Randolph would've remembered, he told himself.

Of course, Randolph was a professional local. He knew his work *and* he knew the land. Ward was winging it. All it had taken was two days to remind him that as great and eclectic as New York was, it wasn't the world. And as tough as New Yorkers were, it was a thick skin they'd developed for specific kinds of challenges. Mountaineering was not one of them. It only just occurred to Ward that he had been so fixated on getting down that he had no idea how he was going to get up again. He had vaguely assumed Randolph could come through the valley and get him. But what if these guys didn't leave? Any of them? One man with an AK-47 was bad. Three or more, even if they were only armed with handguns, were far worse, especially at the fortified end of a path that was barely wide enough for their own ATVs. Even police tear gas might not get them out; not until Randolph found out how far into the mountain that cave went or whether it was ventilated by natural shafts or other openings.

Randolph called around nine p.m. The men had long since gone back inside. Ward hunkered down against the rock, cupped his hand around the phone, and answered with a quiet, "Yeah?"

"You okay?" Randolph asked.

"Yeah," Ward said. He was listening with one ear facing the general direction of the cave. "What you got?"

"A dead end for them," the farmer told him. "According to the U.S. Geological Survey Web site, that cave doesn't have any other naturally occurring opening. That was as of two years ago, and someone would've heard explosions or jackhammering or anything like that."

"I don't think they'd want another opening," Ward told him. "Makes it that much more likely they'd be discovered. How deep does it go?"

"Four hundred meters back before it falls into

a pit. Looks like it was cut by the same waters that carved the valley."

"Okay."

"Hey, you sound funny. You sure everything's okay?"

"Fine," Ward said. "Say, listen. I, uh—Muhammad wasn't coming to me so I came down the mountain to see what was going on."

The silence at the other end was as disapproving as an oath. After a long moment Randolph asked, "Are you safe?"

"Yeah. Got a real good view, too."

"How the hell did you—" Randolph began, then stopped. "Never mind. You pick up anything new?"

"A little. They've got at least one AK-47. Newly arrived, I think. Bayonetted. Three guys, so far, one lamp. I don't hear a generator, so it's probably kerosene."

"Bayonet? Why?"

"So you don't have to put a knife away after stabbing someone," Ward said, still listening carefully for any sound from below. "If you want to make an initial approach, take out a guard before an assault, that's how you do it."

"Jesus."

"Yeah. So I'm thinking this may be a training camp, but I won't be sure until I get a look inside."

"Dammit, John—don't be an idjit! Not a bigger one, anyway! Just hang tight—"

"I can't," Ward told him. "We need to move while they're probably down to just a night watchman. Then it'll be one-against-one."

"One with busted ribs and a coupla years against a kid."

"Hey, the gray hair counts for something," Ward said.

"Yeah, slower reflexes."

"Experience," Ward countered. "And if something happens to me, at least you know what's going down."

"John, I do *not* like this."

"Me neither, but we're low on options."

There was a long silence, then a resigned sigh. "All right. Check in again when you have something."

"Will do."

"Can you e-mail me from that phone?"

"Yeah," Ward said. "I guess texting might be smarter if I can cover the light. And I'll tell you this, you were right about one thing, my friend."

"What's that?"

"It gets real dark out here."

"Just don't do anything *else* stupid, and stay calm," Randolph said. "There are lots of things out there that can make a man jump—owls looking for field mice, bats, possum. A scream'll give you away too."

"I'll bite my knuckles," Ward said.

"Freakin' clown," Randolph said angrily. "This ain't no joke."

"I wasn't joking," Ward said as he clicked off— on Randolph, calling them both "idjits"—and turned back to the cave.

He remained that way for two hours, crouched low behind the rock in an effort to stay warm. A cool wind was coming through the valley and up the mountainside; not only did it cause him to shiver, it shook small branches and leaves, stirred ground cover, and made it necessary to watch the cave rather than merely listen for any activity.

Just before midnight, five men emerged. Ward could see little more than their small silhouettes against the steady orange-yellow light inside the cave. He noticed their arms moving lazily when they moved at all. One man rolled his shoulder in a stretching motion. The men were not wearing heavy garments despite the cold.

You've been working out, Ward concluded. And not just to stay in shape. They could have done that at the local health club.

Four of the men went forward and were lost under the tree cover. There was nothing but blackness and then the sound of the engines starting up. Within moments, four off-road vehicles went tearing along the valley floor—quickly, recklessly. That too, he guessed, was part of the reason they were up here. Learning to master fast approaches and getaways. The sound became an echo and then a hum before it was lost in the turns of the valley.

Ward continued to watch the man who stayed behind. He came out after the others were gone, lit a cigarette, and remained standing in the mouth of the cave. It would be easy enough to take him out with a single shot. This wasn't New York and there wasn't a district attorney to squawk about Miranda rights. But, miraculously, these guys hadn't yet turned him into a murderer.

Besides, he reminded himself, *you can't question a dead man.*

Ward waited another half hour or so until the light went out before rising from behind the boulder. He shook out his cramped legs. It was utterly dark now, darker than a man-made blackout in a hallway in the projects, but he had used the last of the light to study the hundred feet of terrain leading down, and the hundred or so feet that led to the mouth of the cave. He had a course mapped out in his mind; hopefully, if he made any noise, the kid inside would think it was an animal.

At least I'll have a little warning if he comes to check, he told himself. The man inside would have to turn on a light to see.

He took the rifle from his back and started down, using the butt to poke ahead of him for anything that wasn't solid ground. He was making good progress—he had covered about fifty feet, by his estimation—and was feeling pretty good about it when he caught his foot under a root. It snagged just enough to drop him to one knee. He bent to that side, the pain of his broken rib causing him to suck in a long, painful, wheezing breath. It was not the kind of sound made by any nocturnal animal and a flashlight came on within moments. It stabbed the inside of the cave before spearing into the night.

Ward lowered himself to the ground, onto his left side. Gunmen who couldn't see their target tended to shoot high because they shot from the hip or shoulder; this position would present as low a profile as possible.

Each breath was like being stuck with a long needle.

Got to thinking you were Superman, didn't you? he thought bitterly. You *don't need to rest busted ribs—no, not* you*!*

Drawing air deeply through his mouth to keep from moaning, he slowly brought the rifle around with his right arm. He couldn't site it so he just propped it against his shoulder. He didn't relish firing: he would only be able to put a bullet in the vicinity of the man. The kid, in response, could chop about a hundred yards of woodland into splinters.

The light probed the darkness, falling short of where he was. The kid was standing just inside the opening.

Smart, Ward decided. *You don't want to expose yourself to attack from above.*

The question was, how far would the kid go? Would he return to the cave or would he take some kind preventative action, risk spraying the area with gunfire?

Ward heard the distinctive *clack* of the AK-47 being fitted with a loaded magazine. That was followed by the small click of the selector lever being adjusted. The kid was probably going to threaten to shoot and, if no one answered, he'd step out firing in a continuous sweep: up to the left or right, ahead, then up the other side. Overkill was all these young, edgy, inexperienced punks knew. At six rounds per second the odds were pretty fair that one bullet in the volley would hit him. The detective had to get the drop on the guy and there was only one way he could think of. He drew a deep breath and said:

"Guide us to the straight path, the path of those whom You have favored."

They were the words burned in his brain by that scumbag vendor in Battery Park. As Ward had expected, the utterance from the Koran got him a momentary hall pass. Gunmen were unpredictable but Muslims were not.

The kid was silent for several seconds. Then, still inside the cave, he shouted, "Who is out there?"

Ward did not reply.

The young man started forward cautiously. Ward could hear the dirt crunch with each tentative step. He saw the front of his boots emerge from the cave before the young man stopped.

"Who are you?" he repeated. "Answer me!"

Ward was going to have to say something. "It's *me*," he said weakly, not having to fake the pain. "We . . . we were ambushed."

"*What?*"

"The man from New York . . . he was waiting . . ."

That was all Ward said but he was watching the cave intently. He aligned the barrel of the gun with the opening as best he could. If the kid came out to help him, he'd have to shoulder the AK-47 and Ward would have about a second or two.

The young man came outside a few paces but not to help him. The boy covered one ear with his hand. In the other hand Ward saw an additional glow, a small one. He knew what *that* was. The kid was calling someone.

There was no time for stealth or further deceptions. With the boy outside—possibly for better reception—Ward moved to the south a few paces to where he knew there was a tree. He felt his way through the dark with an extended hand and leaned against the trunk for support. He raised the rifle. A hundred feet away, his ear pressed to the phone, the kid didn't hear him.

All he heard was the single shot that struck his shoulder and knocked him down.

CHAPTER FORTY-TWO

The kid landed hard just inside the mouth of the cave. Ward hurried to where he lay writhing and swearing. The detective ignored him for a moment. The phone had dropped behind him, just inside the cave. Ward picked up the device and listened. The wind was howling around him; that was why the kid had risked stepping outside. The mouth of the cave was like a turbine. Ward pushed a palm to his other ear so he'd be able to hear. Because it was late, the call had gone into someone's voice mail; he heard the tail end of the salutation and a familiar, silky smooth voice.

Gahrah, you two-faced prick, Ward thought.

Ward killed the call. Then he composed a text explaining that he'd hit the call button by accident, and signed the kid's name, Saeed, which he pulled from an earlier text. Before sending it, Ward checked the old text further to see if there were some kind of special code. There wasn't. He pressed send. Then he put the phone on a cooler and looked down at the kid.

"How ya doing?" Ward asked.

Blood was pushing through the white shirt, around young fingers which were scratching pitifully at the wound. Ward picked up the AK-47 by the strap, flicked the safety on using his fingernail, and carefully lay the gun over his shoulder. He leaned his own rifle against the cave wall and looked around. He found a bottle of water on a large, oblong crate. He grabbed it and knelt beside the young man. The kid twisted and kicked his feet on the ground in an effort to get away.

"Thirsty?" Ward asked.

"You bastard!" the boy said through his teeth.

"That may be, but I'm all that stands between you and bleeding out," Ward said. "You gonna let me save you or not?"

The kid spit at him. The saliva landed back in his own face.

Ward sat back on his heels to keep his back straight. "You gonna tell me what you were doing up here?"

The boy said nothing.

"Sure, sure. You got pride. I'm impressed. You got a mother, Saeed?"

Fury filled the young man's eyes. Ward didn't know if he took that as a threat or if he was simply offended that an infidel had mentioned the sainted woman.

"I only ask," Ward told him, nodding toward the phone, "because I'll need to know which number to punch when you've headed off to Paradise—which'll be in about a half-hour, I'd say. I'm sure she'll want to know."

The kid looked away. He was huffing hard, trying not to show pain, apparently resigning himself to torture. He was also shivering from the cold; the cave was naturally cooler than the outside and was made even colder by catching the valley wind. But the boy showed no intention of yielding. Ward decided to wait until he had bled a little more, had a little less fight in him, before trying to patch him up—or interrogate him. From what he could see, the wound was high and clean. The detective felt bad, but then the kid was out here waving around a weapon that looked like it had been through a few wars.

Which it probably has, the detective thought. He picked up the kid's flashlight and rose. A kerosene lamp on the floor revealed some of what was in here, none of which was designed to make friends. There was a collection of handguns and rifles hanging from a pegboard, along with knives and even a trio of hand grenades.

"You've made a bunch of back-alley scumbags very happy, haven't you," Ward said. "The question is, why?"

He turned the flashlight on the area below the pegboard. A pair of fold-out chairs served as desks. There was a laptop on one and a Koran on the other. The kids obviously knelt here while working.

"Guess you're used to kneeling," Ward said as he noticed two shelves stacked high with tightly rolled prayer mats. He went over and counted them. There were six on each. "A dozen jihadists."

He shined the flashlight into the darkness beyond. The sight was not unexpected but it chilled him all the same. A rope ladder was strung up one wall, to the cave roof some fourteen feet above. Several feet behind it hung a thick rope reaching halfway to the floor. "Climb the ladder, transfer to the rope, climb down, drop to the floor. Jump back up to the rope, climb, swing like Tarzan back to the ladder, then down." To the left of them was a chin-up bar fixed between two outcroppings of rock. "You got yourself a little terrorist training camp here, don't you?" He continued to explore with the flashlight. Also against that wall were bedrolls, two life-size martial arts dummies—hard rubber torsos and heads mounted on a pole, scuffmarks showing where they'd been struck with blackjacks—and, hanging from hooks, the most chilling sight of all: three sets of street clothes stuffed with straw.

"Scarecrows for bayonet practice," Ward muttered. And for the first time he felt sick. There was a man, a woman, and a child with holes in each.

He turned back to the computers, saw Saeed trying to claw his way to the pegboard. Ward walked over and drove a heel down on the back of his right hand. The young man screamed.

"You practice on *children*, you twisted son of a bitch? You can't afford to let them scream so you cut their little straw throats?"

Ward lifted a heel and broke the man's left hand as the knuckles on his right were turning reddish-purple. Saeed's second scream was more of a loud sob. Ward could've stood there and done that all night, up one arm and down another. But he had other work to do. He went to the laptop, knocked the pack of cigarettes off the top.

"So, families," Ward said. "Is this just a general education or are you planning on attacking families out here?"

The laptop was still on and Saeed was still logged in. Ward was almost disappointed. He had made a bet with himself that he could get the password with kerosene, a cigarette lighter, and Saeed's head.

There were local maps, mostly of Basalt and Aspen, with bookmarked sites for tourist spots. But the biggest file was on the Aspen/Pitkin County Airport.

"You've got photos and schematics but no schedules," Ward thought aloud. "What's that about, Saeed?"

Ward looked through the photos. They were mostly ordinary shots taken inside the terminal, a few exteriors, and then shots of people moving en masse toward exits with security personnel going the other way. He looked at the date stamp.

"Eight days ago," the detective said. There was something bobbing around in his memory—then he remembered. The car rental agent said something about a security scare the previous week.

A test run?

With sudden, stomach-twisting fear, Ward saw dots starting to come together.

He pulled Police Chief Brennan's card from his wallet and, rather than drain his own battery, used Saeed's phone to call her private number.

CHAPTER FORTY-THREE

For the briefest moment, John Ward's New York paranoia struck: he had visions of the few bad cops he had known in his life, in his father's life. He was momentarily gripped with the fear that Police Chief Brennan would answer, "Saeed—is there a problem?"

She did not. She sounded alert as she said, "Bet you have a wrong number."

Ward's throat relaxed. "No, Chief Brennan. This is John Ward and I have the right number."

It took a moment for her to gather her thoughts. "But the wrong phone. Who the hell is Saeed Kamyab?"

"He's a guy who was babysitting what looks like a terrorist training camp up here in the mountains," Ward said.

Again, she took a moment to process that. "In *my* mountains?"

"Buried deep," Ward told her. "It's the reason the Muslims wanted the Randolph place. Not just because it was a high point for a mosque, but because it was a wormhole to this little slice of hell." Ward was looking among the other supplies the men had brought up, packed in a trio of duffel bags. "Look, I can explain that later. I'm in the cave, Saeed is my prisoner, and you have to promise you and the troops won't come rushing up here."

"One thing at a time," Brennan said. "This Saeed—is he hurt?"

"Not a bit," Ward lied. He couldn't tell her the truth. He was betting she'd be forced to send a Medivac chopper up to get him. Seeing or hearing that might scare the others away. He started rummaging through their supplies.

"What's his condition?" the police chief asked.

"Semi-conscious," Ward said as he found what he was looking for: a first aid kit. "Chief, we have a situation. The place is armed for an assault and there are all kinds of images of the Aspen airport on their laptop."

"There was a false alarm there last week," she said.

"I know. I was just looking through the photographs. I have a feeling someone was testing their response apparatus."

"Aspen?" she said. "Why would terrorists strike there?"

"Because—it's *Aspen*?" Ward said.

"Yeah, but it's off-season and tourism is down. Even the glitterati are going elsewhere."

Ward didn't buy that argument. The NYPD ran a focus group on potential terror targets. The majority of respondents said they wouldn't care if celebrities or jet-setters got hit, but celebrities and jet-setters would be all over the airwaves talking about a Vegas or Atlantic City or some other pleasure spot if it did get clocked. It would be in the news for weeks, a jihadist's dream.

"Regardless," Ward said, "there has to be a reason for all the surveillance and we need to find it. Do you have any of the specifics of the alert last week?"

"I'm looking it up now," she said. "Threat analysis from the FBI Denver—terminal evac and flight lockdown triggered by the discovery of a 7.62-by-39-millimeter casing on the floor of the main terminal."

"That's an AK-47 shell," Ward said. "They've got a bunch of those bad boys up here."

"Security cams were unable to ascertain who dropped it or where," Brennan went on. "Early conclusion was that a hunter, probably meeting someone on a flight, had it on his person without knowing. Planes were allowed to take off and the terminal was reopened. Fingerprints turned up negative. Initial judgment stands."

"That's bull," Ward said. "Someone was testing the system. They were exposing the sky marshals on-site. Some of the images here, I saw two civilians with handguns helping passengers out."

They were both quiet for a while.

"Any kind of calendar in the computer?" Brennan asked.

"Nothing that I found. But it doesn't look like we're dealing with a seasoned operation," Ward said. "But they *are* homegrown, which is trouble. And something else."

"What?"

"Saeed was trying to call Gahrah when I stopped him."

"John, that doesn't make any sense."

"Why?"

"Gahrah and his cronies own over a dozen properties in Basalt," Brennan said. "The man's got the stealth *jihad* working for him, and pretty effectively. Why would he do something like attack the airport?"

"*He* may not be doing it," Ward said. "I've never dealt with a criminal enterprise that's monolithic. Maybe there's a radical cleric behind it, the imam here or whoever is funding them. Gahrah may not have a choice when it comes to supporting it."

"All right," she said, thinking quickly. "I need to get some tech guys working on that computer."

"Fine, but in the meantime we've got to shut this training camp down—preferably when a bunch of them are inside. That lessens the chance that they can pull off whatever they're planning at the airport."

"Any idea how many people are involved?"

"They've got a dozen prayer mats, but I only saw five men here tonight. There isn't a helluva lot of room. They obviously come here in shifts."

"You said they've got guns?"

"Plenty, with the serial numbers burned off the ones I checked. You'll have reason to hold them."

"All right. What do *you* want to do?"

"Well, we've only got till sunrise to set something up," Ward said. "Chances are someone will be checking in come morning—sooner, if he was supposed to check in. When they can't raise Saeed, someone'll come and check it out."

"Can you get him to play ball with us, buy us time?"

Ward looked at Saeed. He was barely moving. "I don't think so. Tell you what, Chief. I'll get the laptop to you—"

"How?"

"The kid's Arctic Cat is here," he said. "I can take that and be back before sunup. Why don't you concentrate on the airport angle and—"

"You're trying to sideline me, detective."

Busted, Ward thought. "Not sideline," he said. "Delay. Do you really want to take a bunch of teenagers into custody and question them with their lawyers hovering over you?"

"That's how it's done."

"Right, but I'm looking at bayonet dummies up here—and one of them's a child. Is that a line you'd ever cross?"

"Of course not."

"Exactly. Normally, I'd agree with you. But this isn't 'normally.'"

Brennan did not reply.

"Chief, they're ramping up something deadly and we need to find out what it is."

"John, are you telling me you're gonna work Saeed over?"

"I don't know," the detective answered honestly.

"I was thinking of calling his mom, having her get it out of him. Intel says these kids are more afraid of their mothers than they are of Gitmo."

There was an uncomfortable silence. Ward wasn't sure how far she'd go, even with an attack of some kind in the offing. That was one reason he had not told her where the cave was located. She had to realize that too.

"Bring me the laptop," she said. "And the prisoner."

Now it was Ward who hesitated.

"You took him down, didn't you?" she asked.

"Not entirely," John answered.

"He's wounded. Gunshot. Leg? Shoulder?"

"Shoulder," Ward answered. "He was getting set to fire at me."

"How serious?"

"Clean, through the shoulder. I was waiting for him to pass out so I could patch him up. He was still pretty feisty."

"Christ, John."

"Hey, his fingerprints will be all over the AK-47," Ward said. "I made sure I picked it up by the strap."

"You bring your own evidence bag too?"

"I didn't think this would be a working vacation," he replied.

She laughed a little. "How do I not send a chopper out there to airlift him to the hospital?"

"You wouldn't be able to get a resource of that kind close to this location, even if you could find it," he said. "By the time they trekked here he'd be dead. Truthfully? I'm his best way out. And when I drop him off, it'll be anonymously at the hospital."

"Does he know who you are?"

"Hasn't a clue," he lied.

"All right," she said. "I'll make sure they don't try and ID him until the morning. That'll give us time to look this thing over. Take him first, then get me the laptop. I'll meet you at the station and we'll figure out where to go from there."

"Fine," Ward said. "How's Debbie?"

"Awake and hurting," Brennan told him. "Docs say she'll need some skin grafts but scarring will be minimal."

"On the outside."

"Yeah."

Ward's eyes fell on Saeed. Was he one of the punks behind the home invasion? "Any evidence?"

"Not so far," she said. "The guys who did this worked clean."

"Probably because they were trained," Ward said as his eyes fell on the martial arts dummy. "Right here, I'm guessing."

"The law will see that they get what's coming to them," Brennan said.

"You're wrong about that," Ward replied. "Oh, we'll incarcerate their bodies. But these lunatics don't care. When the judge sentenced the failed Times Square bomber, he ranted about his cause and how others will take his place. The SOB is going to read his Koran in prison because the ACLU will make sure he can, and he'll thump his chest to the grave. Same with these monsters. Meanwhile,

Debbie will never know a night's peace for the rest of her life."

"You may be right," Brennan said. "But our community is as strong as theirs—we just don't show it. The day we do, with a loud voice, every Debbie from here to Kabul will sleep better. I'll see you soon, John." She hesitated, then added: "Nice work."

"Thanks."

The police chief hung up. She had a point. But until the hyphenates got out of the way of a unified America, that was only a local dream. It needed to become part of the American persona once more.

He wanted to be part of that big change, though that would have to wait. Despite what he had told Brennan, he had no intention of figuring anything out with the police chief. He had a better idea.

The detective opened the plastic first aid kit. He pulled out the bottle of zinc oxide, bandages, gauze medical tape, and small surgical scissors. Saeed's eyes were shut and his breathing was shallow but regular. Ward cut open the kid's shirt, poured the astringent on the entry wound—the kid didn't even gasp at that, so he was definitely out—then carefully raised and angled the boy so he could douse the exit wound. He pressed gauze on both sides and fixed them in place with tape. Then he wrapped the bandages around his chest to keep the dressing from moving much. Finally, he propped the boy against the wall to lessen the flow of blood to the wound. It wasn't a great patch job but it was probably better than the young man deserved. He didn't do anything about Saeed's broken hands.

"You'll recover but you won't be cutting any throats," the detective observed.

When he was finished, Ward went to the cooler and found some power bars. He ate one as he got his own cell phone from his pocket. He walked outside and noticed, on a ledge, a small solar panel.

"Al Gore, you're helping terrorists recharge their batteries," he said.

He scrolled to Randolph's number.

"It's about time," the farmer said. "I thought you were going to text me?"

"Not necessary."

"Why?"

"I've been busy," Ward said.

"Doing what? You're also not whispering anymore, so where the hell are you?"

"In the cave," he replied.

"Goddamn, I *knew* you'd try that!"

"I didn't 'try,' Scott. I've got it. It's ours, and it's *jihad* central. The good news is, the bad guys don't know I have it—yet. If we act quickly, we can really do some damage."

"Brother John, I don't know what angel is looking over you but I want him on my side. What's the situation?"

Ward told him about the camp and about the airport. He explained that he was coming back to make the drop-offs but would need some guidance on how to get out through the valley. He said that he was coming right back but had a job for the farmer.

"If it involves payback, I'm in," Randolph said.

Ward assured him it did. He outlined what he had in mind, and Randolph endorsed it enthusiastically.

"You understand, though, that this requires absolute secrecy," Ward said. "The Muslims can't suspect anything."

"They won't," Randolph assured him. "We're gonna show those bastards they aren't the only ones who can wage a stealth war."

CHAPTER FORTY-FOUR

Earl Dickson was too ashamed to call his daughter. Nor did she call him, not that he expected her to. He could not imagine what was in her mind—if anything. Perhaps, like him, she was no longer a human being, but a shell.

He glimpsed from his desk as the van returned to the cleaner. He watched his baby get out, a tiny figure down the main road, followed by the lanky brute who had assaulted her. He saw her drive away again after the van was loaded, the young monster with her. His only consolation was that she would be safe as long as he cooperated.

He executed his responsibilities by rote, and if any of the officers or tellers suspected anything might be wrong, they said nothing. Most were still too surprised, some unnerved, by the hulking presence of the new security guard.

Dickson ignored him. He refused even to look at that creature. He had nothing to fear from the man: the Muslims had already done the worst they could do. And he had been powerless to prevent it except by capitulating.

Again.

You are a father but not a man, he must have told himself a hundred times since the encounter at the community center.

At different times during the afternoon, Dickson went into his locked desk drawer and clandestinely removed the Muslim cash in small amounts. He put them in various trays, unseen by the tellers, as he pretended to count cash-on-hand. Then he personally cut bank checks for that money and deposited them in various accounts.

All of it without emotion. He was numb, dead, beaten.

After the bank closed and everyone went home, Dickson stayed behind to do paperwork, the normal business of the bank. He was deeply troubled by more than just the vulnerability of his family. He realized that the operation was not just about shuffling cash into the system. This was clearly a beachhead. The Fryingpan was handling more cash than they had initially agreed to, and over a longer period. He had gone along with that because the first phase had been successful and the second phase guaranteed more profits. After the initial two million dollars was funneled into the bank, three million more was routed. The service fees were lifesaving for the institution, and the mortgage division profited from the foreclosure purchases the Muslims made. Everything was hidden in MRI dealings, turned into real estate, or stockpiled in safe deposit boxes. His bank was a glorious example of the economic recovery-with-a-capital-R.

Except that it wasn't.

Dickson finished, locked the doors, set the alarm and went to his car. Hamza, who left the bank after banking hours, had stayed in his car in the parking lot. He didn't leave until Dickson did.

This situation was bad but it was going to get worse. Dickson was no longer naive. The operation would be expanded to funnel petrodollars into these accounts. Before long the operation would have to be expanded to include other banks; there was no way one institution could handle all that cash, show so much health, without the FDIC and other regulators noticing. If those banks declined to play, what would the Muslims do?

"They'll buy them," he muttered. "Or they'll have the Fryingpan buy them."

He would rise. He would become a giant in Colorado banking.

And he would be the Muslims' man.

"Why the *hell* didn't you think this through *before*?" he yelled, pounding the steering wheel with a fist.

Because he had been able to look at himself in the mirror when he thought about doing this, but not when faced with failure.

Dickson pulled into a driveway down the street from his home and turned the car around. He pulled to the curb and called his wife. She had been crying.

"Do you know what happened today?" she asked.

"What do you mean?" he answered, not wanting to tell her more than she might know.

"Angie said she got in a fight. She has cuts on her neck and face and her clothes are torn. She came home and shut herself in her room and won't come out."

"It's going to be all right," Dickson said. "I'm going to take care of this."

"You knew?" she said.

"Yes."

"And you're going to take care of—*what?*"

"It's one of the Muslim kids," he said vaguely. "I'm going to see them now."

"Earl, no. Call the police."

"We can't," Dickson said.

"Why not?"

The next sentence snagged in his throat. "Angie found out about the money. She's an accomplice."

His wife was quiet for a moment. When she spoke again her voice was the growl of a lioness. "You said there was no way—"

"There wasn't, and it was supposed to be *over* by now," Dickson said miserably.

"Then how—?"

"John Ward found out," Dickson told her. "He got her involved, had her look in the bundles."

"I knew it, I knew it, I *knew* it!" she hissed. "I knew this would happen! How could I have allowed this?"

"Because you were as scared as I was," her husband reminded her.

"About *money*, about losing our home," she said.

"Not—not like *this*! Earl, we have to stop, get out of it *now*!"

"Don't you think I tried? *This* was the result."

"Oh God," the woman sobbed. "I knew it! Oh dear, sweet *Jesus*!"

There was no point in continuing the conversation. Like everything else in his life, it wasn't going to end well. "I'll talk to you later. The only thing I ask is that you not call the police. Our girl will be safe after tonight."

"Earl, what are we going to *do*?" she asked urgently.

"Just leave it to me."

"No—you have to call the police! They'll understand, about Angie!"

"They won't," he said. "She panicked. She inadvertently sent them to attack Ward, another woman, put them both in the hospital. She's in this now up to her neck."

"Then . . . what?" she said pitifully.

"I said I'll take care of it," he said.

"How?"

"I'm going to foreclose," he said simply and hung up.

Dickson swung by the community center to make sure Hamza's car was there, then headed back to the bank. He went inside and locked the door, but didn't turn on the lights. He went to his desk, unlocked a drawer, took out a .38, and set it on his Fryingpan "We're cookin' up business" mouse pad. If Hamza tried to get in, the Muslim would be a dead man. Sniffing back tears but starting to feel clean for the first time in months, he began going back over the records, documenting every transaction the Muslims and MRI had made.

He would fall but his family would be safe. He'd see to that. He would FedEx the documents to Harold Carey, one of his old college chums who worked at the U.S. government General Accounting Office. The GAO spearheaded oversight of money laundering operations that were being worked through private banking activity. Carey would make sure the file got into the proper hands. Then Dickson would get his family out of town and turn himself over to Police Chief Brennan for safekeeping. She would know what to do about protecting his wife and kids.

It took Dickson hours to arrange the files; they had been scattered throughout the system to prevent anyone from making just such a reconstruction. But he knew where all the cash had gone.

It was nearly 1 A.M. when Dickson left the bank. Still on the lookout for Hamza, he had the .38 in the inside pocket of his suit jacket. He deposited the thick package in a FedEx pickup box across the street at the post office. He was exhausted and emotionally depleted and leaned against the box. He looked out at the dark, deserted street.

"I love this town," he said through tears. "I'm going to miss it." He glanced over at Papa Vito's. He understood now what the crusty owner had been trying to explain to him.

Witness protection.

He was wondering what kind of plea bargain he could engineer, especially if Homeland Security got involved. Maybe they'd want him to keep working with the Muslims.

"That won't happen," he thought. "They won't deal with me if Angie and her brothers are gone, if my wife goes away." And there was no way he was going to expose any of them to the Muslims, their money laundering, or their thugs again.

As he stood there, the banker heard a humming in the distance. It sounded like a lawn mower. He looked to the northwest, saw a single beam of light. It was an ATV doing what it shouldn't be doing, riding on city streets. It was heading in the direction of his house. Was this a changing of the punk-guards, the graveyard shift watching his place?

Dickson felt the weight of the gun in his pocket. He weighed a prospect he had never faced, the idea of an eye for an eye. Shoot out a tire and watch the Muslim bleed. It had a Koranish validity. He rose, driven purely by some uncommon animal id part of him, and walked toward the street so he would fall in the cone of the headlight. This was one way to get into protective custody. He took out the .38, held it stiff at his side. He wasn't breathing, yet, ironically, he felt hyper-alive. His heart was slamming like never before.

The driver saw him and slowed.

Dickson raised the handgun.

CHAPTER FORTY-FIVE

John Ward found the two-seat Arctic Cat relatively easy to handle. Certainly he had expected a tougher ride in the dark, over rough and unfamiliar terrain. Though he took it easy to keep from popping Saeed's bandages, he didn't go so slow as to make the ride comfortable. Now and then during the forty-minute trip the young man would wince and wake and moan; Ward just drove on.

He left the young man, without his wallet, lying on a bench outside the hospital and then blazed the ATV's horn. He watched in his rearview mirror as he drove away, saw an attendant run out. Lacking ID it would take the hospital just a little longer to identify him. Ward needed that time. Next, he sped to the police station and left the laptop on the hood of the police chief's car. He logged onto a radio station, turned up the volume so they would hear it inside, and left. He did not want Brennan following him. Then he sped along Midland Avenue, back toward the plateau and the route to the cave.

As he approached the post office, Ward saw Earl Dickson standing at the curb with a handgun. The detective's instincts took control and he ticked through the threat assessment: he couldn't know it was Ward, he was standing there waiting for someone, and he was armed. Ward saw the gun start to come up. The man wasn't really present; he was on autopilot. He must have snapped or something else might have happened. Ward flicked off the headlight and swerved off the road and over the curb onto the post office lawn. There, he cut the engine, jumped off, and ducked behind a mailbox. It wasn't much protection because the bandages prevented him from ducking very low. But it was better than nothing.

"Earl, it's John Ward!" he shouted. The night remained still and silent. "Earl?"

"John? Oh."

Ward heard him deflate in just the space of those two words. Cautiously, he circled around. The glow of the spotlights at the post office gave him enough illumination to see where he was going. He reached the banker's side and took the gun, put the safety on, shoved it in his pocket.

"Earl, did something happen?"

"They beat her," he said numbly.

"Angie?"

Dickson nodded.

"I'm sorry," Ward said. "Will she be okay?"

"Physically."

Ward looked past Dickson. He expected to see Chief Brennan racing after him any moment, trying to get him before he went up into the foothills. "I want you to go home now. Be with your daughter—"

"I can't," he said. "I—I have to go to Gahrah."

"No, Earl, that's what you *don't* want to do."

"I have no choice."

"You shoot him, they'll take revenge."

"And if I shoot myself?"

Ward didn't see that coming. He had to admit it wasn't a bad plan—ends the laundering and frees the family—though it *was* premature.

"Look, we're *going* to get these guys," Ward said. "I just dumped one of them in the ER and I'm going back to round up the rest."

Dickson regarded Ward. "How?"

"I found a hideout they've been using."

"Take me," Dickson said. His voice had gained sinew.

Ward considered that. "Do you know how to fire the gun?"

"My granddad owned a gun shop."

Ward reached into his pocket, gave it back. "Let's go."

The men jogged to the ATV, which was still running. Ward switched the light back on and Dickson squeezed onto the seat behind him.

"I smell horses," Dickson said.

"It's been—an eclectic day," Ward replied.

Easing over the curb he tore up the road, throwing Dickson back against the seat as he accelerated. The wind rushed hard around them, making it impossible to speak. It was just as well.

Dickson pretty much said it all, Ward thought. *It was long past time to put an end to the bullying*.

Coming down, Ward had followed the route Randolph laid out for him, noting all the landmarks—the fallen aspen that slanted across the mouth of the valley on the eastern side, the boulder shaped like a "U" that marked the start of the old trail, the bat cave that you didn't want to enter unless it was an emergency because you'd break a leg slipping on guano. The return trip was easier. Ward knew there were no major impediments, no disabling gullies, no sudden drops. He saw the distinctive shapes easily in the headlight. In fact, as he ascended, he was able to sneak a look to the south. He smiled slightly when he noticed the lights on the plateau. Scott Randolph was doing his job. Ward wished he'd had time to stop there. In all his years of police work he had never attempted what he was about to do. He could have used a few pointers. In that respect, it was good to have Dickson with him. Even though he spent his days in a bank, he was a local. And locals tended to know things an outsider never could—either a New Yorker or a Chicagoan.

It was almost a comfort to reach the leaning aspen, like coming home to a hotel. He traversed the narrow valley quickly, pulled the ATV into the foliage where Saeed had parked it, and went to the cave. He approached, staying close to the western side. If, for whatever reason, someone were up on the cliff with a rifle and a night-vision site, the overhang would not permit them a shot. He moved in with his rifle at the ready but saw no fresh tracks in the dirt or newly crushed grass.

Dickson followed him in.

"Do you think they have sentries?" the banker asked, jerking his head upward.

"They didn't before," Ward said, "except for the guy I took out."

"You killed one of them?" Dickson asked eagerly.

"Wounded." He added, "Badly."

Dickson grunted. He was looking around. "I can't believe this is out here, though I guess I shouldn't be surprised."

"Why?"

"These higher elevations are not exactly widely traveled," Dickson said. "My dad once told me the CIA had training facilities in the Rockies."

"The CIA?" Ward asked.

"Back in the early sixties, for Tibetans fighting Chinese in the Himalayas," Dickson said. "Camp Hale, I think it was called. I always thought it was sort of an urban myth. Maybe not."

Locals, Ward smiled. *They know stuff.* He was pleased to see life and vigor returning to the banker.

"I wonder if these bastards have a name for this place," Dickson said. "Like Muhammad Base or something."

Ward hadn't thought of that. The idea that an enemy facility on American soil might be named for a radical terrorist made him want to tear the place apart with his teeth.

Reaching the cave, Ward grabbed the flashlight he had left beside the solar panel. Then he went to the cooler where he had left the Muslim's cell phone. It occurred to him that he hadn't gotten the kid's password but he didn't need it. Ward was still able to access the text function. What he saw alarmed him. The detective's lips pursed tightly.

"What is it?" Dickson asked.

Ward looked at his watch. "The return trip took us forty-five minutes," he said.

"What of it?"

"There's a text asking Saeed to confirm that he sent the last message."

"Okay—"

"*I* sent it."

"Can't you send another?"

"Wouldn't do any good," Ward said. "There's another text from someone saying that if he didn't respond they would be taking action."

"Meaning?"

"I guess they'll come to investigate," Ward said.

"When was that sent?"

"Nearly a half-hour ago."

Dickson's expression showed anxiety for the first time.

"They know the trail better than I did, so it may not take as long as it just took me." Ward thought for a moment. Do they stand and fight or retreat to the mountains? He couldn't see that there was anything worth dying for in here.

As he considered the situation the chirping of crickets and the occasional cry of a night bird were consumed by the hum of multiple engines.

Their options had suddenly narrowed to one.

CHAPTER FORTY-SIX

"We've got a serious problem," Ward said into his own phone.

Scott Randolph listened intently as the detective described the situation. He had put the phone on speaker and pulled a map from Dunson's brochure rack so the others in the Dunson ranch house could follow. Gathered there were Matt, Garth and Tessa Dunson, concrete worker Ethan Ford, service station owner Howie Bond, Vito Antonini, and two of the Dunson's part-time hands, twins Noah and Hank Hayden.

As Ward brought them up to date, Randolph pointed out each location. When Ward was finished, Randolph spoke.

"Earl's a good up-close shooter," Randolph said.

"And I'm probably the last person they'll expect to see here," Dickson said without explaining to the others. "I can hang to the side near the entrance, block them in if it comes to that."

"That means I'm the bait who has to hold off their initial approach," Ward said.

"You good with that?" Randolph said.

"Beats retirement," he said.

Randolph chuckled but he was already motioning to the others and jabbing a finger toward the outside as they spoke. The group understood. With Tessa and Garth in the lead, they hurried to the stables.

"We still got four hours till daybreak," Randolph told Ward. "I'm not sure we can give you the full measure of our support till then."

"I've got a feeling we're gonna need some luck holding out until then," Ward replied. "What about the police chief?"

"There's nothing she can do, not there, not now," Randolph said.

"Karma."

"Huh?"

"That's exactly what I told her, only I didn't think I meant it," Ward said. "Any advice? Those motors are getting real close."

"Don't get shot."

"Any *other* advice?"

"We're workin' on it," Randolph said. "I won't call unless I need to. I don't want to give away your position. If we come up with somethin', you'll know it."

"Copy that," Ward said. "Gotta go."

Randolph hung up and joined the others. They were in the barn preparing nine horses. "Garth, go to your compost heap and fill one of those empty feed bags with as many horse patties as you can."

The young man jumped to it without asking why.

Randolph grabbed a flashlight from the wall, one with a leather thong. He tested it then went to the first saddled horse. "I'm goin' up to my cabin. Matt, you've been up there. Can you find it?"

The horse rancher nodded, then said, "Tough ride in the dark."

"Not if I set a good fire on Cabbage Point," Randolph replied, jerking a thumb toward the compost. "That'll light up the whole cliff side."

"Gotcha."

"I want you, Garth, and the twins to meet me there," Randolph said.

"But that's a couple hundred feet above where we need to be," Noah pointed out.

"There's no way we can get to the valley itself, on horseback, at night," Randolph said. He took the bag from Garth, tied it to the pommel, and wrapped the leather thong of the flashlight around his left wrist. That was going to be his headlight. "Gettin' to the bat cave is doable, though. Straight shot round the cliff. I want the rest of you to take whatever weapons you've got and wait there. Between the cliff on one side and the cave on the other we can bottleneck 'em."

"And do what?"

Randolph swung the horse toward the barn door.

"They got AK-47s," he said. "I'd make sure they don't get to use 'em."

CHAPTER FORTY-SEVEN

Ward held a flashlight as he and Dickson walked briskly across the valley. He was looking for a good place to position the banker.

"Tell me something," Ward asked as they walked. "How does the money get into Basalt?"

"I think it comes in by private jet," the banker told him. "I'm not sure."

"Why do you think that?"

"Something Gahrah once said, about a delay caused by weather. It wasn't snowing here, so I figured it was a problem en route."

"Any idea how it's packaged?"

"Inside Korans, I think. They always had stacks of them at the community center."

"Right. Customs wouldn't dare check them without a damn good reason."

The Muslim cash comes in by air, to Aspen, Ward thought. *In hops, no doubt, from Iran to either Germany or France where there's a large Muslim population, then to here. They couldn't risk coming directly from Iran*

*without having the plane dismantled by inspectors. But
if the Muslims are successfully getting it into the country,
why test security response? Why train for an airport
attack?*

Ward's phone buzzed. He was not surprised to
see it was Brennan. He did not take the call; no
good could come of it. Besides, the engines were
quite loud. The echo was still deceiving, but Ward
knew the riders were very close. There was nothing
Brennan could do in time even if there were anything she could do at all.

Ward stopped Dickson and looked left and right.
"You're there," Ward said, pointing to a thick-boled
tree a few paces to the east. "Don't fire unless they
shoot first. You're the ace in the hole."

Dickson nodded.

The detective looked around. He saw a flat boulder a hundred or so yards behind on the same side
of the valley. "I'll be there," he said. "If it does
come to gunfire, we don't want to duplicate our efforts. You cover targets south of your position, and
only south, toward the mouth of the valley. I'll
cover the north, toward the cave. That way you
won't accidentally fire in my direction."

Ward had saved the cave for himself in case it
was necessary to pursue anyone who went inside.
There was one circumstance in which Ward *might*
shoot first: to preserve evidence in case the Muslims decided to torch the site.

Before Ward left, Dickson grabbed his jacket
sleeve. "I want to hurt them."

"We will," Ward promised him. "By winning. We
put holes in 'em only if we have no choice."

Dickson hesitated. Ward wasn't sure the newly energized banker—who was also exhausted—grasped the distinction, but he couldn't fix that now. All he needed was for Dickson to follow orders.

The detective jogged to the boulder, which would afford him a flat, slightly elevated surface on which to take careful aim in the dark.

It was a long three or four minutes before the first of the ATV headlights could be seen. It appeared as illumination from an area outside the mouth of the valley. The light narrowed and intensified until a single beam came around the corner, the cyclopean eye of a monster returning to its lair. Ward was calm, as he often was immediately before a confrontation; it was always the crawling minutes of anticipation that revved him up. His own exhaustion probably contributed to that, now that he had stopped moving, along with the realization that one way or another this situation was about to come to an end.

And how do you want it to end? Ward asked himself. *With prisoners who can use a trial as a platform for radical causes, or as corpses that become martyrs?*

Four headlights followed the first into the valley. The cave was dark and Ward wondered if it was supposed to be. The four bikers slowed as the lead ATV approached. He was still about fifty yards from Ward's position. The first ATV sounded his horn, three short bursts, then waited. After a brief wait he fired the salvo again. The horn almost sounded impatient. The biker revved his engine then cut it. He raised his right arm. The others remained where they were, idling. Ward could not see what he was doing. When a cell phone rang in the cave, he knew the man had called Saeed.

Now they'll know for sure that something's wrong, Ward thought. He had left the phone near the front of the cave, far from the bedroll. Saeed would not have done that. The detective was no longer relaxed.

The lead biker raised his left arm this time. That obviously meant "stay" because he rolled ahead. As the biker sped past, Ward saw something in the young man's hand but couldn't quite make it out. A sawed-off shotgun, it looked like. He saw the other riders pull weapons from the gun scabbards mounted to the back of the vehicles.

The rider stopped just short of the cave. He adjusted his headlight by hand to study the interior. He must have guessed, correctly, that if someone were going to shoot at him, they would have done so already. He also may have surmised that anyone who did so would be subject to withering return fire from the other men.

What the hell is he holding? Ward wondered as he strained to see through the dark. It wasn't a gun; it was long and narrow.

The white light showed the front section of the cave. The man dismounted and stepped in front of it. He was sharply delineated, like a freeze-frame flash snapshot.

Holy crap, Ward thought. *I've got one of them.*

He was gripping what appeared to be a tire iron. That was no doubt the weapon used to crack Scott Randolph across the back of the neck. What's more, he wasn't wearing a mask. He didn't expect anyone to survive this and identify him.

"Who's here?" the Muslim yelled. "Show yourself, wherever you are! You have no way out!"

Ward was pretty sure this was also one of the voices he heard in Debbie's room when they were beaten. He silently apologized to Earl: he wanted to shoot the guy in cold blood himself.

"This does not have to end in bloodshed!" the youth shouted. He reached into his coat pocket, pulled out a .38. "We have money! Come out and talk—"

An echoing crack drowned out the rest of the sentence, or whatever part of it the man completed before hurling himself behind the nearest rock. Ward didn't know if he were hurt or not, but he *did* know the shot hadn't come from Dickson or Ward. It had come from above.

Randolph.

Unfortunately, Dickson didn't know that. The banker fired two shots toward the mouth of the valley, where the other bikers were waiting. Ward saw one of the ATV riders lurch back then slump forward over the low windshield. The other three guns let loose on the tree. Splinters flew and Ward only hoped that Dickson had gotten down low, and fast. Ward had no choice now but to return fire. He swung his rifle around. He didn't have a shot at the leader so he opened up on the others.

Gunfire clanged off the ATVs and sparked off rocks surrounding the cave mouth. There was more than one gun on the valley wall. Ward knew how poor the visibility was from up there but that didn't seem to matter. The shooters up there were pouring it on. All they had to do was aim for the headlights or at the bursts of gunfire coming from that vicinity to keep the enemy ducking.

The gunfire from above continued but the distinctive *barruuuuumm* of the AK-47s on full automatic ceased abruptly. The headlights had either been turned off or shot out; in any case, Ward heard the bikes rev and recede. The cowards were leaving, and a couple of shots from Dickson followed them. At least the banker was all right.

The leader did not follow them. His ATV light was gone but Ward saw him, a dark silhouette against the darker mouth of the cave. He had scurried inside where he couldn't be fired on from above. He probably didn't realize he was still backlit by the faint glow of the kerosene heater pilot lights.

When the gunfire from above fell silent, Ward whistled to get Dickson's attention then shouted toward the mouth of the valley.

"Don't speak, partner. Just stay where you are!" He had not used Dickson's name: the man in the cave had no idea who was out there. Should he find out, he still had a cell phone and could call in retribution against Dickson's family.

As soon as Ward had given the order, he immediately vacated his position, creeping as low as his bandages would allow toward the opposite side of the valley. As expected, the Muslim leader loosed a barrage of automatic fire toward the spot he'd just vacated. It was just a short burst. A moment later, Ward heard sloshing sounds.

Overturning the heaters, he realized. The leader must have noticed the glow.

When Ward reached the other side he followed it toward the cave. In the deep shadows, the man inside couldn't see him. The leader himself wasn't moving. He was obviously afraid that his footsteps on the dirt floor might give him away.

Ward crouched against a tree that had been splintered during the onslaught. He had excellent coverage of the cave mouth. Now, all he had to do was get the Muslim to expose himself.

Ward leaned out as far as he could. "Freeze!" he shouted.

The Muslim fired at the voice but Ward was no longer there. He had withdrawn behind the tree and fired multiple shots to the left and right of where he had seen the burst. Ward heard the man cry out and heard the gun hit the ground. Ward flicked on his cell phone's flashlight app. He shined it toward the cave. The Muslim had landed on his belly, facing in the opposite direction. He had lost the tire iron but was still holding the .38. Ward ran forward, his gun trained on the man. The Muslim was trying to get something from his pants.

"I told you to *freeze,* asshole!" Ward yelled.

The young man withdrew his hand.

There was a cigarette lighter in it. *That's* why he overturned the heaters.

"I die for my people!" the Muslim cried. *"Allah ak—"*

Ward shot him through the arm. "No Paradise for

you, asshole. You're going to the same hospital where you put Debbie."

"*Allah . . . Allah . . .*"

The young man had resolve, Ward had to give him that. His gun arm was unhurt and he tried to roll onto his back so he could fire. The detective had reached him by then and kicked the weapon away.

"Religion of peace like hell," he snarled.

Shouldering the rifle and picking up the AK-47, Ward ran to the ATV he'd left in the foliage. It would have been faster to take the other ATV but he wanted whoever was above to see that it wasn't the terrorist leaving.

Before he started the engine he turned on the headlight and stood in it so they could see him. Then he yelled along the valley, "I'm riding over partner—don't shoot!"

There was no response.

"You can answer now—the danger's neutralized," Ward said with a slight smile.

"Okay!" Dickson shouted. "I won't shoot."

Ward sped to Dickson's position and pulled up without dismounting. "I'm going to follow those SOBs. Wait in the cave and keep an eye on that punk. He's only got two working limbs but they still want to fight."

Dickson nodded. "Thank you," he said.

"For what?"

"For making me feel like a man again," Dickson said.

Ward lay a hand on the man's shoulder then raced off. He had already decided he wasn't going to play nice with the other guys. At four-to-one, he had to lower the odds by any means possible. He would be coming at them from behind and he intended to use that advantage.

Rounding the turn in the mountain, Ward was abruptly forced to change his plans. Two of the riders were racing toward him at high speeds.

What the hell?

They came charging toward Ward from about 400 yards away. He braked on the narrow trail, skidding out of control and riding up several of the smaller boulders to his right, along the mountain wall. He doused the headlight and leapt from the lopsided ATV as gunfire rang from its metal side, ricocheting among the rocks.

Ward returned fire above the oncoming lights, where he expected the riders to be hunched low. The two windshields shattered and he heard the scraping of bike-against-bike as the vehicles collided. The headlights suddenly veered in wildly different directions. He heard an ugly crack as the bikes careened off one another, one propelled to the north against the mountain and one to the south into a gulley. The motors continued to hum but it was the only sound coming from the two wrecks.

Ward ventured from his spot just as a third ATV came shooting up the trail. It weaved left and right for a short distance before slamming into the ATV that had tipped into the gulley. Both vehicles smacked together loudly, their strong chassis preventing them from crumpling altogether. The rider, however, was thrown over the wreckage. He landed on his back, his left side in the ditch and his right side on the trail.

Ward did not hear the fourth biker. He continued forward, the tableau a surreal display of three zigzagging white beams, upended vehicles, and three immobile bodies. The nearest, the one on the road, was peppered with blood.

Why were you coming back? he wondered.

Ward didn't venture too near the ATVs until he made sure there were no sparks or leaking fuel. As he walked back and forth some ten yards from the upended vehicles he noticed two small lights coming toward him.

What now?

They were too high and slow for ATVs. He ducked behind the vehicle that had gone up the mountainside. The lights were bobbing. They didn't seem threatening.

"This is John Ward!" he shouted. "Who's there?"

A woman's voice answered from the gulley side of the trail. "Tessa Dunson and Vito Antonini."

Papa Vito?

Before he could answer, Ward was distracted by a sudden noise in the gulley, a familiar *ca-chunk.* The sound was lost in a loud pop as a flare erupted at the woman's side. Ward instinctively hit the ground, straining the goodwill of those bandages; the Muslim who had been pumping his shotgun from the tangle of ATVs was not so lucky. He was visible now, splayed across the handlebars.

When it became clear the third man either would not or could not move, Ward rose.

"We've got the fourth guy back at the bat cave," the woman said. "He was smart enough to surrender."

"After you shot him," Vito said.

"Yeah, they tend to do that," she replied.

The two horses came into view now, their riders probing the wrecks with their flashlights, looking at them for any sign of life. They saw the third rider bent in an ugly manner beneath his ride. His eyes were open and quite lifeless.

"That expression does not belong to a man who is looking out on Paradise," Tessa remarked.

"No," Antonini agreed soberly. "It's just a dead kid who found a group that let him hate and kill. I seen a lot of that in my life."

Ward was walking toward them slowly, mindful of his ribs. "I assume Randolph and company were up on the cliffs?"

"Yes sir," Tessa said. "He wanted us to maintain a roadblock, but when we heard the ruckus—"

"The flashlights were a good idea, but these guys were nice enough to light the road for us coming in and going out," Antonini added.

"What about the training camp?" Tessa asked.

"Secure," Ward told her.

The detective stopped walking. He was beat. Tessa handed her reins to Antonini and came around the destroyed ATVs. She was carrying a canteen and handed it to Ward. He thanked her and drank, then found a flat boulder to sit on. It was cold. Nothing in Manhattan was ever butt-chilling like this. Heat came from every grate, every sewer. Then again, he never had backup blow someone away like Tessa just did.

Life is a succession of compromises.

Tessa called Randolph to report on the situation. That reminded Ward of the call he had received earlier. Fishing his cell phone from his pocket and finding it intact, he checked the message from Police Chief Brennan. It was a text, and it was not the yelling-at he was expecting.

The message was short and chilling:

Trouble.

CHAPTER FORTY-EIGHT

Ward left on the ATV he'd been riding. The uneven mountain road didn't do his ribs any good, but compared to where he'd been perching, the seat felt comfortable, and it was warm.

He felt bad leaving Tessa and the others to lock down the site. Randolph had phoned to let her know he'd already called Dr. Stone to get him on-site. He knew that transporting the wounded Muslim in the cave, by ATV or horseback, would be problematic. Tessa said he could deal with the others when he arrived.

Tessa also told Ward, as he was leaving, that the cover story was going to be the terrorists attacked them when they discovered the training camp.

"On a night ride?" Ward asked Tessa as he rolled the vehicle back to the trail then walked it through the wreckage.

"On a tip from Scott Randolph that something

funny was going on out there," she replied. "They fired first. We had no choice but to defend ourselves."

"I feared for my life." Ward thought. Well, it was more or less the truth. It was the story he'd give about Saeed. Plus the tire iron would probably link the punks to the attack on Randolph's farm. Then there was the training camp itself, an enemy base on federal land. The boys who survived were not in an enviable legal position.

But Brennan's text message was still front and center in his thoughts as he spit dust and stone and headed back down the trail.

Ward was in the hyper-alert state that comes from no-sleep and a short, intense period of activity. From experience, he knew he had a few hours of good, strong edge left before he crashed fast and hard. Whatever the trouble was, he hoped it was almost upon them or would have the decency to leave room for a power nap.

It was still dark when he rolled into Basalt and drove to the police station. The town seemed even quieter than before; or maybe it was the woozy sense of general well-being that came with waking up from surgery. One tumor, at least, had been cut out.

The door to the station was locked. It hadn't been before. Ward pressed the night buzzer but Brennan was already on her way. She was wearing her uniform and a look of grave concern. She let Ward in then locked the door behind him.

"We under siege?" he asked only half-joking as they walked to the back, to her office.

"We had a deal, I thought."

"The situation evolved."

"No. *You* pushed it. Who do you think you are, Richard the effin' Lionheart, the flaming sword of two cities? You were supposed to take me to the camp."

Brennan was angry. Fair enough. She *was* the police chief. Ward said nothing.

"Dr. Stone called to let me know he was going out to treat a gunshot wound," she went on. "I sent Hawks with him. Then he got word there were more wounds, probable fatalities."

"Muslims," Ward replied. "The first guy was one of the gang that attacked me, and probably Randolph. He was carrying a tire iron—"

"Circumstantial reason to shoot him—"

"*Plus* he had a gun *and* he was trying to torch the place," Ward told her. "The others attacked me. At least two of those four are dead, one of those in an ATV wreck. They were running a terrorist training camp, Chief Brennan. The evidence will back that up. We formed a posse. We took it out."

Brennan looked at him with worried eyes. He didn't blame her. This was popping out of control, bursting the lid she had tried so hard to keep down.

"As a citizen I am relieved," she said. "As the police chief, I cannot condone vigilante action against alleged terrorists."

She was right. She should be arresting him and they both knew it. But he didn't care. What he'd done was *right*.

"I suppose the killings were in self-defense," she went on. "That *is* correct, isn't it?"

"Actually, it is," he replied. "*We're* not the animals they are. Look, I'm sorry if this is going to create problems for the town and for you. But maybe it'll also wake up the nation to a danger in their midst. God knows those guns and training equipment were real, and the desire to draw first blood was strong in those kids. And the money feeding them from overseas, fueling the operation—that was us helping."

"You know where it was coming from?"

"Dickson was in a sharing mood."

"Did you hurt him?"

"Didn't need to," Ward said. "He had his reasons."

Brennan chewed her cheek thoughtfully, then turned abruptly. "Come."

They entered her office. The desk sergeant and a patrol officer just in from his rounds were the only other people present. They followed Ward with angry eyes. It wasn't a look of disapproval but of kids who had been benched during the big game.

"Where are Officers Pawley and Miles?" she asked before entering her office.

"Just got to Elk Circle," the desk sergeant informed her.

"I want an update asap," she said, shutting the door. She went to her desk and flipped open the laptop Ward had taken from the cave. She remained standing. The detective stood beside her.

"First, there's nothing in this computer to tie Gahrah or his community center to the training camp or any other activities," she said. "Unless you've got something else, he and his people are still clean."

"Dickson will pin his ears back," Ward told her.

"What happened to Earl? Why's he suddenly so chatty?"

"They assaulted his daughter this afternoon as a warning."

"Who did?"

"One of the kids, working on orders from Fawaz. He decided to fight them. He had my back in the valley tonight."

She was still stunned. "*Earl* was part of the fire-fight?"

"Up to his assets."

That seemed to soften the police chief's unhappiness with Ward. "Well, that brings us to the second, and frankly, more troubling matter. The laptop *is* full of plans to the Aspen airport." She began clicking through the files. "Also photos. According to the time stamps, they were taken during the evac they had there last week."

"So they *were* behind that," Ward said.

"Apparently, but why?"

"Dickson thinks the money he launders comes in by private jet, packaged inside Korans."

"That doesn't surprise me," Brennan told him. "The private jet, I mean. Aspen runs on jet-setters, and with the sour economy, more and more of them are coming from abroad. Customs is not about to subject them to the third degree." The police chief's phone beeped. She hit speaker. "Go."

"Sir, the officers report that the vehicles are all gone," the desk sergeant reported.

Ward was watching the police chief. Her face seemed to pale a little.

"Thank you. Notify state." She clicked off and looked at Ward. "That, Mr. Ward, is the sound of a clock ticking."

"I don't follow."

"After Randolph was attacked, we collected the license numbers of all the Muslim kids from DMV. Just in case any surveillance video caught them heading to or from the farm. Nothing turned up, but we kept the numbers."

"Five of the kids were up in the mountains," Ward said. He nodded toward the phone. "You just found out the rest of them are not at home. State troopers are going to check the highways."

Brennan nodded.

"But you know you won't find the vehicles because they moved out hours ago," Ward said.

"That's the problem of having a loose cannon," she said.

"You think *I* caused this, that they scattered when they didn't hear from their night watchman?"

"You have a better theory?"

"I do. Today will be a week since the evac. With maybe slight variations, the same crew will be working at Aspen today that were on the ground last week. They will react the same as they did last week. I think you've got this bass ackwards. The Muslims ramped up their activities, against the bank, against me, even hitting Randolph, in *preparation* for today. They wanted to put us in the hospital or on an airplane or in prison."

"Why? In preparation for what?"

"Exactly," Ward said. "They've been running cash successfully through customs for months now.

Private jets coming from different countries where, let's just say, Iranian or Saudi money was bundled in Korans. Jets whose contents get just a cursory look-see at customs not just because the owners are going to spend money in Aspen, but because they're Muslims who'll raise a stink if their books are fingered by infidels. They've got a sweet setup. Why change that now?"

"Because you busted their operation in the valley?"

"We stopped some kids," Ward said. "And maybe Earl can take Gahrah to prison with him. Those are acceptable losses to these guys. There's something else going on here."

"Earl will spill on their airport operation. It can't be that."

"I'm not so sure," Ward said. "What do you know about the imam?"

"Not a lot," she replied. "Low profile here, rarely seen outside the community center. When he was still back in Chicago, he attended one of those Holocaust-as-myth seminars in Tehran, but so did hundreds of other imams who carried that message out into the world."

"Typical," Ward said.

"What is?"

"The anonymity, the blend-in. The imam who shot off his mouth in New York about the Ground Zero Mosque—look at all the bad press he got. The Muslim radicals saw that as a textbook case of what to avoid.

"We did a five-year anti-terror study in New York, all very hush-hush so as not to offend the *New York*

Times," Ward went on. "It told us that unlike imams throughout the Middle East and Far East, clerics in the U.S., Britain, France, and Germany have what they call 'blank-grounds.' They're selected because there's nothing to flag 'em once they get to their new communities."

"So you could have radicals in your community and not know it," she said.

"Not 'could,'" Ward said. "It's insidious. At worst, they want to take us down. At best, too many of them are silent. What we have here, I'm afraid, is one of the former. Who do you know at the airport?" Ward asked.

"Head of Security, Natalie Ford."

"Have you talked to her?"

"Not yet," Brennan said. She looked at her watch. "It's not even four a.m. and I wouldn't know what exactly to tell her."

The desk sergeant informed her that Major Crockett was on the phone.

"Thanks," she said. "Have Officer Webb bring his car around. He's taking Mr. Ward to the airport."

"Not again—"

"I'm not asking you to leave," she said. "You're gonna help me finish what you started. Major Crockett runs the State Patrol, Northwest District. We need eyes at the airport that know who to look for, *what* to look for. I'll call Natalie at home, tell her you'll explain. She's tough, will probably bust your chops. I'm guessing he hasn't slept much the past week trying to puzzle that whole thing out."

"You going to meet me there?"

She shook her head. "I've got no jurisdiction and I've got next-of-kin calls to make here. You want Webb to stay with?"

"Might be useful," he said. "He's seen these kids too, I'm guessing."

She nodded and offered her hand. "I'm still pissed at the way you lied and cut me out, but good luck."

"We'll need it," he said.

"Why? Is there something else you didn't share with me?"

"Yeah," he replied. "There were a lot more pegs on the gun board than there were guns or grenades."

CHAPTER FORTY-NINE

Ward napped for the entire ride—if passing out and then being jarred awake twenty minutes later can be called a nap.

State Police didn't come up with any sightings of the vehicles registered to the community center or any of the kids whose identities were known. Again, not a surprise; if there were some kind of plot against the airport, the perpetrators would either hide the ATVs and steal a car or take public transportation. At this hour, getting any kind of information from bus companies was difficult; no cabs had gone from Basalt to the airport, but that didn't mean anything. The kids could have gone somewhere else first to throw the police off.

"Or they could've had motorcycles stashed in garages for this purpose," Officer Webb pointed out after updating Ward. "They could have trucked them in from out of state and ditched them somewhere close by."

Or they could have thumbed a ride. Or maybe someone drove them. Or maybe they aren't even here and are getting ready for a second-wave attack to retake the training camp.

Ward couldn't think clearly, but that didn't stop him from thinking too much. His brain was foggier than when he'd slumped into the seat.

Ward couldn't believe all that had happened since the last time he'd seen this airport, with its simple chalet-style peaked roof and great glass windows. The first shots and stabbings and beatings against the American homeland had taken place by jihadists. This wasn't a one-time event like the World Trade Center and Pentagon attacks. This was the Boston Massacre, Fort Sumter, the face-to-face struggle that marked the start of the real war. The battle had started with a skirmish on the Randolph farm and raged through the dry cleaning van and then into Debbie's home. It spilled into the cave in the valley and now, here, the finale of Act One was about to take place. Ward felt a kind of tidal momentum wash against his lawman's soul.

"Are you okay, sir?" Officer Webb asked as he parked at the curb.

"Why?"

"You look like you want to bite someone."

Webb—a blond, blue-eyed rookie—had a good eye. Ward did feel himself going feral. "I do, and the enemy's feeling that too. Don't give him quarter."

"I haven't really been briefed," the young man apologized.

"You will be," boomed a voice from behind him.

A man the size of a brown bear was walking through the automatic door. He was followed by two other men, each broad and powerful-looking— but still small beside the speaker, despite the ominous, black AR-15 assault rifles they were carrying. The three men were wearing the sharp cobalt-blue shirts and what looked, in the morning light, to be grayish trousers of the Colorado State Patrol.

"Walt Crockett," he said to Ward. He did not give his rank; there was no need. He wore it on his sleeve and projected it in his voice. He offered his hand which the detective was loath to take; it looked like it could shatter a beer bottle. Ward survived the grip, but just barely. "Troopers Holt and Big Tree," he said, jerking a thumb over his shoulder. The men acknowledged with a nod as their names were mentioned. They did not smile. Their lips did not part. They knew the major was The Major and this was his show. Now Ward knew it too.

"Good to meet you all," Ward said. Webb nodded his own agreement though he seemed a little surprised and intimidated by the breadth and firepower of the men.

"We've got three more men inside," Crockett went on. "This time of day, there's not a lot of traffic moving out. Visibility and line-of-fire are both A-1."

"Is there somewhere we can talk?" Ward asked, noticing a pair of skycaps looking anxiously in their direction.

"The Airport Facilities Manager's office is at our disposal," Crockett replied, leading the way. His two men stepped aside then fell in behind Ward and Webb.

They walked through the brightly lit terminal with its vaulted ceilings and still-shuttered shops. They walked through a wood-panel door that said Authorized Personnel Only. The night crew was still on the clock, consisting of three people. No one was using the office of the AFM. At a signal from the major, only he and Ward went in.

"The tactic is deterrence, then," Ward said as Crockett shut the door.

"You mean the show of firepower?" Crockett said. He set a big thigh on the edge of the desk. "Yeah. Our policy is to discourage terrorists from attacking our airfield. I understand you're here without-portfolio."

There was an edge of disapproval in his voice; it teetered, like a seesaw, with his obvious intention to be a good and professional host.

"If you mean I'm defrocked and unarmed, you're right," Ward answered. "If you mean I'm a guy with experience fighting these thugs, you're also right."

"By 'these thugs' do you mean the alleged terrorists in Basalt or the street vendor in New York?"

"The kids in Basalt," Ward replied. He felt stupid. He hadn't realized he was being brought in this room for interrogation. "And there's no 'alleged' about them. I fought some of these goons in the back of a van."

"Their van, which you invaded," Crockett said.

"Yes, in response to the discovery of a money

laundering operation and a prior attack against one of the townspeople."

"It is believed but not proven," the major pointed out. "I understand there were deaths last night in an operation under civilian control. And one of your team members is said to have shot first."

He felt, at that moment, like he was back in New York being grilled about the Muslim in the park. Major Crockett was twisting everything Brennan had told him so that defense of the homeland was coming across as blind bias and preemptive aggression. "They boxed us into the valley where I had found their weapons cache," Ward said. "The single shot fired at them was a warning."

"Announced as such and preceded by a verbal admonition to lay down their arms, both delivered as per protocol by a deputized officer of the law?"

"No, and I hope this is all part of some cover-your-ass drill so you can testify later that we did the dance, you conducted due diligence. Because the threat is real, major. All these rules you're trotting out—they don't work anymore. They're being used *against* us."

The major rose from the desk. "Thank you for the primer, Mr. Ward." His eyes were steel and his manner was even more formal now that he'd been called out. "You are here to ID any of the perpetrators you may notice from past encounters. We will handle quarantine and neutralization."

"Fine."

"You have no function beyond advisory."

"Okay," Ward said. "Then I advise you to get out

there with your men and start doing a threat analysis."

"Based on what?" Crockett asked him. "We are out there collecting observational data—"

"Based on the fact that we found a terrorist camp not too many miles away and we think this airport is the target. All you're doing is waiting to *respond* to something. That may be too late."

"Do you have some kind of actionable intelligence?"

Do you have any intelligence? Ward wondered. "I'm not following your game plan, Major. Are you telling me we're just going to sit here?"

"We're going to wait here while my men watch for suspicious activity," the major went on. He patted the small radio mounted proudly to his shoulder. "These are new, Mr. Ward. One mile range and maximum clarity, much better than the old hip models. I promise, we'll know at once if anything comes up." He took a few steps toward Ward. "We do not act recklessly. We do not assault innocent citizens of Colorado or their guests."

There was a try-and-rough-*me*-up challenge in the major's expression. Ward was tempted. Instead, he went to the door.

"Where you going?" Crockett asked.

"To wait with Officer Webb."

"You'll wait with me," the major replied. He tapped the radio with a finger. "I may need your input."

Ward reminded himself that this man was small town, by-the-book, with no practical field experience. He didn't know any better. The problem was, there was no way Ward would convince him. The job of intercepting an attack was in the hands of his troopers. He hoped, but doubted, "the book" was equal to the task. The Muslims would know the rules too.

They sat in the office for over an hour. Somewhere in the distance Ward heard sirens. So did Crockett. The major got on his radio to find out what was going on. Before any of the troopers could answer, the door flew open and a woman charged in. She was about forty-five, dressed in black slacks, a blue windbreaker, and a baseball cap with the airport logo. She wore no makeup and locks of platinum blond hair dangled here and there. There were coffee containers in the trash but none in her hand; Ward surmised she had been called in too suddenly to get a cup.

The woman stopped and stared. "Who the hell are you two?"

"Major Walt Crockett, State Patrol," he said, rising. "This is civilian advisor John Ward. You are?"

"Pilar Ireland, the woman whose name is on the door," she said harshly. "I saw your troopers parading through my airport, major. What the hell are you doing?"

"Ma'am, I've established a perimeter according to the provisions of the existing Severe Alert status."

Ward was confused by her confusion. "Police

Chief Brennan was supposed to have called you," he said.

"Who?"

"Basalt PD," Ward told her. "Hold on. It wasn't you Chief Brennan said she was calling. It was Natalie Ford."

"My boss," Pilar replied. "I haven't heard anything from her."

Major Crockett seemed puzzled, but Ward suddenly understood. "You're not here because of *our* threat," he said.

"I was in the shower and I got a text from parking lot security," she told him. "What's *your* situation?"

"Possible terrorist strike modeled on last week's dry run," Ward said. "What happened in the parking lot?"

"Bus fire," she replied.

Those were the sirens Ward heard. His mind was working the new information, the timing, the location.

"You've got an airport fire department," Ward said.

"Yes, and I've also got morning rush about to get underway," Ireland replied. "Two planes are already making their approach."

"Right. Smoke and visibility concerns," Ward said. "I'm betting the wind is blowing in the opposite direction from the landing pattern."

"Yes." Ireland seemed impressed.

"Far end of the parking lot?"

"The farthest," Ireland said. "That's where

the bus terminal is located." Now she was really impressed.

"It's a feint," Ward told her. "They want our assets as far away and as widely dispersed as possible."

"For what reason?" she asked.

"I don't know yet," Ward said as he reached for the door. "But we damn well better find out."

CHAPTER FIFTY

Ward left the executive offices and looked around the terminal. Ireland was beside him, Crockett behind, still in the doorway. Officer Webb was behind him. The state troopers were scattered.

"Can you find out if the bus was parked there all night?" Ward asked Ireland.

"Do you want to know if any buses are on their routes?" she asked as she called the parking lot security officer.

"Not necessary," Ward shook his head.

"What's this about?" Crockett demanded.

Ward didn't seem to hear him. "This new situation is *not* about getting cash into the United States," he thought aloud.

"How do you know that?" Webb asked. ·

Ward seemed startled by the voice. He hadn't realized he'd said that aloud. "The Muslims already have a functioning system, one that was not in any fear of discovery when they rehearsed their attack last week."

"Maybe it's not about contraband," Webb suggested.

"Possibly," Ward agreed. "Major, you should probably get your men off the floor, let things unfold so we can stop it—"

"That's not going to happen," Crockett said sharply. "Don't even *think* of telling me my business."

Ward let it go. One of the things he'd learned dealing with New York politics is it was better to be on the wrong side of a tactic and succeed by chance than fight among each other and fail for sure. But he knew that Crockett's deterrence was no deterrence. Ward had worked undercover long enough to know that more often than not, public displays of security simply redirected the enemy, sent them to where you weren't. They had to be let in and trapped, not bounced back and pursued. He also knew that the bulletproof vests obviously worn by the troopers under their shirts were telling the bad guys where not to aim. It counseled them to get close enough for a head shot.

"That burning bus had just rolled in," Ireland told the detective. "It came from Redstone."

"Which is where?"

"West of here."

"They didn't catch it in Basalt," Ward said.

"Who?" Crockett demanded.

Ward ignored him. "Where's the driver?"

"They can't find him," Ireland replied.

"Crap. Major, have your men check roadsides along the route," Ward said. "I'm betting you'll find the driver and whatever other passengers were on the bus. Hopefully, they're alive."

"Hopefully? You're '*betting*'?" Crockett said. "You better share whatever data you're working off, because you are *not* running this operation!"

Ward turned on him. "You want data? The terrorists are here. You'd do well to *find* them!" He turned to Ireland. "Arrival board?"

"On my computer—"

"No. I want to be out there."

She pointed to the left.

Ward started in that direction and Crockett grabbed his right shoulder with a thick, powerful hand.

"*You* want? *I* want everything you know," Crockett said. "Now."

Ward faced him again. "You're looking for a tall, skinny Muslim about twenty years old. Four or five accomplices, maybe more. Automatic weapons, probably basic scatter tactics for maximum coverage. An attack is imminent. I'd profile the hell out of this crowd as I evacuated the airport. Now, Major—run your team and leave me alone."

Ward pushed the hand off hard and jogged to the board. Ireland and Webb ran with him. Crockett followed at a slow, military run.

Ward scanned the board. Two planes had just landed.

"What are these?" he asked Ireland.

"One's a 737 from Atlanta, the other's a private jet from Philadelphia."

"Passenger manifest on the Philly jet?"

"There wouldn't be one," Ireland informed him. "Only for commercial."

"City of origin?"

"I'll find out." She got on her radio.

Ward was trying to consider all the possibilities. He was thinking aloud again. "If the flight originated overseas we've got to stop them from disembark—"

There was a loud bang, like someone hitting a trash can. It originated far to the right of their position.

"What's over there?" Ward asked

"Baggage claim."

"But there's no baggage yet," Crockett said. He got on his radio to send his men over.

"Just send one," Ward told him. "It could be another distraction, like the bus."

Crockett didn't argue. He ordered a man to investigate and report.

"The plane originated in Paris," Ireland told the detective.

That made sense. France had a huge Muslim population. "What else is in the baggage claim area, something a terrorist would want to take out? Cameras? Security?"

"Yes—" she said. She stopped as though afraid to say the rest.

"What's there?" Ward prodded her.

"The GRS," she said. She was already in motion. Ward and Crockett followed.

"What's the GRS?" Ward asked.

"Gamma radiation sensor," she said. "If there's a threat-level dose of radiation an alarm will sound."

"Unless someone has blown it up," Ward said.

Everyone took a moment to process that information.

"So all we need to do is contain the bags," Ireland suggested.

"Not all, but it's a start," Ward said.

Ireland got on the radio and gave the order to one of her five operations officers, who was just about to call and tell her that someone had detonated what appeared to be a hand grenade in the baggage claim area, right under the GRS.

"Injuries?" Ireland asked.

"Only to the equipment and doors," he replied. "Glass is everywhere. None of the skycaps was injured."

Ireland told him to institute standard lockdown procedure—the gates on all the roads to the airport were to be closed to all traffic except the local police and fire departments. "And get IDs from the drivers before the bar is raised. I want to know we're letting real personnel in."

"Is that the only sensor?" Ward asked when she was done.

"Yes."

"But the door at the gate and the main door are the only exits," he asked urgently.

"For passengers, yes."

Ward turned to Crockett. "You'd better get men to the employee exits. Someone may try to get out that way. Forget the baggage claim."

"Why?" Crockett asked.

"Commercial luggage would have been scanned at the point of departure since commercial and private all goes out the same chute," Ward said. "But not carry-on for a private jet. There are no checks."

Crockett understood. He gave the command.

"Where's the gate for the Philly jet?"

"All gates are that way," Ireland told him, pointing in the direction opposite the baggage claim.

Ward ran toward the gates. The results of the explosion were already being felt. Airport security personnel were heading in that direction and shops and cafés where the gates had come up were not yet open for business. Updates were coming in on Ireland's radio about smoke in the baggage claim area, but no fire. She asked one of the operations officers about the incoming flights.

"We've got the private jet in the SPHR," he said.

Ward shot her a questioning look.

"Screened passenger holding room," she told him. "How many people?" she asked the ops officer.

"Five passengers, three crew."

"We're en route," she said into the radio. "Keep them there until we arrive—"

The pops came from what sounded like every direction at once. The echo of the gunfire blurred into a single drone that enveloped the three. Crockett stopped and listened, trying to get a read on any of the points-of-origin.

"Sir, we've got shooters at security!" a voice shrilled from the major's radio.

The officer ran hard toward the gate, followed by Ward and Ireland. Another radio voice punched through the din but Ward couldn't make it out; there was a burst from behind them and Crockett went down, the legs cut from under him. Ward grabbed Ireland and threw her to the tile floor, himself on top, as he turned to try and spot the shooter. It wasn't difficult. The man was approaching openly, firing semi-automatic bursts from the left hip, swinging the barrel easily from side to side. The airport workers had scattered or gone down, so only store windows, benches, and planters were being struck. In his right hand he held a .45. He didn't need it yet. The handgun was pointed down.

He was near enough so that Ward could see his face.

It was one of the Muslims from the van.

This wasn't how they planned it, Ward thought. They had been expecting to do a repetition of the previous week: get everyone out of the terminal after the blast in the baggage claim area. Ireland's lockdown of the SPHR instead of evacuation had screwed them up. Carnage was Plan B.

Crockett swiveled on his bleeding legs. He had landed on his holstered Smith and Wesson and managed to draw the M&P 40 unseen. The major didn't get to fire. His movement drew the attention of the shooter. The AK-47 spat a short volley and the officer's forearm flopped back, nearly severed in a thick ribbon of blood. The major turned to grab the gun before realizing that his hand was useless.

"Lie still!" Ward ordered Ireland.

Even before the handgun had finished spinning across the floor, the detective was after it. He elbow-crawled behind the major which afforded him a moment's protection. The gunman might have thought he was merely trying to escape. The Muslim was in no hurry as he swung the assault rifle toward him, chewing up the tiles as it stitched a line toward him. Ward reached the weapon but did not pick it up: he flopped his chest on it as he continued forward, toward a green metal trash can. The clanging of the bullets against the iron was painfully loud and Ward screamed as though he'd been hit. The cry was purely reflexive, angry, but the gunman seemed to think he had struck him. The killer turned his fire toward Crockett and Ireland. Ward snaked around the far side of the trash can and shot the man in the belly. The AK-47 spit for a moment longer and then went silent.

Ward jumped to his feet, ran over and yanked the guns from the Muslim's hands. The kid was biting his lower lip, trying not to cry out. His knees were stacked on their sides, curled toward the wound which was just above his belt line. Ward did not consider helping him.

Unless putting a bullet in his black damn heart is considered help, he thought as he ran back to Crockett. Ward lay the guns down and, grabbing the front of the officer's shirt, dragged him behind the trash can. He unhooked the major's radio. He made sure it had a loudspeaker function then slung it around his neck. As he went back to get the guns, he motioned Ireland over. She hurried there on hands and knees.

"Do what you can to stop the bleeding," Ward told the woman.

"What are you going to do?"

"Stop them," he said. He checked the clip and set one of the guns beside her. "When you're finished, I need you to do something."

"All right," she said, though it was as much a question as a statement.

As Ireland used her kerchief and belt to try and stop the arterial bleeding, Ward told her what he wanted her to do. She expressed some reservation about her ability to carry it out. He told her that this was a battle in a war and that we mustn't lose it. She said she'd do what he asked.

The drone of gunfire was converging ahead of him. The Muslims obviously wanted to get someone out of the secure zone. Someone who ordinarily would have been evacuated because of the grenade but wasn't. Someone who obviously was carrying something they didn't want to have checked by customs.

"State patrol, this is Detective John Ward," he said into the radio. "Major Crockett is down. I'm armed and headed toward Gate A." He added, "Don't shoot me."

Ward tucked the handgun in his waistband and raised the AK-47. He walked forward briskly, watching the corridor through the gun sight. His knees were slightly bent, lowering his center of gravity, leaving him ready to absorb the recoil of the gun or move to one side or the other as needed.

There was no one about. He reasoned that anyone who was leaving the area had already done so or had been cut down in the attempt. As he passed a fast food restaurant he found the bodies of two custodians, shot in the chest, lying with their heads toward the gate. A single set of bloody foot-prints lead from the corpses. They had been shot by someone who came through the main entrance, moving in the direction Ward was moving. That meant the shooter's back would be facing him. Ward had never shot anyone who hadn't threatened him, who wasn't facing him. But the two poor souls bleeding out on the tile had been gunned down for a sick religious dogma, not necessity. The detective would have no trouble executing their killer from any direction that worked.

There was motion ahead and the sound of single shots being fired. A figure was crouched behind an overturned desk just inside the security area. A dead Muslim lay facedown on the other side of the table. He had bloody soles.

Ward got on the radio. "Officer at the security table, I'm coming in from behind."

The man did not turn but raised a hand. Ward crouched and ran through the scanner, setting off the alarm. For some reason he hadn't expected a pair of guns to generate the same sound as loose change. Bullets chewed away pieces of the table as Ward slid beside the officer.

"You doing okay, Officer Wister?" he asked, noting the man's name tag.

The young man nodded.

"How many are there?" Ward asked.

"Five gunmen," he said.

That we know of, Ward thought. If the goal was to get someone out of there they probably had someone in reserve. He wouldn't join the shootout unless it was absolutely necessary. Ward glanced at the belt of the dead Muslim. Like the one before him, he had no additional ordnance. Chances were good that if there was a hidden gunman he was the one who had the grenades. They would almost certainly be used to cover the terrorist retreat.

"Where are the rest of our men?" Ward asked.

"At the gate," Wister told him between shots. "If that's their target, we're not letting them in."

"Good man," Ward said proudly. "What about the passengers?"

"The staff has them contained," Wister said. He fired, went on. "We believe the area is bulletproof."

"The enemy is probably prepared for that," Ward said. "I assume those are your guys at the far end?"

"Yeah." The three other state police officers were at counters and benches farther away, obviously having been patrolling nearby when the gunfire erupted. "We've called for backup."

"These guys have to know the cavalry is on the way," Ward said. "Stop shooting for a minute."

The officer obeyed.

"I want them to lay off us," Ward said. "When they do. I'm going to that kiosk." Ward pointed to a coffee stand nearly halfway between the security position and the first gate. Because Wister had a clear line of fire, none of the Muslims were holed up there. Ward handed Wister the AK-47 he'd appropriated. "When I go out, cover me. Let me have your handgun."

Wister handed it over, butt first. The detective made sure both his guns were fully loaded then crouched by the right side of the table and watched the gate to pinpoint every enemy position. When there was a lull in gunfire directed at the table—as expected, the terrorists were concentrating on the three police officers—Ward charged across the open area, maneuvering to the left to keep the kiosk between himself and the gunman who had been shooting at the table. As soon as the Muslim poked his gun from behind the ticket counter, Wister pummeled it with fire from the assault rifle. As expected, the drumming fire got the Muslim's attention. He shouted in Arabic as the side of his ticket booth vanished in a tornado of splinters.

Ward changed his mind. When the ticket booth gunman fell back the detective made that his destination. He didn't dare turn his back so he ran backwards, firing toward the four other gunmen who were behind benches and poles, leapfrogging their way slowly from one to the other.

The bastards' cave training had paid off. One moved, the others covered with crossfire, and progress was being made toward the SPHR. The drawback for them was that, with the exception of the spotter behind the ticket counter, all the Muslims were in the same general area.

Ward fired his handgun left to right then back while Wister, who figured out what he was doing and adjusted, kept firing at the ticket counter. He stopped just before Ward reached it. The detective turned to face the counter just as the Muslim emerged. The detective put a single shot in his forehead as it appeared around the shattered side.

The man dropped on his left cheek, his dead eyes shut. Ward heard more shouts in Arabic behind him, heard Wister fire in that direction, and jumped hurdle-like behind a row of benches as gunfire pinged off the tiles and counter. One of them slashed through his jeans, cutting his leg. He dropped as he landed, ignoring the searing pain as he scrabbled forward behind the counter. He set down the handguns and grabbed the Muslim's assault rifle. He reached for the radio he'd taken from Crockett, didn't feel it, and realized he'd lost it as he jumped the benches.

He needed to let the passengers in the secure area know what he needed them to do, and his voice alone wasn't enough to carry over the gunfire. And there was no time to waste: he had to get to the secure room before the Muslims did. It wasn't only a matter of finding out who was in there. Ward knew there could well be another danger.

There was a lull in the gunfire. A moment later there were cries in Arabic.

They were answered by a shout from the SPHR, also in Arabic.

That's not good, Ward thought. He got on his knees. His leg burned where it had been hit by the ricochet but he didn't have time to worry about the damage. He had to get a message inside the SPHR, so he grabbed the microphone on the counter and switched it on.

"This is the police!" he shouted. "Everyone in the secure area get down *now!*"

His warning came an instant before someone inside began shooting. Screams were barely audible beneath the loud drumming of an automatic strafing the door and the area around it. Ward imagined that was to take out the security personnel, who were probably armed. Their next move would be to the exit.

Then the terrorists out here will do whatever is necessary to get them outside, to hook up with their hole card. Plan B was solid, Ward thought bitterly. Especially because the terrorists were obviously willing to die to carry it out.

Ward had to find that hidden Muslim and take him out.

Going back to the way he had come was too risky, especially if the SPHR gunman suddenly emerged and added more firepower to the assault. Instead, he turned and fired a burst at the plate glass window behind him. It fell in big icelike chunks, crashing inside and outside the single-story terminal. Ducking low, Ward ran down an aisle. The pain in his leg actually helped, burning and sharpening his focus. He reached the window, jumped over a clear section of frame, and landed on the tarmac. He ran back toward the main terminal.

CHAPTER FIFTY-ONE

An assault rifle slung over his shoulder, Hassan Shatri marched boldly through the terminal. He pulled the pin of the hand grenade as he headed toward the security checkpoint. He reached a concrete planter, ducked behind it, and rolled the explosive forward. It hit the tile with the sound of a bowling ball. Wister heard it coming and tried to scurry behind to the other side of the checkpoint. Gunfire from the terrorists cut him down even as the metallic bang of the grenade sent a pale gray cloud of shrapnel in all directions.

Shatri emerged from hiding and followed the sound of gunfire through the tester of acrid smoke. He walked through the dissipating cloud toward the twisted frame of the security gate. Before the state police could fire he had pulled a second grenade from the weapons belt he was wearing. His repeated cries of *"Allah Akbar"* filled the air as he lobbed it, hugging the luggage conveyor for protection. The second grenade exploded and the gunfire ceased. Shatri rose cautiously, swinging the AK-47 ahead. Officer Wister was on his back on the other side of the secure room. He could see Shatri coming and squeezed off several rounds in his direction. They punctured the ceiling without injuring the Muslim, who lay gunfire across the officer's kneecaps, then back across the underside of his throat.

The young Muslim stopped and surveyed the waiting area. He saw a shadow on the floor. It was coming from behind one of the columns near a window. Shatri threw a grenade to the right of it. The man behind the column moved to the left and the Muslim shot him. Shatri had not pulled the pin on the grenade; he recovered it then faced the gate area from the opposite direction. He saw his dead comrades, felt pride for their sacrifice. Soon, if Allah willed, he would be joining them. He looked down at the officers as he walked toward the SPHR, making sure they were dead.

"Bagher?" he called out.

A voice replied from inside the secure area. "I am here."

"It is safe. We must hurry."

The door opened inward. The key the passenger used was still attached, by a long wire line, to the belt of the security officer. The young woman was lying facedown in a wide, crimson pool. The passenger gingerly made his way around it. She looked to Shatri like a fish on a line. Her weight kept the door from closing. Shatri could see passengers lying on the floor, he could hear them sobbing. If he didn't need the two hand grenades he had left, he would use them here. He hated these people, these cowards . . . these infidels.

A young Muslim emerged carrying a Russian MP-446 pistol. He was wearing a white *dish-dash-ah*, a traditional long-sleeved dress, beneath a checkered *shumag* head scarf which was held in place with a thick black band. There were flecks of blood on the hem of the dress. It had been the imam's idea to hide in plain sight, discouraging profiling by appearing to be exactly what police should be looking for. Also, as he had gone through Orly Airport to his private plane, the looks Bagher al-Sanea's wardrobe received distracted onlookers from paying much attention to the thick-ribbed silver suitcase he carried.

"Things did not go as planned?" al-Sanea remarked, anger creasing his round face.

"They were not ideal," Shatri admitted.

An alarm sounded nearby and the newcomer started. He looked around, his eyes settling high on the wooden structural arches. "There are security cameras."

"It doesn't matter," Shatri replied, his own eyes moving from side to side. "Only the package is important."

"There will be more police—"

"And blocked roads, I know. I set a fire earlier so I could steal the keys to a security car parked nearby. It has not been moved. If we approach with the siren on, we will not be stopped. We drew them out last week during—"

A voice from the left said, "That was last week, jerkoff."

CHAPTER FIFTY-TWO

Shatri and his companion shot a look in the direction from which the voice had come.

John Ward was standing inside the exit that led from the tarmac. The alarm overhead was still blaring from having kicked the handle off the keypad-operated door. Air swirled through the door, clearing the smoke of the firefight. Ward stood inside the red metal frame, still as a statue, eyeing the targets through his gun sight. The Muslims were about twenty yards distant. Neither of them moved.

Shatri smirked. "Another game of Chicken?"

"So you're the gang's point man," Ward said. "I figured it was the guy I left lying in his own blood back at the training camp. Saeed. More guts than brains."

Shatri's smirk wavered and he took a step forward. Ward slammed a short burst at the floor and was ready to fire another if need be. The Muslim stopped. The detective knew he wouldn't risk using a grenade for fear of killing his companion. But the terrorist *would* use his body to shield the other man, who would return fire. It was all about advancing the man with the suitcase.

"Here's the deal," Ward said. "You put the case down, I'll argue that you get life in prison instead of the death penalty. The advantage for you is you get to spout your crap for another seventy years or so. The disadvantage is you won't get to kill anyone else."

"Here is my counterproposal," Shatri said. "You go back out the door and you will survive to see your daughter again."

Ward remained where he was, watching the men through the sight of the assault rifle.

"This need not end with your death," Shatri said.

"Shut up. I know your game."

"What game is that?" Shatri asked.

The terrorist's eyes moved along the wide corridor and he shifted slightly from foot to foot. Ward could see that he was starting to get restless, to consider the best worst-case scenario.

"You've got no intention of hurting anyone in Basalt," Ward said. "You're after a bigger target— Denver or your old hood, Chicago. You haven't got a bomb because those are tough to build and smuggle. You've got a radiological container in there—cesium-137 from old Soviet stockpiles, I'm guessing."

The man with the suitcase had started slightly when Ward mentioned the element. The detective had been watching for any kind of reaction to confirm. Cesium was one of the few elements known to be on the loose, ever since the Chechen separatists tried to dirty-bomb Moscow in 1995. The

NYPD had gotten word about five months before that several containers were MPS—Missing, Presumed Sold. The Muslims had set up the cash drop here not just to finance operations but to fine-tune a system of getting contraband into the country. The only impasse was the radiation detectors in the secure area. The evacuation scenario was their way around that. When that failed, they had to disable the device . . . make it *seem* like a mere distraction.

The alarm finally shut off. Even with their ears ringing, the men could hear the distinctive police and fire sirens growing louder. Bordering on anxious now, Shatri made his move. As Ward had expected, he stepped in front of the other man, firing the AK-47. Ward rolled outside the door for protection, but only for a moment; the gunfire stopped as quickly as it had started.

Someone had fired from within the terminal. Ward poked his head in.

Pilar Ireland.

The woman was standing just inside the door of a restroom on Ward's side of the corridor. She had gone there, as instructed, and waited for the passenger Ward suspected was coming.

Ward jumped back inside the terminal. Shatri was on the ground, gripping his side, just below the waist. The assault rifle lay several feet away. The man with the briefcase was still standing. He had turned in the direction from which the shots had come. He didn't raise the handgun.

Ward could pretty much figure out why. The Muslim was planning on getting *something* out of this mission—either killing the woman or trying to open the container, poison the terminal, kill Americans.

Ward was betting he'd opt for the cesium-137. Unlike the Israeli Mossad, terrorists didn't take revenge against people. They lashed out blindly at crowds. To them, it was a numbers game.

The man said something in Arabic. It sounded conciliatory. Maybe he didn't understand English. Maybe he was trying to bargain, buy time. It didn't matter. The assault rifle was the modern Esperanto: everyone understood it. Ward approached, the barrel aimed at the Muslim.

"Drop the gun and put the case *down*!" he said.

The Muslim nodded, dropped the gun. He knelt slowly and lay the case before him, as if he were surrendering.

Suddenly, the terrorist's spindly fingers shot out and popped the latches.

Ward fired.

The man died with *Allah Akbar* on his lips and his heart exploding through his back. He slumped sideways, twitching.

"I got screwed by one Muslim with a briefcase," Ward said. "Never again."

The detective continued toward Shatri. The man was lying between the case and his gun.

Ward kicked the gun away and moved the case several feet away with a toe. Ireland ran to Ward's side.

"Are you all right?" he asked her.

The woman nodded once. Ward noticed her pale face and drooping mouth. She was anything but fine. He was guessing she'd never had to shoot anyone before, had probably put in the job-minimum requirement on the firing range.

"You did good," he assured her.

She nodded again.

"Thing's got a surprising kick, right?"

"Yeah," she said, her voice trembling. "Yeah, it does."

He took the weapon from her and smiled. "Raise your hands and go to the front door," he said. "We don't want anyone shooting you by mistake. Tell the state patrol where we are, that we have wounded and a sealed radiological device, and that the situation has been contained."

She nodded once more, then turned, lifted her hands shoulder high, and set off. Her arms were shaking. Ward watched for a moment to make sure she didn't fall over, but he never let the Muslim out of his peripheral vision. When he was sure Ireland was all right, the detective turned back to the wounded man.

"See her? *That's* what you're facing, little man," Ward said. "Not pretend Americans like you but real ones. Americans who will do whatever it takes to preserve the Republic, even if it's personally distasteful."

"We will . . . overwhelm . . . you . . ." the wounded man said through his teeth.

Ward sneered. "Punk, build all the mosques you want. Truth is, you haven't got a prayer."

Ward heard the clap of footsteps running toward them from the main terminal. He lowered his weapon and lifted his hands as a phalanx of state police surrounded them. Chief Brennan was among them. She smiled broadly when she saw Ward.

"I had a feeling you wouldn't need the cavalry," she said, motioning the police to move on, that he was all right. The state commander acknowledged then indicated how the men were to disperse as they approached the gate.

"The radiological material's in that case," Ward told the officer before he had moved on.

The lieutenant reported the information into his radio as he moved in with his men, after taking a moment to fire a salute at Ward.

"There were other passengers on the private jet," Ward told Brennan. "Better question them."

"They should be okay. We checked them out with the jet lessee. They were all businessmen, legitimate ones as far as we can tell." She indicated the dead man. "This guy was the only one attached to the Chicago crowd."

"I was right," Ward said. "That was the target."

"Appears so," Brennan said. She looked down at Shatri, who was curled like a fetus and moaning. "The EMTs are looking after our people. They'll get to you eventually."

"You're all . . . going . . . to die."

"We can finally agree on something," she replied. "But it won't be now and not by your hand."

More police arrived along with EMTs. Shatri was cuffed and a trooper stood over him with a gun pointed at his head before the medics were allowed to approach.

"Hey, this man needs attention," Brennan said, noticing Ward's leg.

"It'll keep," he assured her. "I don't want this guy bleeding to death until we can talk to him." Ward took one last look at Shatri's pained but unrepentant face. "Lord God, I hope I'm in on the interrogation."

"I don't think that'll be happening," Brennan said.

"Yeah, I know."

"No, I mean—someone's been looking for you." He looked at her. "Who?"

"Guys from New York," she replied. "Your phone's probably dead. They said they left messages, then tracked you to me through your ex-wife."

"Did they say what they wanted?"

She smiled. "Yes. And I have a feeling you're about to break this police chief's heart."

CHAPTER FIFTY-THREE

Brennan was right: his phone was dead. It was not just dead, it was crushed from one of the falls or slams or jumps he had made.

The police chief held off the state patrol commander from questioning Ward until he could call his voice mail. He did that from Director Ireland's office.

The message was from Lee McClure, one of his Organized Crime Control Bureau brothers. Like McClure, the message was short and direct:

"Boss, we found video from skateboarders who were taping their Tony Hawk moves. We've got clear images showing you barely touched the guy. IA has given the footage to the commissioner. It was on the news. The Muslim has disappeared. Welcome back."

Ward sat with the phone pressed to his ear. His body was near exhaustion and the firefight was still singing loudly inside his head. But he knew he would never forget the words, the tone, or the soul-stirring impact of McClure's message. He realized that without the coalition, the brotherhood that was at the heart of him and his work, he would not be going home. Without it, he could never have stitched together the coalition of Americans who had saved countless lives today. Yes, at a price—the price freedom seems to demand from time to time.

Numb in mind and body but full in spirit, he took a moment to call Joanne's cell phone. She answered at once.

"John, are you all right?"

"Yes," he said. "How are you and Megan?"

"Fine," she said. "When I heard the news flash about the airport, I knew." For the first time in a long time her voice didn't sound critical. She almost seemed relieved.

"I want to come and see you once this is all buttoned up," he said.

"You can't, John. I mean, you *can*—but we're in Utah."

"Utah? The state?"

"Yes, John. The state."

"Sorry, I'm a little tired and that was kind of a surprise. What's there?"

"Hunter's parents. We decided to take Megan out of Basalt until this was over."

He exhaled. His chest hurt. His ribs were still not fully healed and he hadn't done them any good today. "Good move. Smart. Can I talk to her?"

"She and Hunter's folks just went north, to Dinosaur National Monument. Meg's teachers are letting her do a video report as part of her schoolwork. I didn't know what was happening with you—I didn't want her sitting around watching the news."

Ward laughed thinly. "That's great. 'Daddy may be dead—let's check out the pterodactyls.'"

"Not fair," she said. "She was very upset."

"Okay. I'm sorry."

"I understand you need to get back to New York," Joanne said.

"Seems so."

"The man who called, McClure, said they knew you were innocent. I guess I should've given you the benefit of the doubt."

"It's okay. It worked out."

Guilt free, maybe, he thought. *But innocent?*

He wondered if anyone in this *jihad*-poisoned world could ever be innocent again. Even young girls like his daughter, provincial girls like Angie, would never feel safe and secure in their own heartland community. To him, that was a greater tragedy than what almost happened here today. A systemic, corrosive plague instead of a one-time punch that could be absorbed.

"Tell Megan I'll come and see her when I can," Ward said.

"She's been wanting to come back and visit you," his former wife said. "Maybe during spring break?"

"Great. I'll try not to get into trouble in April," he promised.

"Cute," Joanne said.

The door opened and a state patrol face peered in. Ward said his good-byes and hung up the phone and stood to face one Colonel Luke Dallas.

"Is every member of the CSP six-foot-four and built like a linebacker?" Ward asked.

"Pretty much," the fiftysomething officer replied. His mouth was lost in his square jaw, but his gray eyes seemed to smile. "I just want you to know that as he was being loaded into an ambulance, Major Crockett made a point of asking me to thank you."

"He and his team did all the heavy lifting," Ward said.

"Detective, I'm told we also have a grip like a bench vise. Care to find out?" He offered a monster of a paw and this: "It's an honor, sir."

Ward shook his hand and it got to him. Everything that had happened, the courage and unity he had seen, ordinary men and police standing elbow-to-elbow to defend their community. He tried to say something but the words snagged in his throat. He thought it instead:

The honor, sir, is mine.

EPILOGUE

It was a short visit, only a day and change, but it was all Scott Randolph could spare. He had a business to rebuild back in Basalt.

But it was a welcome reunion, and the pig farmer had never been to New York. It wasn't nearly as intimidating as he had expected. His late, beloved pigs were louder, sometimes, than the traffic, and the mountains made the buildings look like foothills. What impressed him more was how so many people, all so different, all moving hip-to-hip, got along so well. It was a lesson for the world, he thought.

John Ward had been back a week and on the job for just two days, so he didn't have a lot of time to spend with the man he referred to as his "war buddy." It was an apt description. The events had made the news and the showdowns at the mountain training camp and the Aspen airport had been described as "pitched battles." Ward had declined interviews—he had his job back and didn't want to say anything to undo that—but Police Chief Brennan, Angie Dickson, Scott Randolph and others had finally given up trying to find another way of saying "hero."

"That's what John Ward is," the police chief told Fox News. "He's a bonafide American hero. How else do you describe someone who saved a major American city from a dirty bomb?"

To Ward's surprise, that city was not Chicago. Documents on the dead jetsetter showed that his final destination was Albuquerque, New Mexico. After his arrest, Mahnoosh Fawaz had confirmed that to Homeland Security. The idea was to cause chaos in a border state so that other illegal sympathizers could make their way into the United States—some of them with additional radiological material from the former Soviet Union.

Fawaz had not been a radical sympathizer, he swore, and was cooperating to prove it, he said. He had been in this to build dry cleaning shops across America and become a wealthy capitalist.

No one believed him. But the information he provided proved accurate. As a result, he and his wife were the only Muslims who were not charged with terrorism, aiding terrorism, weapons charges, and money laundering. They ended up in witness protection—somewhere in Mississippi. Ward wondered how long they would survive there.

Earl Dickson was not so lucky. Though he accepted a plea deal to cooperate with authorities, he still faced a minimum five years of jail time. Ward's testimony on his behalf would ensure that the banker would get that minimum as well as a reduced sentence for good behavior. He seemed grateful for that, and for his wife and daughter being kept out of it.

Over drinks the day he arrived, Randolph also assured Ward that Angie and also Deb were doing all right. Before leaving for his New York hearing and reinstatement, Ward only had time to thank the airport team and the training camp posse. Sleep, the media, and the signing of statements and police reports consumed the rest of the twenty-four hours he had left, and made alone-time impossible. Also, he didn't want his presence to draw undue attention to the women. They needed alone-time to recover.

"They'll be okay," Randolph promised. "Both got some steel in 'em, like those pioneers who cut their way through the mountains. That's how we grow 'em out in the shadow of the Rockies."

But none of that was the reason for Scott Randolph's visit. It was all about the early evening on the night of his departure.

Before flying east, the pig farmer had spent a day in his cabin on the Internet, doing research and making connections through mercenary Web sites. He finally found the name he was looking for, got a contact number, and after sunset he was waiting in the alley to pick up his .375 Magnum from Alexander Cherkassov. Police Chief Brennan had loaned him some of the Muslim cash from the evidence locker to make the purchase. And she gave him one thing more from her own personal stash.

Now the pig farmer was standing in an alley admiring a Thunderstorm pistol, a favorite of the Spetsnaz, the Russian special forces.

"Nice," Randolph said as he felt the weight of the handgun in his gloved hand. "How much?"

"Five thousand cash," the Russian told him. He was facing the street so he could look back whenever he heard a car go by.

"Rubles?" Randolph joked.

"Dollars," Cherkassov said humorlessly.

"I wanted a silencer as well," Randolph said.

"Another two thousand."

Randolph handed him the gun then reached into the pocket of his windbreaker and removed a wad of cash. He quickly counted out seventy one-hundred-dollar bills and handed it to the Russian. The Russian gave him the weapon.

"How do you put it on?" Randolph asked.

The Russian turned away. "I do not have time—"

"Another five hundred," Randolph said.

The Russian hesitated, turned back, then held out his hand. Randolph counted out five more bills. Cherkassov screwed in the suppressor, handed the weapon to Randolph. "That's all you needed to do," he grinned. "Easiest money I—"

"The *last* money," Randolph said and shot him through the heart with the bullet he'd loaded while the Russian's back was turned. The bullet he'd borrowed from Chief Brennan and kept in his heel. A heel that did not go through security because Brennan took him to the airport and walked them around the metal detector.

The Russian's chest caved in and he dropped like a deflating used car lot balloon. Randolph dropped the gun on his chest and took the cash from the Russian's pocket. He pulled off a glove, licked a finger, held it under the Russian's nose.

"That's how I tell if pigs is dead," he said.

There was nothing.

Randolph stood and walked briskly from the dark alley. He didn't know if Ward would make the connection for sure; it didn't matter.

This is Basalt's way of thanking you for everything you gave us, he thought as he picked up his carry-on, hailed a cab, and headed for the airport.